HANGING WITH HUGO

HANGING WITH HUGO

Katherine Bolger Hyde

**SEVERN
HOUSE**

First world edition published in Great Britain and the USA in 2024
by Severn House, an imprint of Canongate Books Ltd,
14 High Street, Edinburgh EH1 1TE.

severnhouse.com

British Library Cataloguing-in-Publication Data
A CIP catalogue record for this title is available from the British Library.

ISBN-13: 978-1-4483-1186-6 (cased)
ISBN-13: 978-1-4483-1295-5 (e-book)

All Severn House titles are printed on acid-free paper.

Typeset by Palimpsest Book Production Ltd.,
Falkirk, Stirlingshire, Scotland.
Printed and bound in Great Britain by
TJ International, Padstow, Cornwall.

Praise for the Crime with the Classics series

"Hyde knows how to hook the reader"
Publishers Weekly on *Fatality with Forster*

"Engaging . . . a meaty mystery, and a satisfying conclusion"
Booklist on *Fatality with Forster*

"Effectively blends romance and mystery"
Booklist on *Death with Dostoevsky*

"Lively . . . Campus hijinks and budding romances
complement the fair-play plot"
Publishers Weekly on *Death with Dostoevsky*

"Another winning cozy"
Booklist on *Cyanide with Christie*

"Those who appreciate literary allusions and quaint settings
might enjoy a visit to Stony Beach"
Publishers Weekly on *Bloodstains with Brontë*

About the author

Katherine Bolger Hyde has lived her life surrounded by books, from teaching herself to read at the age of four to majoring in Russian literature to making her career as an editor. She lives in Washington State with her husband and is the author of five previous Crime with the Classics mysteries, including most recently, from Severn House, *Death with Dostoevsky* and *Fatality with Forster*.

www.kbhyde.com

To my fellow members of the Rockaway Literary Wine &
Chocolate Society, for all your insights and support

ONE

Late on a cloudy afternoon in early July, Luke pulled the car into Windy Corner's drive. The distant bells of St Bede's Episcopal Church, ringing for evensong, woke Emily from her two-hour doze. She hadn't slept a wink on the red-eye flight from Manchester to Portland, but as soon as they got in the car to come home, she'd drifted off into dreams that mixed the baa-ing of Lake District sheep with the stiff sea breezes of home.

Their official honeymoon was over, but Emily was glad to get back to normal life in Stony Beach. Traveling in Britain for a month had been delightful but also exhausting; she missed familiar faces and the comforts of home. She knew she wouldn't have much time to rest up, though, because her half-brother Oscar's wedding to Lauren Hsu was due to be held at Windy Corner at the end of the month. Although Lauren had promised to take care of all the work of preparation, Emily suspected that she and her housekeeper, Katie, would come in for a sizable share.

Her suspicions were confirmed on Sunday afternoon in a video chat between herself, Katie, Oscar, Lauren, and their mutual friend Marguerite.

'So here's the thing,' Lauren led off. 'We've got an agnostic American man marrying a non-traditional Chinese woman who is cursed with somewhat traditional parents. I've made it clear to them that we're not doing the whole thing with the private tea party and the procession to pick up the bride and the eight-course banquet with the huge guest list and all the weird stuff you do for good luck. But I've got to throw them a bone of some kind or they won't give us their blessing. Or probably even speak to us ever again.'

Oscar jumped in. 'I don't care about the reception, but for some reason, I've always had my heart set on a church wedding. Not a big fancy thing, just a quiet ceremony in a little country church. Not that I'm religious, but maybe because my parents were never married? I feel like that's the only way it would seem *real* to me.'

Lauren took over again. 'So we thought we'd compromise by having a Christian ceremony at your little church in Stony Beach – what's it called?'

'Saint Bede's.' It wasn't really Emily's church, since it was Episcopal and she was Eastern Orthodox, but she did visit there from time to time when she couldn't get to her parish in Portland. 'Would you like me to make the arrangements with the rector?'

'Please. That would be terrific.' Lauren went on, 'Then we'd have the reception at Windy Corner. I don't have a lot of relatives in this country – only my parents – and Oscar only has you, so we'd invite a few friends from Reed and that's about it. We could have a Chinese banquet catered and do a few things with clothes and decorations, so my parents will feel like we made an effort. Marguerite volunteered to help with the décor.'

Marguerite nodded. She had a flair for such things.

'How does that sound?'

'That sounds . . . doable, I guess. What do you think, Katie?'

'If I don't have to cook at all, the rest of it shouldn't be too hard,' she replied. 'How many people would be staying in the house?'

'Well, the two of us, and Marguerite, and my parents. I think everyone else can make their own arrangements.'

'I'll contact the manager of the Stony Beach Inn,' Emily said. 'Get her to reserve however many rooms you need and arrange for a group discount.' She owned the hotel, so she could call the shots on such matters – that is, provided enough rooms were available during peak tourist season. 'I'd like to let your guests stay free, but with all the taxes and whatnot, that wouldn't work.'

'A discount would be great.' Lauren paused. 'OK if we come down two weeks before the date? We'll have a fair bit to do.'

That would leave Emily and Luke only two weeks in which to settle into their new married life before it got completely disrupted. Oh, well, it would have to do. Once the wedding was over, they could keep the house to themselves for as long as they liked.

'And your parents? When will they arrive?'

'They'd like to come a week before, if that's OK. Ma feels like she has to help even though there won't be much of anything for her to do.' Lauren rolled her eyes.

'Anything I should be aware of for them?' Emily asked. 'Food allergies, mobility issues, entrenched hatred of cats . . .?' She sincerely hoped not the last. She'd hate to have to confine their three cats to her and Luke's private third-floor apartment for the duration. The cats would hate it too – the main-floor library was their domain.

'They're a little picky food-wise, but nothing you can predict.' Another eye-roll. 'My dad's getting kind of creaky in the joints and my mom needs her own bathroom, so if you could give them the ground-floor room, that would be great.'

The Dickens room was the only bedroom on the ground floor, so its bathroom was not shared with other guests, though it did serve as a powder room for everyone in the house. Oscar and Lauren would have the larger second-floor Forster room as usual, and Marguerite always preferred the understated elegance of the Austen room, so that arrangement should be feasible. That left two more guest rooms, Montgomery and Brontë, in case of last-minute additions to the house party. The Dostoevsky room, which Emily had kept shut since one of her guests had died there, was now due to be reincarnated as Luke's private den.

'Sounds fine. We'll expect you . . .' She consulted her calendar. 'Around the sixteenth?'

'Perfect. Thanks so much, Emily. This is going to be great.'

It had better be. Emily had offered her home for the wedding on the spur of the moment last winter, and now she was beginning to wonder what she'd gotten herself into. But Oscar was family – the only family she had left. She wanted to do her best to give him and Lauren a good start.

On Monday morning, Emily called Father Stephen, the rector of St Bede's, to carry out her assignment.

'Father Stephen? This is Emily Richards.' She'd had a month to get used to her new name.

But Father Stephen had not. 'Emily Richards? . . . Oh, *Emily*! How are you? How was your honeymoon?'

'It was wonderful, thank you. But I'm calling to talk to you about another wedding. My brother's. He'd like to hold the ceremony at Saint Bede's.'

A slight pause and a cough, then, 'Why don't we talk in person? Can you come up to the church this afternoon?'

'Sure,' Emily replied, wondering why Father Stephen did not at least ask for some basic information – such as the date – over the phone. But she had no objection to speaking to him face to face.

After lunch, she drove the mile south into town. The little white clapboard church, which dated back to the early days of Stony Beach's founding, stood inland, up a hill from the main part of town, so that it could be seen – and its bells heard – from a distance. As Emily drove into view of the hillside, she noticed something different about the structure, but her distance vision wasn't good enough for her to be sure exactly what. When she rounded the final bend in the road, the difference became all too clear: the church was surrounded by scaffolding, and blue tarpaulins covered the roof. A couple of workmen clumped around on the highest boards, doing she couldn't tell what, but it was making a fair bit of noise.

Emily's heart sank. Oscar's vision of a little country church wedding surely did not include ongoing repairs. If the work in progress involved only the exterior, a wedding might still be possible, though the couple would probably want to avoid taking pictures in the church porch. But if the interior was under construction as well . . .

She parked in the empty lot and walked up the flagstone path, checking nervously for falling equipment heading toward her as she approached the door. Father Stephen came out to meet her.

'Good to see you, Emily!' He took her hand and kissed her on the cheek. 'I'm so glad you could come.' He smiled apologetically, gesturing upward. 'As you can see, we have a bit of construction going on. Let's go inside where it's quieter.'

Quieter inside was a good sign. She followed his black-clad form into the nave.

But as her eyes adjusted to the lower light, she realized the current absence of workmen in the nave was not to be taken as evidence of a lack of work in progress. Scaffolding rose across the stained-glass window behind the altar, and the red carpeting that normally covered the aisle had been pulled up to reveal a badly water-damaged wood floor.

Father Stephen led her to a seat in the front pew. 'I'm afraid we're not in the best shape to host a wedding right now.'

'Yes. I see that.'

'Do your brother and his fiancée have a date in mind?'

'July thirtieth.'

Father Stephen whistled. 'Less than a month. I'm not sure we can be in a fit state that soon.' He ran a finger under his white clerical collar. 'By the original estimate, the work would have been done by then. But we've run into some difficulties.' He shot her a sidelong glance. 'To be perfectly frank, we're out of funds.'

Emily suppressed a sigh. She should have known the invitation to meet at the church forebode the inevitable request for a financial contribution. As the wealthiest woman in town, she was accustomed to being hit up for a variety of civic projects, and in general she was happy to contribute. But the honeymoon had stretched her own and Luke's immediate resources to their limit. Dipping into her invested capital was something she tried to avoid.

'Tell me the situation.'

'The main thing, predictably, is the roof. It's long overdue for replacement. We had a particularly nasty storm last month while you were gone, and the leaks partially flooded the church. Hence the floor.' He gestured toward the aisle with a grimace. 'In that same storm, a branch fell against the window and damaged it.' He indicated the Gothic arch behind the altar, which held a beautiful though scaled-down and simplified imitation of the famous circular rose windows in Paris's Cathedral of Notre Dame. Panes of the intricate, colorful design were broken or missing all the way across the top third of the window, allowing the gray sky to peek through.

'It's the finest window on the Oregon coast,' Father Stephen went on. 'Your uncle Horace's contribution, as a matter of fact. I'd hate to be the rector who allowed it to be destroyed.'

He let his words hang in the air, the request for money unspoken but no less clear for all that. With just the right spice of guilt, since all Emily's money could ultimately be traced back to her aunt Beatrice's husband, Horace Runcible. 'If we had thirty thousand dollars, we could finish all the work within the month.'

Thirty thousand dollars. That would definitely require a dip into capital.

'What about insurance? Doesn't that cover it?'

Father Stephen cleared his throat. 'I, uh . . . I'm afraid I let it lapse. Not intentionally, exactly, but there's never enough coming in to make ends meet. I've already cut my own salary to the bone.'

A glance at his graying, crumpled clerical collar and frayed shirt cuffs confirmed that. Letting the insurance lapse had certainly been unwise, but it wasn't surprising that one man doing the work of a pastor plus that of the nonexistent parish secretary and treasurer would let some things slip through the cracks.

'Have you tried canvassing the congregation? Holding a fundraiser?'

'Both. But you know our parishioners – they're fishermen, hospitality workers, a few small-business owners. They don't have that kind of money between them. We did a bake sale, but it only brought in a few hundred.' He raised his hands and let them fall. 'I'm at my wits' end. And so far, my prayers have availed nothing.' Another sidelong glance told Emily how much he hoped she would be the answer to his prayers.

If it hadn't been for Oscar's upcoming wedding, she would have written him a check for a thousand or so on the spot and considered she had done her part. St Bede's was not her own church, after all. It wasn't even her denomination.

But Oscar wanted to be married here. No other church in town had the right atmosphere. And she would hate for him and Lauren to get drenched if a storm happened to come up on their wedding day.

'I'll give it some thought,' she said. 'I'm not sure what I can do at the moment, but I'll definitely think about it. I'll be in touch.' She stood.

Father Stephen stood to face her and gave her a hug. 'Thank you, Emily. The Lord sent you at just the right time.'

Emily forced a smile. She knew from long experience that God's timing did not often take the convenience of his people into account.

That evening, as they relaxed in the library, Emily talked over her dilemma with Luke. 'Of course, I could pay for the whole business, but it would mean dipping into capital, and you know how I hate doing that. It isn't even my church.'

'Could you pay for just the window? To appease the shade of Uncle Horace?' Luke asked with a grin.

Emily frowned in thought. 'I didn't ask Father Stephen to break down the costs. I'm not sure how much the window alone would be. Not cheap, since it's highly skilled work, but surely the roof would be the biggest chunk.'

She sighed. 'The obvious thing to do would be to hold another fundraiser. But with the wedding coming up, I don't think Katie and I can handle that. Especially after last time.' Emily shuddered at the memory of the first and last fundraiser she had hosted at Windy Corner – a murder mystery dinner on the previous Halloween, to fund the Stony Beach Clinic. The murder part had turned out to be all too real, and Katie had discovered the body. Emily would not put her through something like that again.

'No,' Luke agreed, 'it'd be crazy to attempt an event, especially on such short notice. Sounds like they need the money pretty much immediately if they're gonna finish by the wedding.'

Emily shrugged. 'I expect the guarantee of the money would be enough to keep things going. But still, any fundraiser would have to happen within the month, and you're right – that's not feasible.' She sighed. 'I suppose I'm going to have to bite the bullet and sell some stock.'

'Why does it always have to be you?' Luke asked. 'The town can't expect you to pay for everything that goes on around here.'

She sat forward, meeting his gaze. 'You're right. That church is part of the town's history, and the town should contribute to restoring it. I'm going to have a talk with the Chamber of Commerce. I bet the profits from Pirate Days could be funneled into this project – at least some of them. Let the tourists bear part of the burden.' Pirate Days were due to be held over the coming weekend. She'd have to act fast.

'And I'll talk to Father Stephen about the cost breakdown,' she went on. 'If we can get the window fixed and get some new carpeting to cover up the damaged floor, the interior will be presentable enough for the wedding to go ahead. We'll just have to pray extra hard that we don't get another storm before the roof can be fixed.'

TWO

After breakfast the next morning, Emily called Father Stephen to tell him her plan. He estimated five thousand for the window repair and the carpeting but emphasized that he had not contracted with a repair person yet. 'People with that skill are in big demand,' he said. 'I've asked around, and there's nobody on the coast who's available to do it. We'll have to get someone from Portland or maybe even Seattle.'

'Could you get to work on that? And let me know as soon as you have some figures.'

'Will do.'

Fifteen minutes later, she strode into the town hall and asked to see the mayor, who was also president of the Chamber of Commerce – Homer Babcock. 'I'm afraid he's busy, Mrs Ca— I mean Mrs Richards,' the receptionist said. 'You know Pirate Days are this weekend.'

'That's exactly what I want to talk to him about. It's urgent.'

The girl eyed her uncertainly, but in the end, Emily's standing in the community must have won out over protocol. 'I'll see if he can fit you in.'

She lifted the phone, but Emily smiled and sailed past her. That, after all, is what Aunt Beatrice would have done.

Babcock was just putting down the phone as she walked in. He put on a fulsome smile as he smoothed his nearly nonexistent hair. 'Emily! Delightful to see you! How was your honeymoon?'

'Lovely, thanks. I'm here on another matter.' She helped herself to a visitor's chair without waiting to be asked and plunged in. 'You are no doubt aware that Saint Bede's Church is currently undergoing some very expensive emergency repairs.'

He cleared his throat. 'I think I heard something about that, yes. Such a shame. An historic building, though sadly not much used in these godless days.' Babcock himself was a staunch Baptist.

'Saint Bede's is still a fully functioning parish church, even if the congregation is on the small side. And, as you say, it's an important part of the history of this town, and the rose window is a source of civic pride. That's why I think it appropriate that the town should help pay for the repairs.'

Babcock adjusted his tie to lie straight over his ample belly. 'Well, we could certainly bring up the issue when we have our budget meeting for next year. Though, as you know, our funds are usually pretty stretched.' *Stretched* was an understatement. Last year, the budget's ends had simply refused to meet without a substantial contribution from Emily.

'That will be much too late. The church repairs need to be finished before another storm hits.' The June storm that had damaged the church had been a freak, but freaks could happen at any time. And beginning in October, intense storms were a regular feature of Stony Beach life.

She leaned forward and impaled Babcock with her eyes. 'I want you to designate the Pirate Days profits to help Saint Bede's.'

Babcock's protuberant eyes widened until they looked like painted ping-pong balls. 'You want me to do *what*?'

'You heard me. Or I will have to reconsider the support I've pledged for next year's budget shortfall.'

Emily had never thrown her financial weight around like that before, and she would not have done so now if the cause were not so deserving. But she had to admit it was rather fun to watch Babcock squirm.

'I'll . . . I'll see what I can do. But you realize that money has already been allocated.'

Emily widened her eyes in fake astonishment. 'Allocated? Before it has even been earned?'

He threw up his hands. 'We have a pretty fair idea how much will come in. It varies some from year to year, but the ballpark is consistent. And it's earmarked for . . . well, for a variety of projects around town.'

Emily strongly suspected that variety included the personal pockets of the major organizers. She fixed Babcock with one of Aunt Beatrice's signature glares. 'I'm counting on you, Mayor. Or should I say, Saint Bede's is counting on the town to do its duty to preserve one of its historic landmarks. Shall we say ten thousand?'

Babcock's face seemed to melt before her eyes. 'Ten . . . thousand? That's more than we brought in last year. Total.'

She smiled sweetly. 'Then I suggest you make an extra-special effort to boost the profits this year.'

'Yes, ma'am,' he mumbled, as if she were a strict and demanding mother, although he must be at least her age or older. Emily smiled in triumph. She had achieved the status of matriarch without ever having a child of her own.

Being allergic to crowds, Emily stayed well away from town during Pirate Days. But Luke was on duty the whole three-day weekend. The event was family oriented, and usually there was no trouble more serious than a few parking tickets. But a police presence helped to ensure that would be the case.

He dragged himself home Monday evening, grabbed a cold beer from the kitchen, and fell into his chair by the library hearth. 'Whew! I'm glad that's over.'

'Any trouble?' Emily asked.

'Not a bit. Just a bigger crowd than I've seen in years. We had to get creative about parking.' He shot her a grin. 'One thing I think you'll like. We got Father Stephen to open the Saint Bede's lot and ran a shuttle van from there to downtown. All fees go straight to the restoration fund.'

'That's wonderful! Any idea how much that brought in?'

'Not off the top of my head, but fifty cars at ten dollars a pop for three days adds up to a few square feet of roof, at any rate.'

She leaned over and kissed him. 'It's certainly a start. And it sounds like the mayor won't have to dip into his own pocket to make up the ten thousand I asked him for.'

Luke snorted. 'Any word on a window repair person?'

'Not yet.'

They lapsed into companionable silence, Emily knitting, Luke sipping his beer and looking at the newspaper. They might have been married for five decades instead of five weeks. Emily treasured times like this, knowing they couldn't count on their peace being undisturbed for long. She'd thought they'd have the two weeks before Oscar and Lauren's arrival to themselves with no hassles to worry about, but already the business with the church had gotten in the way.

Tuesday morning, Father Stephen called to say he'd found someone to repair the window. 'He's coming from Portland, and he wants five hundred a day plus expenses.'

'How long does he think it'll take?'

'He couldn't say for sure from the pictures I sent him. Anywhere from a week to a month. He'll have a better idea when he sees it in person.'

Emily whistled. 'Let's pray it's closer to a week. As for expenses, I'll talk to my property manager and see if we can come up with a place for him to stay. Will he be coming alone?'

'He mentioned a wife and a toddler.'

'OK, we'll hope to find a small cottage empty. It's a busy time of year, so send up a prayer about that as well.'

'Will do.' Father Stephen paused. 'Any word on the Pirate Days proceeds?'

'Not yet. It'll probably take them a day or two to figure it all out.'

'Right. We made over a thousand on the parking alone, so we can at least give Adrian a down payment.'

'Oh, that's the stained-glass guy? Adrian what?'

'Hughes. Adrian Hughes. And his wife's name is . . . Polly.'

'I look forward to meeting them. When are they coming?'

'Tomorrow, if we can find a place for them to lay their heads.'

'I'll get on that right away.'

Emily ended the call and placed another to her property manager, Justine.

'You are almost in luck,' Justine said. 'We just this minute got a cancellation on that little cottage on the corner of Third and Ocean. Should be perfect for them. But it won't be open till Friday night.'

Chances of finding anything else in town on such short notice were nearly nonexistent. But the artist was hoping to start work on Thursday. There was nothing else for it. She would have to put the family up at Windy Corner until the cottage was ready. It meant sacrificing her and Luke's privacy, but it was only for a couple of nights. They would probably be nice people, and the toddler would be someone for Katie's sixteen-month-old daughter, Lizzie, to play with. How bad could it be?

*   *   *

The Hughes family arrived just before dinner on Wednesday evening. Katie was busy setting the table, so Emily went to the door to greet them.

On the porch stood a tall, brown-haired young man, handsome in a rough and tousled way with shaggy hair and a few days' growth of beard, holding a couple of large tote bags. Next to him was a brunette who might have posed for one of the pre-Raphaelite painters, incongruously clad in a T-shirt and jeans and holding a child on her hip who looked to be about two. The child sported a shoulder-length mop of blond curls and not a single stitch of clothing – not even a diaper. When it squirmed in its mother's arms, Emily saw that it was a boy.

She blinked away her astonishment and put on a welcoming smile. 'You must be the Hughes family. Welcome to Windy Corner. I'm Emily Richards.' She started to put out a hand, then realized neither of the adults had one free to shake.

The young man nodded. 'Adrian. This is Polly' – he indicated his wife with a tilt of the head – 'and our little guy, Raphael.' Ah, so the pre-Raphaelite connection was not lost on this artistic couple.

'Pleased to meet you. Please, come in.' Emily stood back for them to enter. 'Did Raphael have an accident on the way?'

Polly cocked her head with a questioning look, then laughed. 'Oh, you mean his bare bum? No, he hates clothes – rips them off as soon as we put them on him – so we let him be naked most of the time. You don't mind, do you?'

Emily swallowed. 'Well . . . Is he potty-trained?'

Polly shrugged. 'Mostly.'

'I'm afraid I'm going to have to insist on at least a diaper if there's a chance of accidents. We have some valuable rugs and furniture.' Then she thought of Lizzie. 'And my housekeeper has a little girl. I'm not sure Katie's ready to explain to her why little boys are different.'

Adrian and Polly exchanged a look of consternation. 'We have a few diapers for nighttime,' Adrian said. 'But we can't guarantee he won't pull them off as soon as we put them on.'

'If you'd make the effort, I would appreciate it. It's only for a couple of days – your cottage will be ready Friday afternoon.' Emily wasn't thrilled with the idea of a tiny time bomb running around one of her cottages, either, but at least the floors there would be easier to clean.

Polly heaved a sigh. 'All right, buddy, let's get you presentable for polite society.' She put a slight scornful emphasis on the last words. 'Where do we go?'

Emily led the way to the back of the house, to the Dickens room. 'You'll be in here. The bathroom is right next door. I believe dinner is almost ready. I'll see if Katie has a high chair Raphael can use.'

'No need,' Adrian said cheerfully, setting the tote bags on the bed. 'He can sit on my lap. He eats off our plates anyway.'

Emily had a vision of Raphael as the young, untamed Helen Keller from *The Miracle Worker*, running around the table and grabbing food at will off everyone's plates. At least this child was too short to reach that far.

She backed out of the room with a pasted-on smile, closed the door, and fled to the dining room. 'Oh, my word, Katie, I don't know what I've let us in for. They let their little boy run around completely naked, and I'm guessing they don't much care what he breaks or ruins, either. It's going to be anarchy around here for the next couple of days.'

Katie paused in her napkin folding with raised eyebrows. 'Thank goodness we have the house mostly childproofed for Lizzie's sake. Don't worry, Mrs R. We can survive a mini tornado for forty-eight hours.'

Emily gave her shoulders a squeeze. 'What would I do without you, Katie? Oh, here they come. I'll call Luke.'

She ducked out past the entering Hughes family. Raphael was already pulling at the tabs of his disposable diaper. Adrian, who was holding him, said, 'Not now, buddy. We have to keep it on for the nice lady.' Raphael scowled at Emily, clearly disputing the appellation 'nice lady.'

Emily found Luke in the library and filled him in on the situation with a few whispered words. He laughed. 'Hey, be thankful it's only the kid who's buck naked. Could've been the parents too.' He gave her a quick sideways hug. 'If he gets too obstreperous, I'll arrest him.'

Attempts at conversation over the meal were disrupted by Raphael's intermittent attempts to handle everything on the table and squalls when the sharp knives and fragile crystal wine glasses were gently moved out of his reach. Emily's heart stopped briefly when he grabbed the carving fork off the meat platter and seemed about to plunge the tines into his father's hand. But Adrian had quick reflexes and averted the disaster with undisturbed equanimity.

By the time dinner was finished, the summer sun had set. 'Feel free to join us in the library after you get Raphael to bed,' Emily said, hoping for some undisturbed adult conversation. There must be more to this couple than their laissez-faire parenting.

'Oh, he won't be going to bed for a while,' Polly said. 'He sleeps with us. He'd never fall asleep if we left him on his own.'

Emily's face was getting tired from forcing so many smiles. 'Perhaps you'd all like to settle into your room, then.'

Adrian shrugged. 'Nothing to settle. We left most of our stuff in the car.'

'I see.' She turned toward the library door, then had yet another qualm. 'My three cats live in the library. Is Raphael OK with cats?' What she meant was, would her cats be OK with Raphael on the rampage? Lizzie had learned to be gentle with them, but they wouldn't know what to make of a free-range toddler who might want to poke their eyes or pull their tails.

'Sure, he loves animals. No problem.'

At that Emily was reminded of Katharine Hepburn's line in *Bringing Up Baby*, referring to her brother's statement in a letter that the leopard Baby likes dogs: 'I wonder if he means he eats dogs or is fond of them.'

THREE

Emily found the evening anything but restful, being constantly on the alert lest young Raphael decide to torture the cats or start pulling Aunt Beatrice's delicate old books off the shelves. The library was childproofed only in a relative sense – things that could harm a child had been dealt with, but it hadn't been possible to remove everything a child could harm. Since Lizzie learned to crawl, Emily and Katie together had been training her not to touch the books.

It came as something of a relief when the hall phone rang. Emily jumped to answer it ahead of Katie, who was busy cleaning up.

'Emily? Father Paul here.'

Emily started. She couldn't remember Father Paul, her priest from Portland, ever calling her at home, except once or twice about preparations for her wedding. She hoped he wasn't calling to tell her one of her elderly parishioner friends had died.

He plunged in with no preliminaries. 'Sorry to bother you, Emily, but we've got a bit of an emergency here.'

'Oh? What's up?' Meaning, what kind of emergency could she help with when she was a two-hour drive away?

'I have a couple of new parishioners – a man and his foster daughter. Or ward, technically – he's her legal guardian. He's the salt of the earth, devoted to the girl, but they're being harassed by a social worker who's convinced he's abusing her. I promise you he's not. It's a complicated situation, but I'll let him explain it for himself. The reason I'm calling is I need you to take them in for a while. They need to get away someplace where this social worker can't get to them.'

Emily blew out a heavy breath. More guests. Unrelated to either the wedding or the church repair. And guests with trouble right behind them. Exactly what she didn't need right now.

'I don't know, Father. I've got a young family here for a couple of days, then Oscar and Lauren this weekend to start preparations for their wedding. Plus Marguerite, who's helping out. And then Lauren's parents in another week. It's a busy time and a pretty full house.'

'*Full* full? As in no spare beds?'

'Well, no. I do have two rooms open. But with everything going on, it wouldn't be very restful for them. And I wouldn't have much attention to spare. And if there's trouble . . .'

Father Paul heaved a noisy sigh. 'I wouldn't ask if I had any other alternative. I can only appeal to your considerable compassion in the name of Christ. You may be entertaining angels unawares.'

No pressure there. That was an offer she couldn't refuse. And she had to admit that even a crowded Windy Corner would make the perfect refuge – a big, comfortable house designed for hospitality, relatively isolated, with no public or internet presence. She'd intended the home her aunt had bequeathed her to be a writers' retreat, but wasn't sheltering people in jeopardy an even more worthy use of her inheritance than hosting writers? Heaven knew the writers so far had not proved to be trouble-free.

'No rest for the wicked,' she muttered.

'What was that?'

'Oh, nothing. When should I expect them?'

'Tomorrow, if you can swing it.'

'Any idea how long they'll need to stay?'

'Not really. It all depends on how the adoption case goes.'

'I guess we'll roll with it, then. What are these people's names? And how old is the girl?'

'Moses Valory. It's his given name, but he also took Moses the Ethiopian as his patron when he was baptized last year. The girl is Charlotte.' Father Paul paused. 'I just realized I don't know her last name. Anyway, she's about fifteen, though she looks younger – little waif of a thing. Whereas Moses is practically a giant. He'll need your longest bed.'

All the beds were average length. Moses the Giant would simply have to cope.

'Anything else I should know? Food allergies or anything?'

'I have no idea. But there is one thing. Charlotte doesn't talk.'

'What, not at all? Is she deaf?'

'No, it's nothing like that. It's post-traumatic muteness. I'm sure there's some more technical name for it, but that's the gist of it. Moses will explain when they get there. I'll call him now and give him directions.'

Father Paul rang off. Emily turned to see Luke coming toward her with a questioning look. She answered it with a baffled one of her own.

'It seems we're going to have visitors. More visitors, that is.' She related the little Father Paul had told her about them.

Luke frowned. 'They're not running from the law, are they? You know I can't harbor fugitives in my home.'

Since their wedding, Luke had quickly become accustomed to thinking and speaking of Windy Corner as 'my home.' Technically, it was Emily's house, but in her mind, what was hers was his. She was happy he felt a sense of belonging here, even though he'd had little opportunity to put his stamp on the place.

'I certainly didn't get that impression. It sounds like they're being unfairly harassed. If anyone is outside the law, it's probably this social worker.'

'Hmph. We'll give them a chance, but if there's any whiff of wrongdoing . . .'

'I know. You can't be compromised.' Emily said a quick prayer that it wouldn't come to that. She took pride in her role as hostess, and having to throw out her new guests would certainly compromise that. Surely Father Paul would never put her in such a difficult position.

Emily took in a deep breath to steel herself and found that it brought an unexpected smell to her nostrils. 'Speaking of whiffs of wrongdoing . . . Is that . . .?'

Luke sniffed and narrowed his eyes. 'Weed. Sure is. It may be legal in the state now, but it's sure as heck not legal in this house.' He strode down the hall with a set to his shoulders that meant business.

Emily followed at a distance. His sharp knock at the Dickens room door was answered by a muted scuffle followed by Adrian's voice. 'What is it? We're getting ready for bed.'

'You're going to have to find a different sleep aid. We don't allow marijuana in this house.'

'Oops. Sorry.' Emily heard a feminine giggle in the background, and Adrian snorted as if stifling a laugh. 'It helps Raph get to sleep. But we'll put it out now.'

Emily and Luke exchanged a look of horror. 'You're not giving it to that child to smoke?' Luke said. ''Cause that would be actually illegal. And I do have the authority to arrest you.'

'Oh, no, he doesn't smoke it. He just likes the smell.'

Luke rolled his eyes. 'Well, we don't, so open the windows, will you?'

'Yes, boss.' More giggling, then the sound of old casements creaking open. Gradually the smell began to abate.

Emily retreated to the library, followed by Luke. She leaned into his embrace, feeling overwhelmed. 'What on earth have I gotten us into this time?'

The next morning, Adrian left for the church after breakfast, and Polly took Raphael down to the beach. Emily hoped they had plenty of sunscreen so they could stay out until lunchtime. Although she'd be more comfortable with them out of the house, she hated to think of the little boy burned red from head to toe and everything in between.

She assumed the new guests sent by Father Paul would leave Portland fairly early and arrive before lunchtime, so she planned accordingly. She kept an eye on Lizzie while Katie made up the rooms and started the lunch preparations. Katie had managed well when Lizzie was an infant, but now that she had reached the age of maximum mobility with minimum judgment, Katie found it difficult to accomplish much with her daughter underfoot. But Emily adored the child and was happy to help out.

The doorbell rang shortly after eleven. 'I'll get it,' Emily called to Katie in the kitchen. She scooped Lizzie up and went to the door.

To her surprise, Marguerite stood on the doorstep. '*Allo, chérie*,' she lilted. 'I decided to come early. You do not mind.' This was not said as a question.

Marguerite sailed in with a peck on each cheek for Emily and a smooch for Lizzie. She wasn't especially interested in children in general, but Lizzie's dimpled cheeks and ginger curls were irresistible.

'Look who I met in the drive,' she said, stepping back to wave two more visitors inside. 'Moses Valory and his daughter,

Mademoiselle Charlotte.' She gave Emily a quizzical look. 'You expect them, yes?' This was definitely a question.

'Yes. Father Paul called last night to ask if they could come.' She turned to the visitors. 'Welcome to Windy Corner.'

Although Father Paul had warned her of Moses' unusual size, Emily blinked to hide her astonishment. He must be at least six-seven, black, with massive shoulders that appeared to be all muscle under his light jacket. His clipped iron-gray hair and careworn face suggested he was at least sixty – probably older – but he exuded a feeling of contained power suggestive of a much younger man. Not threatening power, though; his expression was among the gentlest Emily had ever seen, and his voice when he greeted her was soft and low. She thought he had chosen his patron saint well – St Moses the Ethiopian had been a man of extraordinary strength who ultimately chose a life of humble repentance.

'Thank you kindly for having us, ma'am,' he said. 'We were up a creek without a paddle.'

She shook his hand, which was roughly the size of a dinner plate, but he was careful not to crush hers in his grip. 'You're very welcome. I'm happy to be of use,' she replied. She turned to the girl hiding, almost cowering, behind him, and put on her friendliest smile. 'Welcome, Charlotte. I hope you'll treat Windy Corner as your home for as long as you need to be here.'

The girl sidled partway out of her guardian's shadow. She was small and slight, so much so that Emily might have taken her for twelve or thirteen if not for the depth of hurt in her huge, startlingly blue eyes. Her eyes dominated her pale face so that her other features faded into insignificance. White-blonde hair fell in a long braid over her shoulder with wisps flying out around her face and down the braid's length to its straggly end. Her gray T-shirt and jeans were clean but generic and baggy on her fragile form.

Emily extended her hand, but Charlotte retreated again with a tiny shake of the head. The slightest suggestion of a smile indicated she didn't mean to be rude but was simply averse to physical contact with strangers. But then Lizzie smiled at her, and Charlotte's smile spread across her face. She wiggled her fingers in a wave.

Moses waited till this interaction had finished to say, 'I hope we won't have to trespass on your hospitality for long. I'm making arrangements to adopt Charlotte and take her out of state, but Janine is throwing up obstacles as fast as my lawyer can shoot 'em down.'

'Janine is the social worker Father Paul mentioned?'

He nodded. 'The fox in our henhouse. I can't keep her out.'

Emily winced in sympathy. 'I'd like to hear more, but you don't need to tell me your life story standing in the doorway. Bring your things and I'll show you to your rooms.'

Moses hefted a bag over each shoulder and another in each hand without seeming to notice their weight. Emily handed Lizzie off to Marguerite and led the way upstairs to the two rooms that faced the drive. 'Charlotte, this will be your room,' she said, opening the door to the Montgomery room. Charlotte crept out from behind Moses to look in at the quilt-topped white wrought-iron bed, braided rag rug, delicate writing desk, and the semicircle of windows overlooking the sea. Her eyes went even rounder, and she turned to Emily with a face full of wonder, as if to say, *Really? All this for me?*

Emily smiled. 'It's all yours. Please, unpack and make yourself comfortable.' She gestured to the pale-yellow dresser and wardrobe standing against the unbroken wall. 'The bathroom is at the other end of the hall. The toilets and shower are in separate rooms, and there's a lovely big tub if you'd like a soak.' Charlotte answered with a tiny smile.

Moses put two of the bags in the Montgomery room. Emily indicated the door next to it. 'This will be your room.'

He entered and took in the furnishings with a glance that registered the location of the furniture but probably nothing of its appearance. Just as well, since the dark, heavy Victorian pieces with their maroon velvet hangings appealed more to a Goth sensibility; most people would find them depressing.

'Come down to the library when you're ready,' Emily said. 'Katie will have some coffee for you. Oh, and I should warn you – we have some other guests. They're only here for a couple of days, until their cottage comes free.'

Moses' brows rose in alarm. 'May I ask who they are?'

Emily understood this was not nosiness but necessary caution in his circumstances. 'A young family, Adrian and Polly Hughes and their son, Raphael. Adrian is repairing a stained-glass window at the church.'

Moses' alarm subsided but did not disappear. Hopefully, meeting the Hughes family would dispel any fears he might have for Charlotte's safety, though he might share Emily's concerns about them in other respects.

Emily joined Marguerite in the library, where she and Lizzie were entertaining the three cats with catnip mice she had brought them. Cats were Marguerite's greatest and most enduring love; Emily came second, with a long succession of lovers trailing far behind.

To be precise, Levin and Kitty, Emily's matched grays, were being entertained. Bustopher Jones, the feline patriarch she had inherited with the house, opened one eye and sniffed, then went back to sleep. Sleeping was what he mostly did these days. Emily didn't know how old he was, but somewhere north of fifteen was a safe guess.

'Do you want to settle in before lunch?' she asked Marguerite.

Her friend waved a hand. 'That can wait until Katie has time to bring in my bags.' Marguerite was a strong and independent woman in most ways but quite continentally feminine. She expected service, and she got it.

Emily sank into her favorite chair. Marguerite got up from the hearth and sat in Luke's chair opposite. 'And now you will tell me who these people are and why they are here. Especially at this soon-to-be-so-busy time.'

'Honestly, I hardly know myself. Father Paul only said they were being harassed by a social worker for no good reason and needed to get out of town. And I was his only option.'

'What is their connection? They do not seem to be blood relations.'

'He's her guardian, apparently. I don't know the situation. I only know Charlotte doesn't talk due to some sort of trauma in her past. I suppose if she's lost her parents, that could be trauma enough. And Moses looks like a man who's seen hard times, for sure.' Emily sighed. 'They wring the heart, those two, just to look at them.'

Marguerite shrugged. '*Tout le monde* has problems. Theirs may be no worse than most.'

Emily doubted that, but there was no point in arguing with

Marguerite. She saved her compassion for those close to her. 'I'll ask Moses to tell us their story over lunch. Luke can come home so he'll only have to tell it once.'

She texted Luke – a skill she had learned only recently, since he had returned to work and was often not able to take a voice call. Then she glanced out the window and saw Polly coming across the lawn with Raphael, in his natural state.

'I have some other guests here as well, and it looks like they're on their way back to the house.' Quickly she filled Marguerite in on the situation with the church and the Hughes family.

'*Mon dieu!*' Marguerite threw up her hands. 'Are you now running a hotel?'

'It's starting to feel that way.' She heard heavy footsteps on the stairs at the same time as the front door creaked open. She hurried to the hall to make introductions, as each party had the potential to startle the other.

But when she glanced from Polly, just inside the door, to Moses on the bottom step, she saw something she wasn't expecting – a glimmer of recognition in both faces.

'Hey, didn't we run into each other at the Happy Home office?' Polly said in a friendly tone.

Moses nodded solemnly. 'We did indeed.'

Polly shifted Raphael's hand from her right to her left and held out her right hand to Moses. 'Polly Hughes. This is my son, Raphael.'

Moses hesitated before taking her hand and responding, 'Moses Valory. This is my daughter, Charlotte.' He gestured toward the girl sheltering behind him on the stairs.

He mustered a smile for Polly. 'So you were successful.' He nodded toward Raphael.

'Ultimately, yes. No thanks to Janine Vertue.'

Emily's mind reeled. Two groups of people had come to her house from diverse sources and for unrelated reasons, and both of them had dealings with the same obscure social worker? But she should know by now that nothing happened randomly in her life. This coincidence must have a purpose, though at this point God alone knew what it was.

Polly turned to Emily. 'We adopted Raphael a few months ago, and Janine Vertue tried to stop it. She gave us a bad home review. But we managed to get a second review that approved us.'

Emily told herself severely to withhold judgment, even though her first impulse was to think that, in their case, Janine had been in the right.

'Lunch will be ready soon. Shall we wait in the library? Polly, you and Raphael may want to clean up a bit first.' The two of them were covered in sand.

'Sure thing,' Polly said. 'Come on, buddy, we don't want to get sand all over the nice lady's house.' She picked the boy up and carried him toward the bathroom.

Emily led the way to the library. Moses had to duck as he entered to avoid banging his head on the lintel. Charlotte slipped in silently after him. Moses looked around as if unsure whether any of the seating options would hold his weight. Marguerite tactfully moved back to the hearth, and Emily waved him to Luke's chair. He must have fifty pounds on Luke, but she thought the chair was sturdy enough to take them.

Charlotte spotted the cats and gave a little gasp of delight. She made a beeline for the hearth and crouched between Lizzie and Marguerite. Marguerite offered one of the catnip mice she'd brought for Charlotte to dangle before the wildly pouncing Kitty and Levin. But Charlotte preferred to pet the recumbent Bustopher instead. He wasn't the friendliest of cats, but he submitted to her ministrations and even began to purr.

'I see Charlotte and Marguerite have one thing in common,' Emily said in a low voice to Moses. 'They both love cats. And cats love them.'

Moses smiled sadly. 'Yes, ma'am, Charlotte takes to animals like a duck to water. It's only people she's shy of.'

Emily hesitated. 'I'd love to hear your story – as much as you're willing to tell – but my husband's coming home for lunch, and I'm sure he'd like to hear it too. I don't know if you want to tell it in front of Adrian and Polly, though.'

Moses sighed. 'It won't come as any big surprise to them, given what they've been through. And you have a right to know who you've taken under your roof.'

FOUR

L uke got home just as Katie rang the gong for lunch. He greeted Emily in the hall with a quick kiss. 'Sorry for cutting it fine. Couldn't be helped.' Stony Beach presented fewer challenges to a lawman than most places, but even so, Emily knew that unpredictable hours went with the territory.

'They're in the dining room. Come in and I'll introduce you.'

The others were already seated, but Moses stood as Luke came in. Emily saw her husband's eyes widen. Luke was six-two and solidly built; it wasn't often he met a man who dwarfed him. Moses, for his part, practically quailed at the sight of Luke's uniform. Apparently, Father Paul had not mentioned to Moses that he'd be staying in the home of a lawman. Emily hoped this wasn't an indication he had anything to fear from the law.

Katie served a welcome-to-the-coast meal of seafood stew, salad, and fresh sourdough bread. Emily noted gratefully that she had avoided serving anything that would require sharp knives. But hot stew presented problems of its own. Adrian had returned for lunch, and it took both parents to keep Raphael from tipping Polly's steaming bowl into her lap. They seemed too preoccupied to be curious as to why Moses and Charlotte were there, which was perhaps just as well.

Charlotte watched them, fascinated, as she picked at the salad and bread. Moses, on the other hand, ate half the round loaf and bowl after bowl of stew, only pausing to be sure everyone else had enough.

Emily felt compelled to create some kind of conversation, so in a lull of toddler-wrangling she asked Adrian, 'What do you think of the window, now you've had a chance to evaluate the damage?'

He shrugged, his mouth full of bread. After chewing for a bit, he said, 'It's pretty extensive, but I don't think it will be too difficult to fix. The hardest part will be matching the glass. The older the glass is, the harder it is to find the same colors and texture. Father Stephen has good close-up photographs of what it's supposed to look like, so that helps.'

'Any idea yet how long it might take? I don't know if Father Stephen told you, but we're hoping it will be done in time for my brother's wedding on the thirtieth.'

Adrian whistled. 'That's what, two weeks?' He took a bite of stew and chewed meditatively. 'Could be a close thing. But I'll do my best.'

Emily could only hope he was more organized and diligent at his job than he appeared to be in his personal life. It wasn't unlikely; she knew other artists who saved all their focus for their work.

After Moses had eaten the stew tureen dry, Katie brought in coffee and a bowl of mixed saltwater taffy for dessert. Raphael grabbed a handful of taffy, and the young family excused themselves. Emily was relieved to have some privacy for the necessary conversation with Moses.

'Are you ready to tell us your story, Moses?' she asked, forestalling Luke, who had opened his mouth presumably to ask the same question. Questions from Luke to a stranger – especially when he was in uniform – tended to sound like formal police interviews, and she certainly didn't want Moses to feel he was under interrogation. Even though, in a sense, he was.

Moses nodded, wiping his mouth, then took a long drink of coffee and plunged in. 'I run a shelter-slash-workshop in Portland for women who need a hand up in the world. Maybe they've been in prison, maybe they're tryin' to escape drugs or a pimp or an abusive relationship, maybe they're just down on their luck. We don't ask questions. We give them a room, childcare if they need it, and a job to do, so they can save up for a new start.'

He paused for a sip of coffee, and Marguerite put in skeptically, 'Are not such shelters usually run by women?'

Moses nodded. 'They surely are, ma'am, and mine is too – I'm offsite most all the time. I misspoke – I should've said I *founded* it. Anyway, a couple years ago, a woman named Faye came to us with her little girl. They were runnin' from a guy she was mixed up with who was violent to Faye. And to Charlotte . . .' He closed his eyes and took a breath. 'Well, I don't want to say what he did. But it started when she was 'round about six years old.' He cut his eyes toward Charlotte, who was busy selecting taffy flavors from the bowl. 'Suffice to say, he was the reason she stopped speaking.'

Emily took a shuddering breath. That poor girl. All the tender compassion in the world might not be enough to undo the hideous work of such a man. She glanced at Luke, whose face was white, his jaw tight. Whoever that man was, he should be thankful he wasn't in the room with Luke at this moment. A glance at Moses told her he had noticed Luke's reaction as well. His tense shoulders relaxed a tiny fraction.

'What happened? Where is Faye now?' she asked.

Moses glanced at Charlotte again. 'She died a few months ago. Cancer. She had no family, nobody in the wide world she could trust but me. She asked me to take care of Charlotte.' He heaved a deep sigh. 'Naturally, I agreed. I already loved her like my own. I started the adoption process, and that's when Janine Vertue walked into our lives. That damn boyfriend of Faye's hired her to do a home study 'cause he wanted to adopt Charlotte himself. She took one look at my girl and knew right away she'd been abused. Then she took one look at me and made up her mind I was the one who'd done it.'

Everyone at the table took in a sharp breath – except Charlotte, who was chewing taffy with closed eyes and a blissful smile.

'Couldn't you set her right?' Luke asked. 'You knew who the real perp was.'

Moses' nostrils flared, the first sign of anger Emily had seen him display. 'Well, sir, he's a plausible bas— character. Plus, he's white. He wrapped Janine 'round his little finger in no time flat and convinced her I was the villain before she ever laid eyes on me. Said I'd stolen Faye from him just so's I could get at the child. And Charlotte couldn't speak up to set her right.' His fists clenched on the tablecloth, then relaxed. 'Thank God, Janine couldn't get any actual evidence, since it was all a pack o' lies. Faye had made me legal guardian, so Janine couldn't justify taking Charlotte away from me, but she's done everything she could to block the adoption. And she stalks us, day and night, trying to catch me in some fiendish act.'

He stretched his arms out, pushing against the table, and the sleeves of his chambray work shirt rode up to reveal what Emily thought at first was a watch. Then she looked closer and saw it was a tattoo of a watch with no hands.

She was confused until Luke said quietly, 'No doubt she used the fact you've been inside against you. That alone could make it pretty hard to adopt.'

Moses stood abruptly, pulling down his sleeve. 'I should've known I couldn't keep it hidden. But I didn't know I was comin' to a lawman's house.' He turned to Emily. 'Thank you kindly for your hospitality, ma'am. I guess Charlotte and I will be on our way.'

'But why?' Emily was dumbfounded. 'Have we offended you in some way? Or is it the Hugheses? They won't be here long. We certainly haven't asked you to leave.'

'I didn't give you a chance, but you were going to. Weren't you?' He directed the question at Luke.

Luke stood to face him. 'Mr Valory, in my town we don't judge a man for what's happened in his past. And we sure as heck don't judge him by the color of his skin. Unless you are currently a fugitive from justice, you are welcome in my home.' They locked eyes until Moses blinked and hung his head. 'Now please sit down.'

Moses sank back into his chair. 'I beg your pardon, sir, ma'am. I'm a law-abiding man, have been for donkey's years, but I still run into white policemen who are ready to assume the worst based purely on the way I look.'

'That's understandable,' Luke said. 'I know there's a shameful lot of racism in law enforcement still. But you won't find it in my town.'

Moses nodded his thanks.

'Now, if you feel comfortable telling us, we would like to hear what happened . . . donkey's years ago.'

'Yessir. You've earned that.' He scrubbed his hands over his face. 'It was only a misdemeanor – petty larceny – but it happened in Mississippi, and they slapped on extra charges and put me away for twenty years.' He shook his head. 'I was only a kid, eighteen years old. I stole a chicken to feed my little sisters. But I stole it from a white man, and I got twenty years. And I served every last minute.'

He turned to Luke with a pleading expression. 'Ever since

then, I've been as clean as new snow. Somebody was good to me when I got out, gave me a new start, and I swore I'd spend my life trying to pass that on. I got out of the South, made a little money, founded the shelter. But all that don't count for chicken-shit when a black ex-con wants to adopt a white girl.' Tears came to his eyes as he said, 'All I care about now is to honor my promise to Faye to keep her little girl safe, and make sure she has some kind o' decent life after I'm gone. But it looks like the world's not gonna let me do that.'

After lunch, Emily pulled Luke aside. 'I'm convinced Moses is on the level. Are you?'

'I'm inclined that way, but I want to check him out. I'll run him through the system when I get back to the office. You think he's always had the same name?'

'Father Paul said Moses was his given name as well as his baptismal name, so at least it hasn't changed for that reason. He seems like a straight-up kind of guy to me.'

Luke nodded. 'Let's hope so.' He gave her a kiss. 'See you tonight.'

That afternoon, Emily decided she'd given Mayor Babcock plenty of time to tally the proceeds from Pirate Days. Any delay and he might start to get creative with his accounting. Unwilling to leave all her oddly assorted guests alone in the house, she called him at his office.

'So, Homer, how did we do?'

His voice came back with what Emily suspected was a forced heartiness. 'Made your ten thousand with a few dollars to spare.'

'Excellent! Have you made arrangements to turn it over to the church restoration fund?'

He cleared his throat. 'I was just about to do that. This afternoon.'

Emily wondered how long he would have dawdled if she hadn't called. 'Good. I'll let Father Stephen know to expect it.' That should keep Babcock true to his word.

Next she called Father Stephen and gave him the news. His sigh of relief was audible over the phone.

'Oh, Emily, I can't tell you how glad I am to hear that! That should be enough of a deposit to allow the builders to go on with the roof.'

'Don't forget we also need to do something about the floor before the thirtieth.'

'I won't. But if we don't get the roof secure, another storm could damage the flooring all over again.'

'True.' Emily did some quick mental calculations. 'I can get you another installment at the end of the month when my July rents come through. Then we can figure out some way to cover the rest.'

And meanwhile, pray for a miracle.

When Luke came home at the end of the day, he found Emily alone in the library. He sank into his chair with the grunt of one who's beginning to feel his age. 'He checks out,' he said. 'Moses Valory, all the way back to his birth certificate. Put away, like he said, on what looks like trumped-up charges – resisting arrest, assaulting a police officer, loitering, threatening behavior, you name it, all tacked on to the original petty larceny charge. Served twenty years – no time off for good behavior, though I'd be willing to bet he deserved it.' He ran a hand over his cropped gray hair. 'Nothing on him since then. Not so much as a parking ticket. Just like he said, clean as new snow.' He grinned at Emily. 'You've got a one-hundred-percent verified innocent victim on your hands.'

'On *our* hands, I hope you mean,' she replied. 'I'm going to need your help if the social worker finds them and it all hits the fan.'

'You know it, beautiful. I'll be there for you and for them.'

The presence of Moses and Charlotte seemed to have a subduing effect on the Hughes free spirits, and the household made it through to Friday with only minor damage caused by Hurricane Raphael. Emily began to breathe more freely in anticipation of clearer weather to come.

But late Friday morning, Emily got a call from Justine, her property manager. 'Bad news, I'm afraid,' she said. 'The cottage that was supposed to be ready this afternoon? Something's gone wrong with the plumbing. I've called every plumber in town, but nobody can get there till Monday.'

Emily's stomach sank to her toes. A whole weekend with the Hughes family – and Oscar and Lauren would be arriving on Sunday. 'How bad is it? Will Monday be enough?'

'There's no water to the kitchen at all. From my limited knowledge of plumbing, I'd guess that could mean anything from turning a valve to a whole-house overhaul.'

'And there's nothing else available?'

'There is another place due to be vacated Monday morning. So no matter what, you'll only have to get through the weekend.'

Emily blew out a heavy breath. 'OK. Go ahead and book the Hughes family into that second cottage just in case. And keep me posted.' If the plumbing problem proved to be on the larger end of Justine's spectrum, that could eat a large chunk out of Emily's profits for the month and hence out of what she would have available to contribute to the church repairs.

Adrian was working at the church, so when Polly and Raphael came back from their wanderings for lunch, Emily broke the news. Polly looked slightly pained, presumably because she'd been looking forward to the greater freedom they would have on their own in a cottage. Though Luke had already made it very clear that freedom would not extend to smoking of *any* kind indoors.

Moses and Charlotte had spent most of their time at Windy Corner so far secluded in their rooms – presumably to give Charlotte a chance to acclimatize – but now they ventured downstairs. The Hugheses kept to themselves except for meals, and Friday afternoon and evening passed pleasantly enough, with Charlotte still nervous around the adults but entranced by Lizzie and the cats. Moses surprised Emily and Marguerite by suggesting a game of Scrabble – which he won.

Emily began to think this situation might work out reasonably well – although there was still the wedding to add into the mix. Oscar and Lauren were due on Sunday afternoon, and then she suspected chaos would once again reign – though from Monday on it should be a more adult, more controlled, better-smelling chaos than before.

FIVE

Saturday was Luke's usual day off provided nothing extraordinary came up. Lately, he'd been using his free time to fix up the former Dostoevsky room as his own den – or man-cave, as he would have liked to call it, but Emily wouldn't hear of it. 'There are no caves in my house, thank you very much,' she said. 'It's your room – you may use it as you like and call it what you like, as long as that doesn't include the word *cave*.'

'You've been calling it a den. A den and a cave are pretty much the same thing, at least potentially. Both places an animal might live.'

Emily was caught off guard, but only temporarily. 'I married a man, not an animal. I hope. How about we call it your hideaway? That's essentially what it's for – you hiding out from my feminine rooms and bookish guests.' She softened that with a kiss. The fundamental differences between them might cause the odd bit of friction, but they were a big part of what had attracted them to each other in the first place.

So it was decided. The room was Luke's hideaway, and he was redoing it to hold his beloved seventy-two-inch TV, antique gun collection, and leather-working tools and supplies. This didn't require major structural work, but it did entail building some custom storage. And that meant noise.

'I'm not sure how well Charlotte could stand my construction noise,' he said to Emily as they finished breakfast. 'She's so fragile, seems like all that banging and sawing might get on her nerves.'

Moses turned from the sideboard, where he was replenishing his coffee. 'You got some kinda project going on?'

'Yeah, building some shelves and stuff in the back room on the second floor. You think it'll bother Charlotte too much? I can always do it another time.'

'Nah, we don't want to put you out. She can hang out down

here with the cats and the baby, and she'll be happy as a clam. Matter of fact, I wouldn't mind helping you, if you could use an extra pair of hands. I get fidgety if I don't have something physical to do.'

'It's a deal,' Luke said. 'Work always goes better with two.'

Luke had already prepared the boards for the shelving in his improvised garage workshop. They were cut and sanded, ready for mounting. But some of them were six feet long, and Luke was glad to have another man to hold one end. First, however, the curved wooden brackets needed to be mounted. Getting those exactly level across such a distance was a challenge in itself.

Luke took a finish hammer and tapped across the back wall, listening for the studs and marking them as he came to them. Then he handed a bracket to Moses along with one end of the longest level he could find.

'I want these about three feet up,' he said. 'I've got that marked, but in an old house like this, you can't be sure the floor isn't warped, so we'll have to level each bracket.'

Moses nodded in understanding and placed his bracket at the far set of markings.

'You done this kind of work before?' Luke asked.

'Oh, yeah. Learned carpentry inside. Became a builder when I got out. Worked up to running my own company.'

'In that case, you'll be telling me how to do things right. I'm just a weekend warrior.' Luke placed his bracket and said, 'OK, let's fasten these down.' They pulled out their screwdrivers and screwed in unison, leaving some play in case of adjustments. Luke laid a shelf temporarily across the two brackets and set a pen on it to see if it would roll.

'Looks good,' Moses said. 'We can tighten these up.'

'You build that women's shelter yourself?' Luke asked.

'Sure did. Not *all* by myself, o' course – it's a good-sized place – but my company did it, and I was hands-on all the way.' He finished screwing in his bracket and reached for another one. 'That was a while ago, though. These days, I mostly do management and let the younger guys take the load.' He shot Luke a grin. 'You ever do anything besides law enforcement?'

'Did a stint in the army, right out of high school. Then got trained and started working as a deputy. All I ever wanted to do, really. Keeping people safe.'

'It's an honorable occupation, sir. I just wish more of your kind took it seriously. Lot of them seem to want to keep *themselves* safe and to hell with everybody else.'

'Unfortunately true. But I like to think the honest ones will act like the leaven in the lump, and one day we'll turn the balance.'

Moses nodded as he leveled his second bracket. 'I surely hope to live to see that day.'

Emily was grateful the two men were working together. It should serve to dispel any lingering doubts Moses might have about Luke's intentions toward him. After the men disappeared upstairs, Emily went to join Charlotte and Marguerite in the library. Marguerite was reading some ponderous tome – Victor Hugo's *Nôtre-Dame de Paris*, it looked like – and Charlotte, as predicted, was playing happily with Lizzie and the cats. Emily sat in her accustomed chair and picked up her knitting. After spending several months making gifts for all and sundry, she was working on a fall sweater for herself – her own design in graduated shades of brown, with a different stitch pattern for each color.

Charlotte glanced in her direction several times, each glance lingering longer than the last. Finally, she got up and shyly approached Emily's chair, eyes fastened on her flying fingers.

'Do you want to see what I'm doing?' Emily asked, turning her work so the girl could see it more clearly. 'I'm knitting. Making a sweater.' Charlotte's fragility and lack of speech made her seem so much younger than she was that Emily had to resist the impulse to talk to her as she would to Lizzie.

Charlotte put out a tentative hand to stroke the soft yarn – a scrumptious blend of wool, cashmere, and silk. She smiled and stroked again, then mimed an approximation of the motions she'd seen Emily make.

'Would you like to learn how to do this?' Charlotte nodded enthusiastically. 'I'd be happy to teach you. Let me go get some different needles and yarn. I'll be right back.'

Most of her supplies were in her third-floor sitting room. Emily trudged up the stairs and sorted through her leftovers for a heavier-weight yarn that would be easier to learn on. She preferred lighter weights and smaller needles for herself, but she had some cream-colored worsted she'd used for Luke's wedding gift – an authentic Aran fisherman's sweater. It wasn't as soft as what she was working with now, but combined with size eight needles it would make a good learning sample.

She returned to the library and sat on the loveseat, where Charlotte could sit next to her. She cast on a few dozen stitches in the worsted yarn, then handed the needles and yarn to Charlotte and took up her own, showing the girl how to hold everything to throw in the English style. 'Knitting is based on two kinds of stitches – the knit stitch and the purl stitch. Let's start with the knit stitch. We can break each one down into four mini-steps. Like this.' She resisted the urge to use the mystery writer's mnemonic she'd learned from a previous retreat guest: 'Stab it, strangle it, hang it, throw it off the cliff.' Charlotte didn't need any reminders of violence in her new hobby. Instead Emily went with the traditional rhyme:

In through the front door – (insert the point of the right needle through the front of the stitch).

Once around the back – (loop the working yarn around the needle).

Peek through the window – (pull the needle with the yarn around it out through the original stitch).

And off jumps Jack! – (slide the old stitch off the left needle).

Charlotte followed Emily's movements closely and picked up the rhythm with remarkable speed and accuracy. They worked together for several happy hours, at the end of which Charlotte had created a fairly neat garter-stitch square. Lunchtime was approaching, and Emily needed a break from sitting in one position, though Charlotte's attention and energy had not flagged.

'Would you like to continue this and make a scarf?' Emily asked her pupil. 'Or I could teach you to purl and you could try something different.' Charlotte nodded eagerly. With a wistful look she reached over to stroke Emily's sweater-in-progress again. 'I know – how about we get you some yarn and needles of your very own? You can pick out the color and fiber you like best, and we can find a simple pattern for you to start on.'

Charlotte clapped her hands, then suddenly leaned over and kissed Emily's cheek. Immediately she pulled back into herself, sheltering in the fetal position as if frightened by what she had done.

Emily's eyes welled as an unexpected tenderness flooded through her. She lightly touched Charlotte's shoulder and smiled. 'It's all right,' she said. 'We're friends now.' Charlotte relaxed a fraction and gave her a tiny nod.

'This afternoon, we'll go see my friend Beanie at the yarn shop. You'll love her.' Emily hoped that was true – Beanie could be a bit of an acquired taste, but Emily had an instinct that there was something in her Charlotte would respond to. And it certainly couldn't hurt the girl to have a friend nearer her own age.

After lunch, Emily drove Charlotte to downtown Stony Beach, a mile or so south from Windy Corner. 'Downtown' was rather a glorified term for the three blocks of businesses lining the highway, but it had to be called something. Since this was a Saturday at the height of tourist season, they had to park on a back street instead of right in front of the store.

The shop's front window held an ever-changing display that reflected the character of the coming season instead of the current one, since many people didn't knit fast enough to keep up with the change of weather. For July, Beanie had created a spindly tree with skeins of various mouthwatering autumn-colored yarns hanging from it like falling leaves. Underneath, miniature sweaters with pumpkin and apple designs adorned doll-sized scarecrows, while an elaborate lace shawl in shifting tones of gold, orange, and rust formed a backdrop. Arching over the display was the name of the shop, Sheep to Knits.

Charlotte stood transfixed in front of the window until Emily grew impatient. 'There's lots more inside,' she said, leading the girl in.

'Hey, Emily!' called a voice from behind the counter. 'Long time no see!'

The voice belonged to a young woman with spiky black hair and numerous tattoos and piercings. She was clad in a black tank top and leggings, over which looped and spiraled an immeasurably long swath of knitting composed of multicolored swatches in widely varying colors and stitch patterns made of every yarn Beanie had ever sold. The end swatch – elaborate cables in a bulky forest-green wool – was growing under her needles as they spoke.

'I brought a new friend to meet you,' Emily replied. 'Her name is Charlotte, and she doesn't speak. She's just learning to knit, but she's picking it up super-fast. I want her to find some yarn and a pattern to make something she'll love.'

Beanie slid her work back from her needle tips and tucked the end into the front of her eccentric garment. 'Hey, Charlotte. Let's see what we can find for you.' She looked the girl in the eyes for a moment, then gave Emily a nod that spoke understanding. 'I bet you'd look terrific in this mauve.' She led Charlotte to a table piled with balls of an alpaca-cashmere blend that gave a whole new meaning to the word *soft*. She held a couple of balls under Charlotte's chin and turned her to face the mirror. The color did indeed light up the girl's face.

Charlotte stroked the yarn with rapture, then turned to another table. Apparently she wanted to see all her options before making her choice. Emily approved.

While she was browsing, Beanie asked in a low voice, 'What's her story?'

Emily hesitated only a little before answering. She knew Beanie's interest arose from compassion rather than mere curiosity. 'She's an orphan. She was abused by her mother's boyfriend for years. Her mother's dead now, and a good man wants to adopt her, but the system's getting in the way.'

Beanie's eyes narrowed. 'I know all about the *system*.' To Emily's questioning look she replied, 'I was in foster care for most of my childhood. *Been there, done that* doesn't begin to cover it.' She walked over to the rack of patterns Charlotte was now perusing, pulling out one, then another that were all far too advanced for a raw beginner.

'How about this shawl?' Beanie said. 'It's not too hard, but it's super pretty with these colors fading into each other. Do you like that look?'

Charlotte's eyes lit up. She took the leaflet and held it to her chest, then looked around at all the yarn.

'I know what would be perfect for this,' Beanie said, leading her to a wall that held hanks of speckled and variegated hand-dyed yarns. Together they picked out three skeins in tones that covered the gamut from pale blue to deep violet. Charlotte hugged them all close and came up to Emily with an expression like a puppy asking for a treat.

'Those look lovely,' she said. 'I'll be happy to buy them for you.' She took it for granted that Charlotte would have no money of her own – not because Moses would be stingy with her, but because she might not know how to handle it. She probably never went shopping – or anywhere, for that matter – by herself.

Emily added a set of needles in different sizes and a kit with some basic tools, so that Charlotte would be equipped to continue on her own once she and Moses had settled elsewhere. The total came to well over two hundred dollars, but Charlotte's beaming face was all the thanks she needed.

Seeing that Charlotte responded well to Beanie, Emily followed an impulse. 'Why don't you and Ben come over to dinner one night next week?' she asked the shop owner. Then she had a momentary qualm. 'You are still together, aren't you?'

Beanie laughed. 'Oh, yeah, me and Ben are tight. Don't tell him I said so, but I think he's *The One*.' The two made something of an odd couple – Ben, the studious, straitlaced, classics-loving bookstore owner and free-spirited Beanie, who wrote vampire and zombie fiction in her winter spare time – but they seemed to complement each other rather than clashing. Like Emily and Luke. 'Monday OK? That's our closing day.'

'Perfect. Oscar and Lauren will be here by then – they're getting ready for their wedding on the thirtieth – and Marguerite's here already, so we'll have a full table.' And, Lord willing, the Hugheses would be gone.

'What a merry party we shall be!' Beanie quoted with another laugh. Jane Austen was the one author they agreed to love – though Beanie also enjoyed her *Pride and Prejudice* with zombies.

Beanie started to load all the purchases into a plastic bag, then stopped, looking Charlotte in the eye. 'You need a real knitting bag of your own.' She led Charlotte to a rack of patchwork bags, each one unique and beautiful. 'Pick one. It's on me.'

Charlotte's mouth made a perfect O as she looked her thanks at Beanie, then went through all the bags on the rack. At last, she chose one in tones of pink, blue, and purple that featured flowers and butterflies among its prints.

Emily said sotto voce, 'Beanie, are you sure you can afford to do this? Let me at least pay cost.'

Beanie shook her head firmly. 'I made those bags myself. I can afford to give one away. And I can't imagine a more worthy recipient.' She helped Charlotte stow her new tools and yarn in the various custom pockets and compartments inside the bag.

Charlotte fairly danced out of the store and back to the car, swinging her patchwork bag full of goodies. What a lonely, deprived life she must have led up to now, despite Moses' best efforts. There was only so much an older male guardian could give to a growing girl.

While they were in town, Emily thought she might check on Adrian's progress with the window. 'Do you mind if we swing by the church for a minute?' she asked Charlotte. 'You can stay in the car if you want to.'

Charlotte looked apprehensive but nodded, so Emily turned up the hill. As they approached the church, she could see Polly and bare-bottomed Raphael playing on the lawn near the apse. There was no scaffolding at this end of the building – it was all inside so Adrian could work on the window from there – but Emily couldn't help worrying about falling roof tiles and other hazards to unprotected people on the ground. She debated saying something to Polly but decided her duty of care did not extend that far, and Polly would be unlikely to listen to her, anyway.

But Charlotte had spotted them too, and when Emily parked, she looked eager to join them. Emily put a hand on her arm before she could get out of the car. 'Be careful, Charlotte. If you're going to stay outside, don't get too close to the building. It's not safe with the men working on the roof.'

Charlotte nodded, though Emily couldn't be sure she understood the danger; the hazards she'd learned to be wary of came from the deliberate actions of men, not from accidents. Emily crossed herself, committing the girl to God's care, and went inside to talk to Adrian.

He stood high on the scaffolding, and Emily couldn't see clearly what he was doing. She didn't want to startle him, so she sat in a front pew and waited until he stepped back a pace from the window. 'Hello,' she called. 'How's it going?'

Adrian turned and looked around the nave before he spotted her. 'Oh, hi, Emily. I'm still in the prep stages – removing broken panes, measuring and tracing the spaces that need to be filled in. I have to say, it's an honor to be working on such a masterful piece. I hope I can do it justice.'

Emily was more encouraged by his self-doubt than she would have been by over-confidence. 'I just want to say, although you know how much I hope this can be finished for my brother's wedding, it's more important that it be done carefully and well. I wouldn't want you to think I was trying to rush you.'

'No fear. I wouldn't let you rush me. If I take on a job, it's going to be done right, however long it takes.'

Emily was relieved to learn that Adrian's casual attitude toward life and parenting did not extend to his work. 'Good. Is there anything I can do to facilitate?'

'Not at this stage, but thanks. I'll let you know.'

She left the nave and went around the building to collect Charlotte. The girl was sitting in the grass a good twenty feet from the building, collecting tiny white wildflowers and weaving them into a chain. When she saw Emily, she leaped up and ran to hang her completed chain around Emily's neck.

Emily felt tears start to well in her eyes. She was beginning to understand why Moses was so devoted to this girl. 'Thank you, Charlotte. That's so sweet. Are you ready to go, or would you like to make one for yourself as well?'

Charlotte dropped her eyes with a little smile and shook her head, then skipped off toward the car. Emily wished she could keep the flower chain forever, but she knew it would wilt before the day was out. It was as fragile as the girl who'd woven it.

SIX

S unday dawned to a settled rain that lasted all day. Adrian couldn't work since the church was in use for services, and Raphael seemed to find Emily's spacious mansion too small to contain his two-year-old energy. By mid-morning, both his parents looked frazzled from chasing him around the house trying to prevent him from breaking anything. Katie kindly – and bravely – stepped in and invited them to bring the boy to her apartment over the garage to play with Lizzie for a while.

Luke and Moses continued their work on Luke's hideaway. Marguerite seemed content to remain immersed in *Nôtre-Dame de Paris* while Emily taught Charlotte how to cast on, do the purl stitch, increase and decrease, and work the simple lace pattern included in her shawl design. Charlotte picked up each new skill as if she had instinctively known how to knit all her life and had only been waiting for needles and yarn.

In the early evening, while the others were resting or cleaning up for dinner, Oscar and Lauren arrived and joined Emily in the library. 'So what's happening here?' Oscar asked after their initial greetings. 'I saw some unfamiliar cars in the driveway on the way in. Don't tell me you have other guests besides all of us wedding people.'

Emily blew out a breath. 'I'm afraid we do have some unexpected guests, yes.' She wasn't quite ready to break the news of the church damage to Oscar, so she started with Moses and Charlotte. 'Father Paul asked me to take in a foster father and daughter who are sort of seeking sanctuary from an overzealous social worker. Marguerite's here already too, so we have nearly a full house.'

At Oscar's worried look, she hastened to add, 'Don't worry, I saved the Forster room for the two of you. And Dickens will be open for your parents when they get here, Lauren.' The elder Hsus weren't due for another week. That should be enough time for Katie to air out the room and remove the olfactory as well as the physical evidence of the Hugheses' occupancy.

Oscar's face cleared. 'That's a relief. I know it's presumptuous, but I've come to think of the Forster room as mine, as if I'd grown up here. Of course I'd give it up if I had to – but I'm glad I don't have to.'

Emily smiled, touched that Oscar thought of Windy Corner in some sense as home. She could hardly have taken that for granted, since she and her half-brother had not known of each other's existence before last Christmas, and Windy Corner had been her own home for only a little more than a year.

'They'll all be down in a minute for tea, so I want to warn you – the girl, Charlotte, doesn't speak. It's a trauma thing. She was abused by her mother's boyfriend for years.'

Lauren the psychology professor's ears pricked up at this. 'Oh, really? I find that fascinating. The muteness, I mean, not the abuse. God, how awful.' She shuddered. 'So who's this guy she's with now?'

'His name is Moses. He was a friend of her mother, who died of cancer a few months ago. Before she died, she asked him to be Charlotte's guardian. He founded the shelter where they were staying after they left the abusive boyfriend.'

Lauren frowned. 'And you're sure this guy is OK? Not just picking up where the previous jerk left off?'

'I'm sure. You'll see when you meet him. He's quite an unusual person. But the social worker had the same thought you did – that's why they're hiding out here.'

Emily steeled herself for the other revelation she needed to make. 'We have some other guests as well. Connected with . . . Well, there's a bit of a wrinkle with the church.'

Oscar sat forward with pinched brows. 'Don't tell me it's already booked for that day?'

'I'm afraid it's worse than that. There was a freak storm while Luke and I were away, and the church was pretty badly damaged. The roof gave way, the church flooded, and the rose window in the apse was hit by a falling branch.'

Oscar swallowed and gripped Lauren's hand.

Emily hurried to mitigate the damage. 'Repairs are underway, and we have every hope things will be in reasonably good shape by the wedding. But you may have to put up with a bit of scaffolding and general discombobulation.'

Oscar leaned back against the loveseat, eyes closed. His constitution had never been up to much in the way of handling shocks.

Lauren stroked his hand and said, 'Hey, don't panic, babe. It'll be all right. I'm sure Emily has everything under control. We'll still get married, even if it's under a leaky roof. Or, worst-case scenario, in a different church.'

Oscar pulled himself together and sat up, giving Emily a pale smile. 'Let us know if there's anything we can do to speed things along.'

Lauren asked Emily, 'What does all that have to do with the people staying here?'

'They're the stained-glass repair artist and his family. They came from Portland, and I couldn't get them a cottage right away, so they're here through tomorrow. You'll meet them at dinner.'

She was about to give Oscar and Lauren further pertinent details about the Hughes family when the hall door opened and Moses came in, followed by Charlotte, with Marguerite and Luke bringing up the rear. Emily stood to make the introductions, ignoring the dumbfounded looks on the bridal couple's faces. Moses must be used to that sort of reaction to his appearance by now.

'Moses, Charlotte, I'd like you to meet my brother and my soon-to-be sister-in-law – Oscar Lansing and Lauren Hsu.'

Moses gravely shook their hands, his huge palm swallowing Lauren's tiny fingers. She was even smaller than Charlotte, barely reaching Moses' midriff. Charlotte, however, cowered behind Moses as if all the ground Emily thought she'd gained with her over the last few days had been lost. Then it occurred to her that the girl probably had an aversion to men in general. She'd been shy of Luke, too, at first. Possibly Oscar even reminded her of her abuser in some obscure way, though he was as mild-mannered and affable a person as Emily had ever known. She would just have to hope that his kindness would win Charlotte over before long.

Before Emily could get back to her warnings to Oscar and Lauren, Adrian, Polly, and Raphael came in. Emily made the introductions, and the adults shook hands. Lauren attempted to shake Raphael's hand as well – she believed in treating even the smallest children with the respect due to adults. But he only scowled and slapped her hand away. She pulled back with a shocked expression, but Polly said calmly, 'He doesn't like strangers touching him without permission.'

'I wasn't touching, I was offering. He could have simply said no,' Lauren muttered. 'He didn't have to hit me.'

That episode cemented a standoff between the two young couples. At dinner, Lauren maneuvered herself next to Charlotte and made persistent attempts to draw her out, using every trick in the book to elicit a response. But Charlotte only seemed to become more withdrawn.

After dinner, over coffee in the library, Emily hinted to Lauren that a more subtle approach might be more effective. 'I'm teaching her to knit, and she's warming up to me. I don't know that she'll ever speak to me, but at least she's starting to come out of her shell.'

Lauren sighed theatrically. 'Yeah, I guess I was coming on too strong. Being all psychologist-y. I'm just super interested in what makes kids go mute like that, and what brings them out of it. The theory is they stop talking because they think they have no voice, in a figurative sense, or they think their literal voice has caused harm to themselves or someone they love. So, theoretically, they should start talking again when they think it's safe to use their voice and they'll be truly heard.'

'I don't think that's a situation we can create for Charlotte,' Emily said. 'I don't think she'll feel safe until Moses' adoption of her goes through and the crazy social worker is no longer a threat. Or anyone else, for that matter. There's not much we can do about that – except help her feel safe while she's here.'

Safety, however, was not to be easily found.

Monday morning was particularly fine, and Moses and Charlotte went for a walk on the beach. When they returned, Charlotte was even paler than usual. Her eyes held a haunted look, and she was shaking so badly she could hardly walk, even with Moses supporting her. Moses kept a strong but gentle arm around her, but his face was like thunder.

'Janine,' was all he would say until he'd settled Charlotte in her room and Emily had brought her a restorative cup of cocoa.

Moses joined Emily in the library. Oscar, Lauren, and Marguerite were holding a wedding confab with Katie in the dining room, and Luke was at work.

'You saw Janine? Here?' Emily asked Moses.

He nodded, then scrubbed his hands over his face. 'I don't know how the hell she found us,' he said. 'Nobody knew where we were going except Father Paul, and he wouldn't tell. She must've followed us all the way from Portland. But why wait four days to show herself?'

'Did she show herself intentionally? Or did you just run into her?'

'Not even that. We'd been walking north on the beach, then we turned to come back. And we saw her – like she'd been following us. The minute we turned, she spun around and hightailed it off toward town.'

Emily's heart sank. All Charlotte's progress undone in one stroke.

'So you think Janine's here to continue her stalking rather than confront you directly?'

'That's what it looks like. Though what she'll do now we've seen her is anybody's guess.'

'Maybe there's something Luke can do to discourage her. Charge her with harassment, perhaps.'

Moses looked up at her with a glimmer of hope. 'He'd do that for me?'

'Of course.' His surprise bewildered her. 'It's his job to protect the public, after all.'

He nodded. 'That's a fact, ma'am. It's just that I haven't run into many lawmen who saw me as someone to protect. More often I'm seen as a threat for them to protect the public *against*.'

How very sad that his words were true.

'Will Charlotte be OK?'

'I hope so. She's scared, but it's not like she saw Terry or anyone from the past.'

'Terry?'

'The lowlife who abused her. Seeing him would bring it all back big as life. Janine is a threat, but more of a potential one, if you know what I mean.'

Emily nodded. 'She doesn't cause a post-traumatic reaction.'

'Exactly.' He glanced at her sideways. 'How do you come to know about all that? If you don't mind me asking.'

'I used to be a college professor. We were trained in how to deal with students in various sorts of distress. Not as professionals, you understand – there were counselors and medics on staff for that – but enough to know what kind of help the student might need.'

In fact, Emily had experienced a post-traumatic reaction herself the previous winter while visiting the campus, when a situation with another professor had vividly recalled an episode of abuse from her student days. Her sympathy with Charlotte ran deep.

At lunch, Emily told Luke what had happened. 'Is there anything you can do?' she asked him.

'Not officially, unless she actually does something threatening. It's not illegal to walk behind somebody on the beach. But if she comes to the house or accosts them in the street, let me know and I'll be right there.'

'At least come home early if you can. I have a bad feeling about this.'

'Will do. Things have been pretty quiet in town – I should be here for tea at the latest.'

He made it barely, with no time to change out of his uniform before tea was served. They all gathered in the library, including Charlotte, who was feeling more like herself – at least the more subdued version of herself – after a couple of hours working on her shawl. Polly and Raphael were still there, since their cottage had only just become available and Adrian had taken their car to work at the church. Katie's mouthwatering scones and delicate cakes were vanishing quickly when the doorbell rang.

Emily froze. It was late in the day for a delivery person, and unexpected visitors were rare in this isolated spot. The chances of this one being unwelcome were high.

Luke stood. 'I'll get this.'

Emily waited a moment, then followed him as far as the office doorway, where she could see and hear without being obtrusive. Naturally, she trusted Luke to handle Janine – if this *was* Janine – on his own, but she was curious to see the woman for herself.

Luke opened the door to reveal a nondescript-looking woman in her late forties – the sort who gets described by witnesses as medium height, medium build, medium coloring, to the lawman's eternal chagrin. To complete the picture, she wore an ill-fitting skirt suit in an indefinable color somewhere between gray, green, and brown.

'I want to see Charlotte,' she said without preamble. 'I know she's here. You have no right to keep her from me.'

She tried to push past Luke into the hall, but he stood his ground. 'Now, just a minute. This is my house, and you're trespassing. You haven't even identified yourself.'

She gave an impatient shake of the head. 'Janine Vertue, social worker.' She gave her title as if it were *Queen of the Universe*. 'I represent Terry Garner, Charlotte's stepfather. The person who should rightly have custody of her.'

Luke raised an eyebrow. 'I understood Terry and Charlotte's mother were never married.'

Janine waved a dismissive hand. 'Common law marriage. Makes no difference under the law.'

'But Moses Valory is Charlotte's legal guardian. That counts for at least as much. His claim is perfectly valid, and you have no proof of wrongdoing on his part. You need to leave Moses and Charlotte alone.'

Janine stomped her sensibly shod foot. 'Mr Valory is abusing that girl, and I will not rest until I get her safe.'

Luke shook his head. 'Then you'd better leave her where she is. She couldn't be safer than with Valory. Garner's the one who abused her. If he hadn't terrified her into muteness, she'd tell you that herself.'

'Nonsense. Terry Garner is a good man who has Charlotte's best interests at heart. You've been duped by that smooth-talking monster Valory. You know he has a record?'

'He told me. That was a long time ago, and a minor offense at that. He's a different man now.'

She hmphed. 'You've known him, what, three days? You have only his word that he's changed.'

'Actually, I did a thorough background check with all the police resources at my disposal. But you have only Garner's word that Valory *hasn't* changed. In my world, a man is innocent until proven guilty. And you have no shred of proof that Moses Valory is mistreating that girl in any way.'

Janine's eyes narrowed as she poked a finger at Luke's chest. 'I *know* he's guilty. And I'll get my proof. It's only a matter of time.'

'I can't stop you from investigating, but if you come on to my property again or bother Moses or Charlotte in any way while they're under my protection, I'll slap harassment charges on you so fast you won't know what hit you. And furthermore, I'll fix it so you can never work as a social worker again.'

Emily suspected that last was an empty threat, but Luke's uniform might give it a bit of credibility.

Janine drew herself up to her full unimpressive height and tugged her jacket into place. She seemed about to take a parting shot when her focus shifted off Luke and her mouth opened in indignation. Emily followed Janine's gaze to see Polly and Raphael crossing the corridor.

'What are *those* people doing here?' Janine demanded.

Emily decided it was time for her to come out of hiding. 'That's hardly your business, Ms Vertue. Those people are my guests.'

Janine blinked as she took in Emily's existence. 'But I know them. I did a home study to block their adoption of that little boy. Those people are not fit parents! Do you know they smoke *pot* in their home?' She said 'pot' in a whisper, as if it ought not to be mentioned in polite society.

Despite her sympathy with this particular concern, Emily the hostess felt obliged to defend her guests from any immediate attack. 'Apparently they got another study and the adoption went through. They won't be smoking anything while they're staying with me.' Anything *more*, at least, but Janine didn't need to know about that early episode.

Janine's bulldog scowl was worthy of Winston Churchill. 'They'd better not, or they'll be hearing from me. There's such a thing as child endangerment, and I won't stand by and watch it happen. What kind of place are you running here, anyway?'

She looked around as if expecting to find more offenders crawling out of the woodwork. Disappointed in this expectation, she turned back to Luke and Emily and shook her fist in their faces. 'You haven't heard the last of me.' She stalked off down the drive, presumably to whatever unobtrusive spot she'd left her car in.

Emily turned to Luke, wide-eyed. 'Whew!' she said, putting her hands on Luke's chest. 'What a virago! But you handled her beautifully.' She reached up for a quick kiss.

Luke grinned. 'Thank you, ma'am. So did you. But I'm very much afraid she's right about one thing – we haven't seen the last of her.'

Emily sighed. 'I'm glad the Hugheses are leaving tonight. And I hate to say it, but maybe it would be better for Moses and Charlotte to move on.'

Luke shook his head. 'She found them here – she'd only find them again somewhere else. Better here where I can keep an eye on the situation. I'll find something to arrest her for if I have to.'

Moses spoke from the library door. 'Thank you kindly, sir. I do think this is the best place for us to be, as long as you'll have us. She can't draw this out forever.'

SEVEN

After tea, Adrian, Polly, and Raphael took themselves off to stay in the cottage that was finally ready for them. The parting was cordial on all sides but with a strong undercurrent of mutual relief. On Emily's side, the relief was partly due to the fact that Raphael had done little damage during his stay – he'd broken only one item in the Dickens room.

'I'm glad he broke that godawful seagull lamp,' she told Katie after they were gone. 'I think it was Uncle Horace's choice, and Aunt Beatrice probably hated it as much as I did. Now we can toss the fragments in good conscience.'

Everyone breathed easier in the young family's absence, though Emily was concerned about what might happen to the cottage she had sent them to. Luke had lectured them sternly about both the laws against using marijuana in a vacation rental and Emily's own nonsmoking-of-*anything* policy, and they had verbally agreed, but Emily didn't trust their compliant smiles. She feared the paradoxical but common psychological effect that since they weren't paying to rent the cottage, they would be less concerned with taking care of it.

Ben and Beanie arrived at seven that evening for a pre-dinner sherry. For the occasion, Beanie had shed her never-ending-swatch garment in favor of an actual dress, also knitted but of a consistent color and pattern and only a little eccentric in shape. She looked quite nice on the arm of her tall, lean, handsome black boyfriend, Ben.

Charlotte rose to meet Beanie with a smile of delight. Emily expected her to quail at the sight of Ben, but she only looked at him shyly from underneath her lashes as Beanie introduced him. Emily said to Moses, who stood near her, 'I'm surprised she's not afraid of him.'

'It's 'cause he's a brother,' Moses replied. 'She gives all black men the benefit of the doubt because she trusts me. And he's got a nice, gentle way about him.'

Emily, watching Ben greet Charlotte with a friendly smile, had to agree. She introduced Moses formally to the new visitors, and Ben and Moses immediately fell into conversation. Charlotte dragged Beanie to the loveseat to show off her progress on her shawl.

'Hey, dude, you're doing great!' Beanie said. Emily could never get used to girls calling each other 'dude,' but the usage seemed to be here to stay. 'Look at this, Em. Her stitches are so even, and I don't see a single mistake. You must be a great teacher.'

'On the contrary, I have a great student. I've never seen anyone pick it up so fast.'

Beanie looked at Charlotte, who was beaming and blushing under this praise. 'Then I bet you're naturally artistic. Do you do any other kind of craft?'

Charlotte held out her left palm flat and mimed drawing on it with her right.

'You draw? Do you have any work here you could show us?'

Charlotte nodded eagerly and pointed to the ceiling.

'It's up in your room?' Emily said. 'Why don't we go up and take a look?'

Emily and Beanie followed Charlotte up the stairs, with Lauren tagging along. Emily suspected Lauren hoped to analyze Charlotte through her artwork. Oh, well, it couldn't hurt as long as she didn't let her 'subject' know she was doing it.

Charlotte took a sketchbook out of the drawer of the desk and opened it on the bed, where they could all see. She paged slowly through, giving them time to appreciate each drawing before moving on to the next.

Emily was no expert, but it seemed to her the girl was remarkably talented. She had drawn portrait after portrait of Moses, not posed but engaged in ordinary activities – cooking, working on his computer, standing at prayer. Not only were the likenesses spot-on, but she had captured his gentleness, his deep sadness, his love for Charlotte herself and her reciprocal love for him. These portraits alone would be enough to refute Janine's accusations in the eyes of any sensible judge. No girl could feel such deep affection and trust toward an abuser.

Interspersed among the portraits were sketches of what must

be Charlotte's home neighborhood – people on the street, close-ups of cats, dogs, pigeons, and squirrels. No landscapes, though; it seemed only animate creatures interested this artist. At the end of the sketchbook – which was in fact the beginning, since she had opened it from the back – were a few portraits of a woman lying in bed, looking ravaged by sickness but still with the light of love in her eyes. No doubt Charlotte's mother, Faye, as she approached her end. The one picture with no people or animals in it was of a cemetery with a fresh grave and a newly carved stone that read, *Faye Lovelace, beloved mother. September 22, 1990, to April 10, 2022. Memory eternal.*

So young. And such a hard life she'd led, full of betrayal and heartache as well as violence, illness, and pain. Emily sent a silent promise to Faye's spirit that she would do all in her power to see that her daughter's life would be better from now on.

'Charlotte, these drawings are wonderful,' Emily said. 'You're very talented. Have you had lessons?'

The girl shook her head wistfully. No doubt lessons would be most welcome as a way of developing her natural gift.

'Maybe Moses can arrange that once you get settled.'

Charlotte nodded, smiling. She turned to Beanie, who was full of admiration as well.

'Not much fodder for analysis here,' Emily said in a low voice to Lauren.

Lauren shrugged. 'Maybe not. But I'd be willing to bet there's an older sketchbook somewhere with much scarier stuff in it.'

'You're probably right. But let's not press her to show it, OK?'

Lauren hesitated, then nodded reluctantly. 'I guess that could be counterproductive as far as her recovery is concerned. Though it could be useful in making the case against her abuser – if she drew him as clearly as she did Moses.'

'That's possible. I'll ask Moses about it. I don't want to rifle through her things on the off chance.'

The dinner gong sounded. Charlotte carefully closed the sketchbook and put it away, and they all went down to the dining room.

Emily placed Moses next to herself at the dinner table. When the buzz of conversation had become general, she said to him,

'Charlotte showed us some of her sketches – beginning with her mother's death. She's incredibly gifted.'

Moses nodded. 'Indeed she is. When we get settled, I'll get her some lessons so she can make the most of her gift.' He sighed. 'So many things I want to do for her, but we've got to get the adoption through first. Then maybe she can heal, even start talking again. She's been out of school for two years – they couldn't cope with her muteness. I do what I can for her, but I'm no scholar. She needs so much more.'

'Like a woman's influence,' Emily said gently. 'At her age, it's so important to have a role model of one's own gender.'

He nodded sadly. 'That too. I've seen how she's warmed up to you, and I'm grateful. But you likely won't be in our lives long-term.' He sighed. 'I'm too old and ornery to get married, and neither of us has any female relations. But maybe I can hire somebody. Do they still have governesses these days?' His wry smile told her he knew the answer was no.

'God will provide. Maybe you'll meet a nice babushka at whatever parish you end up in.' Emily gave his hand a quick squeeze. 'There's something else I wanted to mention about those sketches. The ones of you show so much love between you. Surely they could go some way toward proving you're not abusing her?'

He raised a skeptical eyebrow. 'I'm not sure a court would look on a bunch of drawings as proof.'

Emily felt her way carefully. 'I did wonder if there might be other drawings from longer ago – some that might be seen as evidence the other way. Something involving Terry.'

Moses gave a convulsive shudder. 'If she ever did do any sketches like that, I haven't seen them. I think Faye must've destroyed them. Or else they got left behind when she and Charlotte escaped from his place. They had to light out in a hurry with not much more than the clothes on their backs. Stands to reason, if Terry had found anything incriminating to himself, he would've burned it.'

'I can see that. But afterwards, at the shelter – could she have done something then? As a way of processing what she'd been through?'

'Now, that I don't know. I'd have to check with the women

who run the shelter. I don't think it's too likely such things would've been kept. But I can ask.'

Emily hoped this line of investigation would prove fruitful. Charlotte might have lost the power of speech, but there could still be a way for her voice to be heard.

On Tuesday, Oscar and Lauren went out to research possible caterers. Emily wasn't familiar with nearby Chinese restaurants; she hoped they would get lucky. If not, the whole bicultural wedding plan could fall on its face. Gourmet Chinese food was not in Katie's repertoire.

Moses and Charlotte again ventured on to the beach. This time, Moses told Emily afterward, they saw Janine before she saw them. Moses decided he'd had enough. Charlotte was coping now that the first shock had passed, so Moses simply kept to his course, which took them right past Janine and on into town. They browsed the gift shops and came home with several trinkets that seemed to bring Charlotte joy.

Nevertheless, Moses was fuming when they entered the house. 'That damn woman followed us all through town,' he told Emily through gritted teeth. 'What does she think, I'm going to do something to Charlotte right there in public view? The woman's insane, I tell you. Completely irrational.'

Emily's instinct was always to look for the best in people, to try to find some way to explain, if not justify, even the worst or oddest of deeds, but in this case she came up blank. She had to agree there was something not quite sane in Janine's behavior.

'Why do you think she's taking this so far?' she asked Moses when Charlotte had gone upstairs to stow her new treasures. 'A rational person, in the face of a complete lack of evidence of wrongdoing, would simply conclude she'd been mistaken and file her report to the court accordingly. Wouldn't she?'

Moses shrugged. 'You'd think. I didn't know Janine before Terry put her on to our case. She may have been rational then. But he's turned her somehow.'

'Do you think she has feelings for him? Is that what this is about?'

'It's possible. All I have to go on is what Faye told me about him – I've barely seen the man myself. From what she said, he had some kind of almost hypnotic hold over her. If he could do that to one woman, I reckon he could do it to another. All it takes is for her to be lonely and desperate, and I can easily believe Janine was that.'

'So Faye was lonely and desperate when she met Terry?'

He nodded. 'She was only nineteen, trying to raise a two-year-old on her own. She had some money from her parents, but they'd died and she had no emotional support at all. Terry was older, seemed mature and stable on the surface. He made her feel like the only woman in the world – flattered her, bought her gifts, paid her all kind' of attention, promised to love Charlotte as if she were his own. Faye couldn't resist the idea of having someone to take care of her and her baby.'

'Of course. Any woman would feel that way in her position.'

'Right. But after they moved in together, the lies began. He stole and wasted her money, never did a lick of work, drank, ran around with other women – you name it – all the while telling Faye she was the center of his world. Finally she began to suspect all was not as it seemed – and that's when the beatings began.'

'Was that before or after he started abusing Charlotte?'

'After, but Faye didn't know about it at the time. He was slipping her sleeping pills so she wouldn't wake up when he went into Charlotte's room. And he must have threatened Charlotte, maybe saying he'd hurt her or her mother if she told her what was going on. That's ultimately what made her stop talking – she figured if she didn't talk at all, she couldn't accidentally slip and give the secret away. At least, that's what Faye surmised.'

'So how did Faye find out what was going on?'

'She took Charlotte to a doctor when she first stopped talking. She was about twelve at that point. The doctor couldn't find any physical cause, so he sent them to a psychiatrist. The psychiatrist told Faye that kind of thing usually results from trauma or abuse. Charlotte hadn't been through any sudden traumatic event, and Faye knew *she* sure as heck wasn't abusing her own daughter – so that left Terry. And since the girl wasn't covered in bruises all the time, she figured it had to be . . . the other thing.'

Emily tried to imagine how it must have felt for Faye as a

mother to realize she'd been exposing her daughter to such horror. It beggared the imagination.

'She questioned Charlotte till she could tell she was on the right track. Then she got the both of them the hell out o' there. She could put up with anything herself as long as she thought she was in a good situation for Charlotte. But the minute she realized Terry was destroying the girl, she took off and came to us at the shelter.'

Emily sat silent for a minute, digesting all this. 'It's hard to understand how it all could have gone on for so long. I've never had children and have only been married to two decent men. I guess there must be psychological factors at work that aren't obvious from the outside.'

Moses nodded. 'Believe me, Miss Emily, I see this kind of thing all the time. Women who still claim to love their husband, still believe he loves them, even after he's beaten them nearly to death. Women who refuse to believe the evidence of their own eyes that their kids are being assaulted every night by their own father or stepfather. God knows what it is they think they're hanging on to, but there's something about the situation that makes it seem scarier to leave than to stay. Or, in some cases, just plain impossible.'

'*C'est vrai, ma chérie.*' Marguerite spoke up from the corner of the window seat, where she had apparently been absorbed in Hugo, unnoticed, the whole time they were speaking. 'I myself was once such a woman.'

Emily was dumbfounded. '*You*, Margot? But you're so strong, so independent.'

'*Oui*, I am now. But recall, you did not know me when I was *une jeune fille influençable*. My parents divorced when I was small, my father vanished from our lives – I had no man to love me. The first man who came along and claimed to adore me, I was as putty in his hands. He beat me, cheated on me, used me shamefully in every way – but afterwards he would grovel at my feet with flowers and gifts, begging my forgiveness. For five years I took it, telling myself he would change, he would love me again. *Dieu merci* I never conceived a child or it might have been longer.'

The thought of her dear friend going through all that wrenched Emily's heart. 'What finally woke you up?'

'I found him in bed – *my* bed – with another woman. Before that, I had only suspected he was cheating; *then* I knew. And it was as if the scales, they fell from my eyes, and I saw him for the *fils du diable* he was. I shook the dust from my feet and never looked back.'

So many things about Marguerite made sense in the light of this revelation: her hard, apparently self-centered veneer; the way she played with men, which sometimes verged on cruelty; her refusal to commit to a romantic relationship. Emily got up and crossed the room to give her friend a hug. 'Oh, Margot. I had no idea.'

Marguerite gently pushed her away. She was not a hugger at the best of times. 'It is all a long time ago. I never think of it.'

Which accounted for how withdrawn she'd been all through this visit and for her cool, distant attitude toward Moses and Charlotte – their predicament reminded her of a time in her life she preferred to keep buried. Of a person she had once been but had vowed never to be again.

Moses stood and bowed to Marguerite with his hands crossed over his chest, the way Orthodox parishioners bow to each other at the service of Forgiveness Vespers at the beginning of Lent. 'I beg your forgiveness, ma'am, on behalf of my entire gender.'

Marguerite was too astonished to respond, but Moses didn't seem to expect a response. He quietly turned and left the room.

EIGHT

Wednesday was another fine day, and everyone dispersed to various pursuits. Oscar and Lauren went to Seaside to shop for wedding favors. Moses and Charlotte went out, not disclosing where. Emily invited Marguerite for a walk on the beach, feeling it was too long since they'd had a heart-to-heart.

Marguerite looked at her suspiciously. 'You will not try to make me talk about my feelings, *chérie*? You must promise me never to allude to what I spoke of yesterday.'

'I promise. You can tell me all the Reed gossip, or we can talk about the wedding plans, or we can silently commune with the wind and the waves. I just want to spend time with you before you have to go back.' The Reed semester would begin the last week of August, and the teaching staff needed to be on hand well before then.

They walked in silence for a few minutes, letting the ionized sea air revitalize their systems. Emily was now afraid to speak lest she inadvertently touch some hidden nerve. But Marguerite eventually led off with, 'And how are you finding married life, now that you have had a taste of normality?'

Emily barked a laugh. 'Normality? I don't think we know what that is. We had less than two weeks between coming back from our honeymoon and Moses and Charlotte landing on our doorstep. But it's good, even so. It's not like when we were teenagers, all over each other all the time; it's more like we've been married for years but had to live apart for a while, and now we're slipping back into a familiar groove. We're comfortable with each other.' At Marguerite's raised eyebrow she added, 'Not boring comfortable. Happy comfortable. Like the way I want to feel for the rest of my life.'

Marguerite heaved a sigh. 'If I am honest, *chérie*, I envy you. I am getting weary of hopping from bed to bed. If I could find a man like Luke – not exactly like Luke, *tu comprends*, but, as it were, the Luke for me – I think I might be ready to settle down myself.'

Emily rejoiced to hear at last the words she'd longed to hear from Marguerite ever since their friendship began. Her mind whirred as it spun through the list of all the eligible men she knew. Unfortunately, the list was not long. Marguerite wouldn't go for anyone much over fifty, and most single men of appropriate age were single for very good reasons. She knew a couple of widowers at St Sergius who would make great husbands, but they would want to marry Orthodox women. The chances of atheist Marguerite converting were slim indeed. But possibly not much slimmer than the chances of her wanting to settle down.

Absorbed in these thoughts, Emily didn't notice Moses and Janine until they were in earshot. She jolted into present reality to see Charlotte sitting on a driftwood log high on the loose sand, absorbed in sketching, while a short way down the beach, near the water, Moses and Janine faced off. Janine was like a chihuahua to Moses' great Dane, yapping furiously in screechy tones and hopping up to wave her finger in his face while he stood boulder-like, occasionally booming out a reply as his expression grew more intense. Any minute now, Emily thought, he might open his mouth and swallow her.

Emily touched Marguerite's elbow to steer her toward Charlotte, so they could plant themselves in her line of sight in case she should slacken her focus and glance in the combatants' direction. As they passed within comprehension distance, Emily heard Moses say, 'I'm warning you, Janine. One last time. My patience is exhausted. I will keep you and Terry Garner away from Charlotte no matter what I have to do.' He leaned down and spoke right in her face. 'No. Matter. What.'

Emily saw Janine pale and go still for a moment. Then she threw out what appeared to be her favorite exit line – 'You haven't heard the last of me' – and stalked off. Emily turned to Charlotte to give Moses a moment to compose himself.

Charlotte was so intent on her work that she didn't even notice when Emily and Marguerite crossed through her line of sight to whatever she was sketching. 'Hi, Charlotte,' Emily said, and at last the girl looked up – startled at first, then smiling as she recognized them. 'What are you drawing?'

Charlotte tilted her sketchbook for Emily to see. In the fore-ground, comically rendered gulls and sandpipers pecked in the sand for crabs as a golden retriever ran after a Frisbee off to the left and two children erected a sandcastle on the right. No quar-reling adults were to be seen. This was a picture of Charlotte's ideal world.

'That's wonderful,' Emily said. 'I love what you've done with the birds. They practically come off the page.'

Charlotte gave a shy smile and returned the sketchbook to her lap. Moses came trudging through the loose sand toward them. 'Almost finished, sweetheart? We should get going if we want to be back for lunch.' He gave Emily and Marguerite a look that implored them not to mention – even not to have heard – his final words to Janine.

Emily made a show of looking at her watch. 'Oh, goodness, you're right. We'll just have time to wash the sand off our feet if we start now.'

Charlotte added one final touch, then closed her sketchbook and stood. She slid her small hand into Moses' huge one as they set off toward Windy Corner.

They got back and cleaned up with minutes to spare before the lunch gong. Oscar and Lauren had returned and were waiting in the library, communing with their phones. Oscar looked up at their approach.

'Hey, Marguerite, did you know we're getting a new prof in art history?'

'*Ah oui?*' Marguerite's tone was that of one for whom new professors had long ceased to be of much interest. Though often male and single, they were usually fresh out of grad school, penniless, knowing nothing of the real world. Marguerite liked her men suave and *distingué*. Or, occasionally, young and extremely fit, which professors rarely were. Grad school didn't leave a lot of time for body-building.

'Take a look. He might be your type.' Oscar handed her his phone. Emily peered over her shoulder to see a handsome, well-dressed man with salt-and-pepper hair, a nice, natural smile, and a spark of humor in his gray eyes. The photo caption read, *Welcoming Art History Professor Julian Wallingford.*

Marguerite raised her eyebrows. '*Pas mal*,' she said. 'No doubt married. Why was he not tenured somewhere else?' She handed the phone back to Oscar, who scrolled to skim the new guy's CV.

'Apparently his old college gave up the ghost. Couldn't survive the pandemic.' He scrolled farther. 'And he's single. Widowed, grown kids.'

Marguerite's face betrayed nothing. 'We shall see whether he is up to Reed standards.'

Up to your *standards, you mean*, Emily thought. Perhaps there was hope for her friend's future after all.

Luke came in as Katie rang the gong. Emily pulled him aside as the others went into the dining room. 'I think it might be time to file harassment charges,' she said, sotto voce. 'I saw Moses and Janine quarreling on the beach just now.'

He frowned. 'Safe bet she started it, you think?'

'I don't know – I came up to them as it was ending.' She bit her lip, wondering if she should tell Luke what she'd overheard. Maybe wait to see if it proved necessary. 'You'd have to ask Moses.'

At that moment Moses entered the hall. Luke touched his arm. 'Just a minute, Moses.'

The big man stopped with a glance at Emily. Immediately she felt guilty for mentioning the quarrel, but she had only been trying to help, after all.

'I understand you had a run-in with Janine this morning.'

Moses nodded reluctantly.

'If she accosted you, we have grounds to file for harassment. I already warned her to stay away from you.'

'Yes,' Moses said. 'It would be good if she stayed away from us.'

That could be taken two ways. Good for Moses and Charlotte, or good for Janine. But that hardly mattered. Clearly the action was necessary.

'Come to the office with me after lunch,' Luke said, clapping Moses on the shoulder. 'We'll get her off your back.'

They had just left the lunch table when the doorbell rang. Luke was on his way out with Moses, so he answered it.

At his 'Can I help you?' Emily came into the hall, knowing Luke wouldn't want to be detained by anything trivial. But the two people standing on the porch did not look trivial.

An Asian man and woman in late middle age, the woman even shorter than Lauren, the man about Emily's height, both neatly but unremarkably dressed, the man holding two suitcases. Emily turned to whisper to Lauren, who was about to enter the library, 'Lauren! I think your parents are here early.'

Her eyes widened, and she looked past Emily to the door. 'Holy crap,' she said in a low voice. 'This is not what I planned.' She pulled herself together and went to meet them. 'Ma! Pop! You're early. I said to come on Sunday the twenty-fourth.'

The woman's mouth was set in a firm line. She opened it to say in lightly accented English, 'You said the twentieth,' then set it tight again.

'No, Ma, I said the twenty-fourth. But you're here now.' She turned to Emily and the two men. 'Hsu Li' – she indicated her father – 'and Hsu Lin, this is our hostess, Emily Richards. Her husband, Lieutenant Sheriff Luke Richards, and their guest, Mr Moses Valory.'

Luke and Moses inclined their heads. Mrs Hsu had to bend her head nearly backward to look Moses in the face. Her perfectly controlled mouth dropped open.

Luke tipped his cap, which he'd put on in preparation for leaving. 'Pleased to meet you folks. Welcome to our home. I hope you'll excuse me, but I've got to get back to work.' He shot Emily a look that said *Good luck with this* and made good his escape.

Moses dipped his head again and followed Luke. Emily put on her most gracious smile and said, 'Welcome. Please come in. Leave the bags – Oscar or Katie will get them.'

'I will take them myself,' Mr Hsu said firmly. 'Please, where is our room?'

'Right this way,' Emily said. 'I'm afraid it's not made up yet, since we weren't expecting you till Sunday. But you can leave your suitcases, at least.' As they passed the dining room, she signaled urgently to Katie, who nodded and headed for the linen closet.

Mr and Mrs Hsu stepped over the threshold of the Dickens

room and stopped, looking around with downturned lips and pinched nostrils as if they smelled something unpleasant. Emily sniffed surreptitiously but could smell nothing out of the ordinary. Some lingering odors from lunch, perhaps, but that had been a delicious cheese fondue. Perhaps they didn't like cheese.

Mr Hsu set down the bags and turned to exit the room. 'Are you hungry?' Emily asked. 'We've finished lunch, but I'm sure Katie can warm something up for you.'

'We have eaten,' Mr Hsu said. 'We would like only tea.'

Emily quailed. Tea they had aplenty, but was any of it Chinese? And did anyone in the house know how to prepare it properly?

'Please wait in the library,' she said, indicating the door. 'Here's Oscar. He'll introduce you to the others.' Oscar stood in the doorway with his mouth open like a codfish, silently appealing to Emily for help. Tough beans. They were his in-laws-to-be; he could deal with them.

She waited till they had entered the library, then pulled the door shut behind them. 'Lauren!' she said in an urgent whisper. 'What do they expect in the way of tea? And can you produce it?'

'Don't worry about it,' she said. 'In their world, there's tea and *Tea*. *Tea* is made from green China leaves prepared in the traditional fashion. That's what they have at home or when visiting friends. Plain old tea is whatever Americans serve. They know not to expect too much.'

'That's a relief. Plain old tea Katie can manage. You'd better go in and play cultural liaison or something.'

'Or something.' Lauren rolled her eyes. 'Like the dutiful daughter, a status I have irretrievably lost by getting engaged to a non-Chinese man.' She took a deep breath and went in.

Emily went into the Dickens room, where Katie had the bed half made. 'I'll take over in here, Katie. They want tea. Whether they want anything with it is anybody's guess – they said they'd eaten, but maybe some shortbread wouldn't go amiss?'

'Sure thing,' Katie said with a grin. 'This is going to be an adventure, I can tell already.'

An adventure. That was the way to look at it, but Emily wasn't sure she had enough energy to be that positive. A minefield was more what it looked like to her.

She finished making up the bed and looked around the room. It was clean and neat but lacked any of Katie's usual welcoming touches – flowers on the dresser, mints on the pillow, and so forth. Those would have to wait. In the bathroom, she set out fresh towels and checked the supplies of tissues and toilet paper. At least the basics were covered. She didn't want Lauren's parents to feel unwelcome, but when you arrived four days ahead of schedule, you had to expect a little less than perfection.

Leaving the bathroom, she nearly bumped into Katie bearing the tea tray. She'd set out a plate of homemade shortbread and enough cups for everyone so it would seem as if this were a normal thing, tea after lunch. Katie stepped back for Emily to precede her into the library.

She walked into dead silence. Whether she had chanced on a break in the conversation or it had never gotten going in the first place, she preferred not to know. She would simply play the gracious hostess, and her guests could respond as they pleased.

'Here we are,' she said brightly as Katie set down the tray on the round table in the bow window. 'Tea and some lovely home-made shortbread in case you're peckish at all.' She began to pour, and Lauren hurried to hand out the cups. Emily was pretty sure Chinese tended to drink their tea undoctored, but perhaps that only applied to properly prepared *Tea*. 'Do they take anything in it?' she whispered to Lauren.

'Perish the thought,' she said. 'And no shortbread. None for me either, in their presence. But Oscar takes milk, sugar, and anything sweet that's going. As I'm sure you know.'

Charlotte had come to hover at Emily's elbow, no doubt over-whelmed by these new people – one of whom was a man and neither of whom was particularly friendly. Emily had already noticed that Charlotte took milk and sugar in her tea as well.

Last of all, she poured cups for herself and Marguerite, both with milk but no sugar. Feeling she'd done enough hostessing for the time being, she went to sit by Marguerite on the window seat. 'What do you think of our new guests?' she asked her in an undertone.

Marguerite raised an eloquent eyebrow. 'I think Lauren is going to have her hands full. And perhaps you, *chérie*, as well.'

NINE

Once her parents had finished their tea and unpacked their things, Lauren seemed at a loss how to entertain them. Emily suggested she show them the rest of the ground floor and the garden.

Mrs Hsu was unimpressed by the garden but seemed enamored of the parlor, which was decorated in a more formal and feminine style than the library. Since the room was rarely used, Emily jumped at the chance to suggest they consider it their personal sitting room for the duration of their stay – except for the day of the wedding, when it would be needed for banquet seating. They bowed their thanks in unison as if this were no more than their due.

The couple sat there the rest of the afternoon, Mrs Hsu engaged in some elaborate embroidery on red satin and Mr Hsu reading a Chinese-language newspaper. Lauren set out supplies in the dining room and had all the other women in the house busy making wedding favors. These consisted of a miniature photo of Oscar and Lauren in a silver-tone frame, accompanied by a tiny bottle of bubble juice with their names and the date on it and a couple of fancy chocolates, all wrapped together in stiff scarlet paper tied with a gold bow. Charlotte worked quickly, neatly and with obvious enjoyment; Marguerite was competent if perhaps a little bored; but Emily felt as if she were all thumbs. The various items refused to stay together in a neat grouping long enough for her to tie them up. She produced one lopsided favor to Charlotte's three perfect ones.

Oscar, meanwhile, had the job of collating all the RSVP cards and coming up with a final count for the banquet. Emily wished she could trade tasks with him. Every once in a while, Lauren would pop into the parlor to ask her parents if they needed anything. The answer was always no.

Thus, the hours between lunch and Windy Corner's official teatime were made to pass. Emily felt irrationally as if she had been given a taste of what it was like to be in prison.

At last, Luke and Moses returned, looking frustrated. Emily met them in the hall. 'What's wrong? Couldn't you get a warrant?' she asked.

'Nope. Damn judge is on vacation,' Luke replied. 'You'd think they'd get somebody to cover for him, but that's Tillamook County for you. Supply won't be in till morning. Still, Moses has done all he needs to, filled out the paperwork to press charges. Got it right here – charges of harassment against Janine Vertue, signed by Moses Valory.'

The parlor door into the hall was open, and suddenly Mr Hsu burst through it to stand in their midst. 'Did you say Janine Vertue?'

Luke stepped back, blinking. 'Yes, sir. She's been giving Moses here a world of grief.'

To Emily's astonishment, Mr Hsu drew himself up and spat on the tile floor. 'I curse that woman's name. Every day when I burn incense to my ancestors, I ask them to curse her. She is evil, I tell you. If you can bring that woman to justice, Mr Sheriff Richards, I will bless you and your house forever.'

Luke stared at him, wide-eyed and speechless. Emily stepped forward. 'Why don't we all sit down and you can tell us about why you hate her so much?' She ushered the men into the parlor, where Mrs Hsu stood by her chair, shaking. Mr Hsu took her hand and eased her back down.

'It was many years ago, when we had first come to this country. Lauren was small, just beginning school. She did not know the games the children play here. They were rough, and she would often fall and hurt herself. The school counselor did not understand and thought we were beating her.' His eyes filled. 'Beating our own beloved daughter! The counselor told those people – what are they called?'

'The CPS,' Moses put in. He had plenty of experience with Child Protective Services, no doubt.

'Yes. And they sent Janine Vertue to investigate us.' He looked as if he wanted to spit again, but the room was carpeted and he restrained himself. 'You must understand, we were new here, we had little money and less English. We lived in a house with several families. It was crowded, but it was clean. We all had clothing and enough to eat. We had our papers. We all worked hard, saving for homes of our own. But Janine Vertue came into that house and saw a filthy den of foreigners. She turned up her nose, as if we were all drug addicts and prostitutes who cared nothing for our young ones. She filed a scathing report and nearly succeeded in having our Lauren taken away from us – and the other children in the house as well.'

He paused, his hands shaking. Now it was Mrs Hsu's turn to comfort him. She stroked his arm.

'We were lucky enough to find an advocate, one of our own people who had become wealthy and powerful and understood our situation. He was able to stop her and keep our children safe. But ever since then, I have cursed that woman with every waking breath.' He stared imploringly at Luke. 'Please. She must be stopped.'

Luke looked Mr Hsu in the eye. 'I give you my word, I have every intention of doing just that.'

He turned to Moses. 'You won't need to go with me tomorrow. I'll get the warrant in the morning and go straight to her hotel to arrest her. I already found out she's staying at the Stony Beach Inn.'

'She doesn't seem to be spending a lot of time in her hotel room,' Emily said. 'You'll probably find her lurking near Moses and Charlotte.'

Moses cleared his throat. 'As a matter of fact, I have a little errand to run in the morning. Might take me most of the day. Could I ask you to watch over Charlotte, Miss Emily, ma'am?'

'Of course. We'll have another knitting lesson. Provided Lauren can spare us from the wedding preparations.'

She stood and led the others into the library for tea. 'What's on the agenda for tomorrow, Lauren?'

Lauren glanced cautiously at her mother, then replied, 'We were going to shop for stuff for the decorations. Marguerite has some great ideas.' She hesitated, then said, 'Want to come along, Ma?'

Mrs Hsu, having regained her self-possession, gave a firm nod. 'I must be sure you choose the proper colors. They must be red and gold.'

'You be OK on your own, Pop? Or do you want Oscar to stay with you?' Lauren asked.

Her father waved his hand. 'Do not worry about me. I am not a child. I can occupy myself without a minder.'

Lauren dropped her eyes. 'Of course you can, Pop.'

'Well, then, Charlotte,' Emily said to her with a smile, 'I guess it'll be just you and me. We'll have a grand old time.'

The others went their respective ways after breakfast – Mr Hsu going off apparently to walk on the beach – and Emily and Charlotte settled down in the library to knit. Emily showed Charlotte some new stitches she needed for the next section of her shawl. They worked for a couple of hours, but then Charlotte grew restless. She put down her work, went to the bow window, and gazed out longingly.

'Maybe you'd like to go into town,' Emily said. 'I don't think we need to worry too much about Janine at this point. Luke's probably found her by now, or will soon.'

Charlotte nodded eagerly.

'We could hit some of the shops and then go out to lunch. I'll tell Katie. Since there's only the two of us, I'm sure she'd enjoy a little break.'

Emily went to the kitchen, where she found Katie sitting at the table with her head on her arms. Katie was hardly ever to be seen sitting down during the day. Emily touched her shoulder.

'Katie? Are you OK?'

She lifted her head to show Emily a pale face with shadows under her eyes. 'I don't feel so good,' she said.

Emily sat across from her. 'You're not coming down with something, are you?'

'I don't think so. I've been feeling out of it pretty often lately.' She colored slightly. 'As a matter of fact . . . Don't tell anybody. I haven't done a test yet, but I think I might be pregnant.'

Joy flooded Emily's heart. Another little Lizzie! Or perhaps a brother for her instead. 'Katie, that's wonderful! You are happy about it, aren't you?'

'I'm sure I will be when I stop feeling ill all the time. And Jamie will be thrilled. He wants a big family.' She dropped her head again. 'Right now all I want is a nap.'

Emily squeezed her arm. 'You go right ahead and take one. I came in to tell you Charlotte and I will be out for lunch anyway.'

Katie dragged herself to her feet. 'Thanks, Mrs R. Jamie's working from home today, so he's watching Lizzie. I might be able to get a little rest.'

Emily floated back to the library, her mind full of the implications of Katie's probable pregnancy. A baby would be delightful, but with two little ones, would Katie be able to carry on as housekeeper? Adjustments would need to be made, at the very least. And in the near term, what about the wedding and the extra guests? If Katie continued to feel poorly, they might need to get someone in to help her until all the visitors were gone. Emily was so preoccupied that she didn't immediately notice that Charlotte was not in the room.

When the fact did sink in, she went to the foot of the stairs and called. Charlotte had probably gone up to get a jacket or change into outdoor shoes. But of course there was no reply. Emily mounted the stairs and checked first Charlotte's room, then the bathroom. No sign of her anywhere.

Puzzled but not yet worried, Emily went back down and checked the parlor and dining room. No Charlotte. Back in the library, she went to the window and noticed that the French doors on to the patio were ajar. Charlotte must have gone outside.

At that moment, panic began to set in. If she'd gone out of her own free will, fine; she was probably in the garden somewhere, or waiting at the car. But what if Luke had not yet caught up with Janine, and Janine had found Charlotte alone instead?

Emily flew out the door and around the house, calling 'Charlotte?' at the top of her lungs. No response, of course, but no sign of the girl's presence, either. Emily raced up the drive toward the road, assuming Janine would have brought her car if she'd planned a kidnapping. But she saw no car. It had rained overnight, so if Janine had concealed her car in the trees near the drive, it would have left tracks in the mud. No tracks were to be found.

She paused to catch her breath, then ran in the other direction toward the beach. She raced down the stairs at the end of the lawn and plowed through the loose sand to the tideline. There she stopped and shaded her eyes to scan the beach in both directions. She saw a couple of lone dog-walkers and a few family groups, but no one that could be Charlotte. How could they have gotten away so fast?

Emily grabbed handfuls of her hair and groaned in frustration. This was all her fault. She should never have left Charlotte alone. But she'd had no reason to think the girl would wander off, or that Janine would dare to kidnap her. She pulled out her phone to call Luke, but he didn't answer. Maybe that was a good sign. He might be in the middle of arresting Janine, and Charlotte would be safe.

She took several deep breaths, trying to clear her mind. Panicking was useless. Where might Charlotte be if she had left of her own accord? There were nooks and crannies along the beach where she might not be visible from this vantage point. Maybe she'd returned to that driftwood log where she'd sat sketching the previous day. At least that was a place to start.

Emily set off southward at a normal walk, having used up her energy for running. How far had that log been from the house? Maybe as much as three-quarters of a mile – it had taken them all a good fifteen minutes to get back to the house from there. But it wasn't all the way to downtown; the beach would have been more crowded there, right next to the big hotels.

As she walked, Emily scanned the beach to her left, away from the water, glancing occasionally toward the waves as well. She had no idea whether Charlotte could swim. Fortunately the water was quite shallow for some way out, and today it was calm, with no surf to speak of and certainly no sharks or undertow. Even if Charlotte had gone wading, she shouldn't be in danger of drowning unless she acted very foolishly indeed. Emily trusted Charlotte's sense of self-preservation more than that. And if the girl was in fact with Janine, the last thing the woman would want to do was to hurt her physically. Janine was convinced she was destined to be Charlotte's savior.

At last Emily came level with what she thought was the log where she'd seen Charlotte the day before. She hadn't paid much attention to landmarks, having no thought of needing to find the place again. But she'd walked about fifteen minutes, this log seemed the right size and shape, and there was nothing similar nearby. However, the log was empty of Charlotte.

Only when this hope was disappointed did Emily realize how much she had counted on finding the girl there. Now her leads were exhausted. She was pulling out her phone to try Luke again when suddenly she saw a slight blonde figure hurtling toward her across the sand. She slid the phone back into her pocket, and in moments Charlotte was in her arms, shaking and sobbing, clinging to Emily as if her life depended on that contact.

Emily shushed her and smoothed her hair until the girl's shudders subsided a bit. Then she held her out to look into her face and asked, 'Charlotte, what is it? What's wrong?'

Charlotte could only shake her head, wide-eyed. Up till now, they'd communicated fairly well with only Emily speaking, but that method seemed to have exhausted its usefulness. They would have to play twenty questions.

'Did you see Janine?'

Charlotte shook her head, then nodded, then shook it again.

'You did see her?' Emily ventured. 'But that's not all?'

This time she nodded emphatically.

'Did Janine try to take you away?'

Negative shake.

'Did she talk to you, make you afraid?'

Another shake.

'Did you see someone get hurt?'

Slower shake of the head. The girl was getting visibly frustrated, but Emily was out of guesses. 'She seems to be gone now, at any rate.'

Charlotte nodded, her body drooping.

'Then let's get you back to the house.'

The supply judge didn't show up at his office until ten, and then he had a long line of people waiting to see him. So Luke didn't get his warrant until close to noon. Not wanting to waste any time, he drove straight to the Stony Beach Inn.

He knocked on Janine's door but got no answer. Before embarking on a search for her all over town, he checked with the desk clerk just in case. The clerk was a college kid who lounged behind the desk playing on his phone. Luke highly doubted he ever noticed anything, but he had to ask.

'Have you seen Janine Vertue go in or out this morning?'

The kid pulled an earbud from one ear and squinted up at him. 'Who?'

'Janine Vertue. Room twenty-two. Short, dumpy middle-aged woman with brown hair. Not dressed for the beach.'

'Oh, her. Yeah, I saw her come in a little while ago.'

On a gut prompting, Luke asked, 'Was she alone?'

'Yup.' The kid swiped his phone and grinned. 'Unless she had Harry Potter with her. Wearing his invisibility cloak.'

Haha. 'And she hasn't gone out again?'

'Not that I saw. But I couldn't swear to anything.'

'Thanks.' Luke went back up to room twenty-two and knocked again, this time louder. 'Janine?' he called. 'Sheriff Luke Richards. I know you're in there. Open up.'

No answer.

He tried the door, but of course it was locked. These doors locked automatically.

At least it was unlikely she could have escaped via her second-floor balcony. She didn't seem like the athletic type. Either she'd gone out again without the clerk noticing, or she was hiding in the room.

Down to the desk again.

'I need you to let me into room twenty-two. I have a warrant for Ms Vertue's arrest, and she's not responding.'

The clerk glanced at Luke's badge and shrugged. He unlocked a drawer, pulled out a keycard, and handed it to Luke. 'This should do ya.'

Luke rolled his eyes. Not that he wanted the guy to be obstructive, but this was plain laziness. He grabbed the card and headed up the stairs one more time.

He swiped the card in the lock of room twenty-two, and it buzzed open. 'Sheriff here,' he called as he walked in. 'Don't try anything funny, Ms Vertue.' He hardly expected her to be armed or trained in self-defense, but you never knew.

A quick glance revealed an empty room. He checked the closet, under the bed, behind the curtains, on the balcony. Nobody.

Then he pushed open the bathroom door, which stood slightly ajar.

Janine Vertue's body hung from the high metal shower rod, a rolled-up sheet knotted around her neck. A single glance told Luke she was dead.

TEN

Luke pulled out his phone to check the time – twelve twenty-five – and to call it in. He noticed several missed calls from Emily. As soon as he'd reported the death and arranged for a medical examiner and a crime-scene team, he called her back.

'Hey, I must've been driving or something when you called. What's up?'

'Everything's OK now. I lost Charlotte for a while and kind of panicked.'

'Lost her? What do you mean?'

'Well, I haven't been able to get the whole story, for obvious reasons. We were about to go into town together, but apparently while I was talking to Katie, Charlotte decided to go for a walk. I thought Janine had kidnapped her and I panicked, but then I found her alone on the beach. She got more than she bargained for. She seems to have seen Janine, and for some reason, it really spooked her – much more than seeing her before.'

'Not having Moses with her would be enough to spook her, wouldn't it?'

'Maybe. But it seemed like more than that. Like something happened.'

'Was Janine with someone?'

'I don't know. I didn't pursue that possibility.'

Luke ran a hand over his hair. 'Can you try to get it out of her? It could be important. Crucial, even.'

'I'll try, but why is it such a big deal?'

'Because Janine is dead.' He heard Emily suck in her breath. 'Could be suicide – too early to tell – but if Charlotte saw her with anyone, it might be the person who killed her.'

'You didn't . . . find her—'

'On the beach? No. In her hotel room. At least Charlotte didn't see *that*.'

'Thank God.'

'What time period did you lose her for? You remember?'

'Oh, gosh, I wasn't paying attention. I guess it was around eleven, eleven fifteen, when I realized she was missing. It probably took . . . oh, fifteen or twenty minutes for me to find her? Maybe as much as half an hour.'

So Emily had found the girl maybe as late as eleven forty-five. That left a possible short window for Charlotte to be involved. He would have been happier to be able to rule her out from the start. 'Best not tell her for now. Might make her clam up completely. Wait till I get home, or at least till Moses gets back. I could be late, though.'

'All right. I'll do my best.'

Luke put his phone away and pulled out a pair of latex gloves. The crime-scene team wouldn't want anything disturbed, but at least he could look. He took pictures for his own use of the body in situ and of the tub, floor, and shower rod. A light dusting of sand appeared here and there on the bathroom floor. The bathmat showed faint marks that could have been from shoes, but it was hard to tell. On the rim of the tub he could make out what might be a shoe print, but again, it was indeterminate, at least to the naked eye. The body, he noticed, was in stocking feet, the toes just grazing the top of the tub.

He moved into the bedroom area, looking for anything odd or out of place. What immediately struck his eye was that the bed was completely disheveled – spread and pillows on the floor, blanket askew. The top sheet was missing – that must have been what was used to make the noose. Other than that, the room barely looked lived in.

Taking pictures of the bed, he nearly tripped on Janine's sensible low pumps – sensible for the city, anyway, though not for the beach – which had been kicked off next to the bed, then covered by the discarded spread. The lower parts of the uppers and heels were covered in sand, though the soles had been wiped clean – probably on the lobby doormat. Was a suicide more likely to die shod or barefoot? He didn't know. Under the circumstances, barefoot seemed plausible. Unless she'd walked in already determined to do the deed, with her method all planned out, kicking off her shoes would have been a reflex action. But the same applied if she'd let in her murderer sometime after she came in.

He moved to examine the door and lock. They had still been

functioning when he got there, and he saw no sign of forced entry. So either someone had conned the clerk out of the master keycard or Janine had let her murderer in. If murderer there was. He checked the balcony door and railing as well. No indication of any unauthorized entry by that route.

He looked around at her possessions. Her suitcase was open on the luggage rack with items folded neatly inside. Her toiletries were lined up along the back of the sink, and a spare skirt and jacket hung in the closet niche. Next to the desk, a closed brief-case sat on the floor, and a precisely aligned stack of half a dozen file folders lay on top of the desk next to a closed laptop. The nightstand held only the hotel-provided clock radio and the TV remote.

Luke crossed the room to the desk and flipped through the file folders. All the papers seemed to relate to Moses' case. He opened the laptop, and it came to life without requiring a password. That was careless for a public servant. He looked at each of the recent documents and emails, but none of them contained anything that could be construed as a suicide note.

If she had taken her own life, she had no one close to apologize to and no concern for whether someone else might be blamed for her death.

Luke had concluded he couldn't do anything more without compromising the scene when a knock came at the door. Dr Sam Griffiths stood there with a line of techs in bunny suits trailing after her.

'Come on in, Sam. She's in the bathroom.'

Sam grunted her acquiescence. She wasn't loquacious at the best of times.

Since the space was tight, Luke waited in the bedroom while Sam did her thing. She came out to him after some minutes and asked, 'OK to take her away?'

He nodded. When the mortuary assistants had come and gone, wheeling their blue-bagged burden, he asked, 'Any ideas?'

'Looks like death by hanging on the surface, but don't quote me yet. Too soon to say whether it was suicide or murder. Probably rule out accident.' She gave a little smile. That was as close as Sam got to humor. 'As to time of death, I'd say within an hour before you called me.'

Luke nodded. 'That fits with what the desk clerk said about when she came in. Thanks, Sam. You'll let me know when you have more?'

'Course.' Sam didn't normally do autopsies, but the regular pathologist was on vacation and she had agreed to fill in, no doubt hoping she wouldn't be called on. She collected her gear and went out.

Luke said to the team lead, 'I need to see the briefcase, files, and laptop when you're done printing them. And her phone, if she had one on her. The rest can go in the lockup for now.'

Luke's deputies, Pete and Heather, were waiting outside the room for their assignments. He filled them in on what he knew about the victim and her movements. 'OK, Heather, I want you to talk to the desk clerk and see if you can get him to remember anything more about Janine's comings and goings and anyone who may have come in with her or visited her.'

Heather was an attractive young redhead, and he hoped her feminine wiles might help jog the clerk's memory.

'Especially try to pin him down on when Janine came in this morning. Oh, and find out if anyone else borrowed his master keycard. Pete, I want you to check the other guests on this floor, if any of them are in, then go to the beach and see if you can find anyone who saw Janine down there this morning. Especially anyone who saw who she was talking with.' He blew out a breath. 'Meanwhile, I'd better find out if she has any next of kin.'

As Luke was on his way out, the desk clerk called to him. 'Hey, Sheriff? What's going on? What's with all the dudes in white trooping through?'

Luke pivoted and went up to the desk. 'Janine Vertue is dead. Don't let any cleaners or other staff or guests into room twenty-two until further notice.'

The kid's eyes went wide and his mouth dropped open. He pulled himself together with a visible effort, then a strange light came into his eyes that Luke couldn't quite pin down.

'Wow, a dead woman in our hotel! Freaky!' He said it with a note of glee mixed in with the horror. Luke concluded he was looking forward to spreading the story on social media and grabbing his fifteen minutes of fame. 'Did she have a heart attack or what?'

'I can't disclose the details at this time. And not a word or a picture from you to anybody, you understand?' Luke gave the boy his best intimidating-lawman glare. 'No social media. No gossiping with friends. No nothing. Or you will be prosecuted for obstruction of justice.'

The clerk's eyes went wide again and he swallowed. 'Right, Sheriff. You got it. Mum's the word.' He made a zipping motion over his lips.

Luke held his glare a moment longer for emphasis. 'One of my deputies will be down in a minute to ask you some more questions. I need you to give her all the help you can. Got it?'

The kid nodded vigorously. 'Got it. Will do.'

Luke headed for the door. He wasn't at all sure the kid would cooperate, but he'd done all he could short of confiscating his phone, for which he had no real justification. Social media could be useful for investigation, but most of the time it was the lawman's curse.

After Luke's news and the girl's own experience on the beach, the idea of taking Charlotte to town was a non-starter. Emily settled her in the library with her knitting and went to the kitchen to see what she could rustle up for lunch. For two or three? Mr Hsu was still out, and she had no way to predict when he would return.

While she was pulling sandwich ingredients out of the fridge, Jamie came in the back door. Katie's husband of four months was at all times sweetly solicitous of her welfare, but most of the time his concern was superfluous since she was well able to take care of herself. At the moment, however, Emily was grateful Katie had him on her side.

'Hey, Jamie, what's up?' she asked, continuing her task.

'I wanted to ask if you could possibly do without Katie for dinner tonight. She's feeling pretty rocky, and I think she needs the rest of the day off.' His fair, freckled face blushed purple as he said – in a whisper, although no one else was in earshot – 'She did the test. It was positive.' Then he couldn't contain himself any longer. A smile lit up his face as he practically shouted, 'We're going to have a baby!'

Emily dropped her fixings on the table and gave him a hug.

'Oh, Jamie, I'm so happy for you! That's wonderful. Of course we can fend for ourselves tonight. I'll dig out some leftovers, or maybe Oscar can pick up takeout on his way back from Cannon Beach.' Then she remembered the Hsus. She couldn't feed them leftovers. Takeout it would have to be.

Jamie continued to glow, and Emily could see he wanted to talk more about his big news. She did some mental arithmetic. 'So Lizzie will be, what, around two when the baby's born?'

He nodded. 'Pretty close. Katie figures she's about six weeks along, so we're looking at early April. Lizzie's birthday is April sixteenth.'

'What are you hoping for – a boy or a girl?'

'Yes!' he said with another huge grin. 'Honestly, I don't care. Of course, I'd like a son eventually, but we hope to have a bunch of kids, so it doesn't matter if we start out with a girl. Lizzie's a joy, and it'd be fun for her to have a little sister so close in age.'

'I would have liked a sister,' Emily said wistfully. 'Especially after my mother died. But it wasn't to be.' She smiled. 'I have Oscar, and he's all the sibling I need.'

Jamie checked his watch. 'I'd better get back. Lizzie will be waking up from her nap, and I don't want Katie to have to get out of bed. Thanks for understanding about tonight.'

'Of course. Give Katie my congratulations when she's awake.'

Tonight's dinner should pose no great difficulty. But what about all the nights to come? Today's indisposition was likely to be repeated from time to time throughout the pregnancy, and eventually Katie would need at least a decent maternity leave if not a change of career.

But Emily had more immediate problems. The first was dinner. She called Oscar and filled him in, telling him only that Katie was indisposed. Nor did she mention Janine's death. Both good news and bad could wait to be told in person.

'So the bottom line is, can you pick up some takeout for us all?'

'Sure thing,' he said. 'It'll give us the chance to test one of the restaurants we're considering for the catering. It's right nearby.'

One problem solved. That left only the death. But that was

Luke's issue to deal with, not hers. Maybe this time – since the body had not been found on Windy Corner property, as others had been in the past – it would not become her problem as well.

ELEVEN

L uke went back to his office and called his nephew Colin, who was a detective in the Portland police department. He'd been promoted, in fact, since Emily had helped him solve a murder at her college the previous winter and his lazy, incompetent boss had retired.

'Richards,' Colin answered his call.

'Hey, Colin, it's Luke.'

'Uncle Luke! Good to hear from you. Is this business or pleasure?'

'Business, I'm afraid. We've got a victim here – not sure yet if it's murder or suicide, but she's from Portland, so I'm hoping you can help me track down her next of kin. Maybe get some background on her into the bargain.'

'Sure thing. Not *too* crazy busy here right now. What's the name?'

'Janine Vertue. That's Vertue with an E.'

'Any reason to think she's got a record?'

'Not a criminal record per se. May've been some complaints filed against her over the years. She was a social worker. Took her job a bit too seriously, if you know what I mean.'

Colin groaned. 'One of those who want to remove every kid with a few bruises?'

'Exactly.'

'OK, I'll see what I can do and get back to you. How's Emily?'

'She's fine, but we've had a whole passel of unexpected company unloaded on us while we're getting ready for her brother Oscar's wedding. Kind of a circus around here.'

Colin laughed. 'I'm sure she can handle the juggling act. Give her my love, will you?'

'Will do.'

Luke drummed his fingers on the desk, trying to think what he could do while he waited on everyone else – his deputies to report back on their interviews, the crime-scene team to sort out their forensics findings, Sam to do the autopsy, Colin to find out whatever he could on his end. One thing Luke did have was a fairly narrow window for the time of death – eleven twenty to twelve twenty, assuming Janine was already dead when he first knocked at her door and Sam's initial guesstimate was correct. No reason it shouldn't be – the body'd been in a controlled climate with no unusual conditions, and the closer to the time of death it was examined, the more accurate the estimate could be.

He also had at least a few people – maybe as many as six – who could be said to have wanted Janine dead. And most of those people were staying in his own house. Time to check some alibis.

But a quick call to Emily revealed that out of the four possibles staying at Windy Corner, only one was currently there. Moses had not returned from his mysterious errand, Mr Hsu had never come back from his walk, and Mrs Hsu was still out with the wedding shoppers. An interview with Charlotte was hardly likely to be productive; he would have to leave her to Emily.

Just as Luke was about to start pacing in frustration, Pete and Heather returned.

'What've you got for me?' he asked before they'd even shut the door behind them.

'Pretty near damn-all,' said Pete. 'Nobody home on her floor of the hotel. On the beach, a couple people remembered seeing a woman who wasn't dressed like a vacationer, but nobody saw her talking with anyone.'

Luke let out an oath. They'd have to rely on Charlotte after all. 'Heather? Any joy?'

She shook her head. 'Danny – the desk clerk – couldn't say what time the victim came in; "a little while" before you showed up was the best he could do. When pressed, he admitted it was probably closer to half an hour than an hour. He did say "some dude" came in a little while later. He didn't recognize the guy as a guest, but he couldn't say anything else about him either. I got the impression he barely glanced up from his phone when Mystery Man came in.'

She perused her notebook. 'More comings and goings, but all families and groups, people staying there. Danny was pretty vague. Also, he left the desk unattended once or twice to go to the restroom, so anybody could have walked through then. One thing he was positive about, though – he didn't give the master keycard to anyone but you.'

'And the card was locked up when he got it for me.' Luke rubbed the back of his neck. 'So she must have let him in. If there was a him. Well, that's something.'

The door opened again, and a crime-scene tech entered bearing a large evidence bag. 'Here's the stuff you asked for,' he said.

Luke crossed the room in two strides to take the bag from him. 'Great, thanks. Anything you can tell me at this point?'

The tech shook his head. 'We got lots of prints, some DNA, some shoe impressions and fibers. All need to be processed.'

'Of course. Thanks, Nate.'

Luke took the evidence bag into his office and took out the briefcase, which now contained the file folders and laptop, along with the victim's purse and phone. 'Here, Pete, you look through these papers, and Heather, see what you can get off the laptop. It's not protected. I'll tackle the phone.'

He turned on the phone – an older iPhone model – and a number pad stared back at him expectantly. He tried 0000 and 1234, then pulled her ID out of her purse and tried her birthdate. No luck. Luke was no expert on unlocking phones. He sprinted to the door, calling, 'Nate? Hold up!'

Nate had been arranging items in his trunk and had not yet left. Luke panted up and thrust the phone at him. 'Here. Give this to the tech guys. I need it unlocked ASAP. And charged while they're at it.'

'Got it.' Nate put the phone in a small evidence bag and added it to a box of sundries. 'What about the laptop?'

'I checked it out back in her room. Not password protected, unless somebody turned it all the way off?'

'Nope, we didn't do that. I'll take care of this for you right away.'

Of course, 'right away' meant after a twenty-minute drive to Tillamook, plus time to unload all the evidence they'd collected, before Nate would finally remember about the phone. If Luke was lucky, he might hear back from them before nightfall.

He went back in and hovered over Heather's shoulder. 'Anything?'

'Nothing obvious yet. She seems to have used this mainly for work. My guess is the interesting stuff is all on her phone.'

'Keep looking.' She gave him a look to say, *What do you expect, boss? I've been in here two minutes.* He gave her a wry grin and turned to Pete. 'Anything there?'

'Same as Heather – nothing obvious yet. Give us a chance, boss.'

'I know. I'm just restless.' He stood for a moment, hands on hips, rocking from toe to heel. 'I'm gonna head home, see if anybody there has anything to tell me.'

Both deputies looked at him questioningly, and he realized he'd never had the chance to fill them in on the victim's connections with his current household. 'OK. I know some stuff about this woman you two don't know yet. Better do an incident board.' He pulled a whiteboard into the center of his office and beckoned Pete and Heather to join him.

He didn't have any photos yet, so he wrote the names, each enclosed in a circle – Janine Vertue in the middle, with Moses Valory, Charlotte Lovelace, and Terry Garner radiating out from it to the left. On the right, he wrote Hsu Li and Hsu Lin, then Adrian and Polly Hughes, all with question marks. As he spoke, he pointed to the various names with the marker.

'Janine Vertue was a social worker hired by Terry Garner to block Moses Valory's adoption of Charlotte Lovelace. Garner claims Valory is abusing the girl – she's mute, by the way – but Valory says Garner was the abuser during his long relationship with Charlotte's mother. Who is now deceased.' He drew a little headstone with the word 'Faye' next to Charlotte's circle, with a dotted line connecting it to Garner.

'Valory and Charlotte are currently staying at Windy Corner to get sanctuary because Vertue was hounding them. To wit, one warrant against her for harassment.' He pulled the now-irrelevant warrant out of his shirt pocket, waved it in front of them, and slapped it on his desk.

'This couple' – he indicated the Hugheses – 'had a grudge against Vertue because she tried to block their adoption of their little boy. They were successful in the end, so a murderous desire for revenge seems unlikely. But she did know they were here, and if she'd caught them out in some infraction, like smoking pot in front of the kid – not an implausible scenario, I'm sorry to say – she could've threatened them with reprisals.

'These people' – Luke pointed to the names of Lauren's parents – 'have a more tangential connection, as far as I can tell. Years ago – twenty, twenty-five, I'd guess – she tried unsuccessfully to have their daughter taken away from them. They've never forgiven or forgotten, though I have no reason to think they ever pursued Vertue or had any idea she was down here when they came. Their daughter is about to marry my brother-in-law, and all four of them are also currently staying in my house.'

Pete and Heather stared at him wide-eyed. 'Holy crap, boss,' Pete said. 'This is as bad as those other times when people actually got killed at Windy Corner. Except you weren't officially living there then.'

Luke nodded. 'My wife does seem to be a magnet for trouble. I don't want to think about why.'

'Maybe because she's so good at solving it,' Heather put in. 'I don't just mean good at detective work, but good at making peace between people. She can't rest until everyone's happy – except the murderers, of course. And even them she seems to regret not being able to save.'

Luke gave a little smile. He'd never thought about it that way, but that was a pretty good description of his Emily – and a big part of what he loved about her. If it meant they would periodically have a houseful of suspects and witnesses, well, that was the price he'd have to pay.

'I do believe you're right, Heather. But as you can see, this all puts me in a bit of an awkward position. I'll need your help to get all my guests cleared, if possible, as soon as we can. And that needs to start with getting their alibis.'

By the time Emily returned to the library with the tray of sandwiches, Charlotte had fallen asleep on the loveseat, her knees pulled up to her chest and her knitting dangling from one hand. Emily retrieved the work and made sure all the stitches were safely on the needles before laying the bundle neatly in Charlotte's bag.

She sat down at the table in the window to eat, since her hunger had reached the point of shakiness. Charlotte might wake up any minute or sleep for hours. Emily knew from experience that the kind of high-adrenaline experience she'd had that morning could leave one thoroughly exhausted, and Charlotte wasn't strong at the best of times.

Emily thought back over their conversation – if it could be called that – when she'd found Charlotte on the beach. Her having seen someone with Janine would make perfect sense, and Emily was annoyed with herself for not having thought of it at the time. She blamed the stress of believing Charlotte lost, which must have addled her brain. Come to think of it, she could use a nap herself.

She finished her sandwich, covered the remaining ones so they wouldn't become a cat snack, moved to her favorite chair, where she could stretch out with her feet on the hassock, and permitted herself a doze.

Some unknown amount of time later, she woke to see Charlotte at the table, eating with gusto. The girl smiled at Emily with her mouth full and rubbed her tummy with a crumb-covered hand. Emily was no kind of cook, but apparently her sandwiches at least were satisfactory.

She moved to sit at the table across from Charlotte. Best not to interrupt her with questions. Eating would impede any attempts at sign language, and the upset of remembering whatever had happened could interfere with her digestion. Emily got her own knitting out and sat with the girl in companionable silence.

Her mind drifted to the for-now-forbidden topic of Janine's death. What would it mean for Moses and Charlotte? Would their difficulties be at an end, or would Terry simply hire someone else to pick up where Janine had left off? Surely another social worker would see the situation rationally and conclude that since Moses was the legal guardian and Charlotte was clearly happy with him, his adoption of her should be allowed to go ahead. But Emily couldn't help worrying that as long as Terry was in the picture, Charlotte would not be truly safe. Terry had always been the ultimate threat, not Janine.

Charlotte finished her lunch and sat looking out the window, an unreadable expression on her face. Emily wished she could open a window into the girl's mind. The closest thing to such a peek she'd found so far was Charlotte's drawings. Perhaps that was the key to finding out what had happened on the beach that morning.

'Charlotte, do you think you could draw a picture for me?' she asked.

Charlotte nodded abstractedly. Perhaps she didn't realize exactly what Emily was asking for. She left the room and came back in a few minutes with a mostly blank sketchbook and a pencil. She flipped past the picture Emily recognized – of the birds, dog, and children on the beach – and turned to a fresh page. Then she cocked her head at Emily as if to ask, *What should I draw?*

'Could you draw what happened on the beach this morning? When you saw Janine?'

Charlotte's eyes widened and she pushed the sketchbook away from her with a vigorous shake of the head. Too soon. Emily could only hope time would make it easier.

She patted Charlotte's hand. 'It's OK, honey. I understand. It's too scary now. Maybe later.'

Charlotte nodded, her face turned away.

'Why don't you draw the cats for me instead?'

Charlotte perked up at that, picked up her sketchbook and pencil, and went to sit on the loveseat, where she had a clear view of the three cats cleaning themselves on the hearth. In a moment, she was completely absorbed.

TWELVE

I t was nearing the usual teatime, though Katie was not around to prepare it, when the others began to trickle back. Mr Hsu returned first. He came in the library French doors, nodded to Emily, and went through to the bathroom, whence she shortly heard the shower running. Perhaps he'd been on the beach all this time, maybe even wading. The picture of upright, proper Mr Hsu dabbling his toes in the waves and getting nibbled by sandcrabs afforded Emily a much-needed giggle.

After him came Moses, who entered through the front door and came into the library to make sure Charlotte was all right. She jumped up and clung to him as if she'd feared she'd lost him forever. Moses looked quizzically over her head at Emily.

'Charlotte had a little adventure this morning, right before lunch,' Emily said. 'She disappeared for an hour or so. I was afraid Janine had kidnapped her, but I found her alone on the beach. Charlotte was distraught, though – she'd seen something that terrified her, but she couldn't tell me what it was, other than that it involved Janine in some way.'

Moses grimaced and held the girl tighter. 'That woman has gone too far,' he said. 'Didn't the sheriff manage to serve those charges on her?'

Emily shook her head. 'He didn't get a chance.' She couldn't say more within Charlotte's hearing, and she thought Luke might want to break the news about Janine to Moses himself, so she stopped there.

Moses held Charlotte a moment longer, then said, 'Sweetie, I'm beat. I need to go lie down for a bit, OK? You're fine here with Miss Emily.'

Charlotte nodded, reluctantly let him go, and returned to her sketching.

A few minutes later, the whole wedding-shopping party returned, laden with bags of various sorts and sizes. Marguerite's and Lauren's string-handled white shopping bags bore the logos of several upscale fabric and knickknack shops and offered tantalizing hints of red and gold trimmings, while Oscar's bags were of plain brown paper and seemed to be full – not, as expected, of little white boxes wafting tempting odors – but of raw vegetables and other, more arcane ingredients. Mrs Hsu came in unburdened but sailed directly toward the kitchen, beckoning Oscar to follow.

He paused to answer Emily's questioning look. 'She insisted on cooking,' he whispered. 'We couldn't talk her out of it. You wouldn't believe the stuff she bought. It's enough for the wedding banquet. And no shortcuts, either. We could be waiting all night.'

Emily put a hand to her eyes. 'I hope she finds Katie's kitchen suitably equipped. Katie never does Chinese, so I don't think we have a wok or a rice cooker or anything like that.'

Oscar shrugged. 'I guess she'll just have to cope,' he said. 'It was her idea.' At a peremptory call from the kitchen, he hurried to deliver his burdens.

Lauren and Marguerite were already unloading their purchases, to Charlotte's mute but evident delight. Long swaths of shiny red fabric were followed by yards of metallic gold ribbon and several banners, all bearing the same Chinese character – stacked rectangles and lines, in red lettering on white. 'We had to get these printed specially,' Lauren said.

'What does the character represent?' Emily asked.

'Double happiness,' she replied. 'You can't have even a hybrid Chinese wedding without it. Supposedly it ensures we'll have a long and joyous union.'

'I know a better way to ensure that,' said Emily, thinking of things like mutual forbearance, loyalty, trust, and, most importantly, prayer.

'Liling!' came a shrill voice from the kitchen. 'You come in here and help me right now!'

Lauren grimaced. 'My Chinese name. I'm the prep slave for tonight's production. I'll see you in a few decades.' She vanished toward the kitchen as Oscar came out, pausing to give her a kiss for luck.

Emily helped Marguerite refold the fabrics and ribbons to stow them away until wanted. Charlotte reluctantly watched the pretties go and then returned to her drawing, which seemed to be nearing completion.

Luke came in as Emily was wondering how she could provide tea for all these people with Mrs Hsu in full and imperious possession of the kitchen. She decided to serve sherry instead, along with some butter cookies that were kept in a tin above the liquor shelf for emergencies.

Luke came up to her as she was pouring sherry into Aunt Beatrice's cut-crystal glasses, pausing to wonder whether it would be appropriate to offer any to Charlotte. Probably not.

'Hey, beautiful,' he said, giving her a surreptitious kiss. 'Everybody here now?'

'I think so. Mrs Hsu and Lauren are in the kitchen, emphatically not to be disturbed. Mr Hsu, I believe, is finishing up a shower, and Moses is resting in his room.'

'Hm,' he said. 'All the people I need to check on are unavailable. Except Charlotte. Did you manage to make any headway with her?'

'No. I tried – I suggested she sketch what she saw this morning, but she's still too frightened. She's undergoing some cat-drawing therapy right now.'

'OK. I'll take the back-door approach.' He strode over to where Oscar and Marguerite were sitting on the window seat. Emily followed, bearing sherry and cookies.

'I've got some news for you folks,' he said, sitting down next to Oscar.

'Good or bad?' Oscar asked.

'Depends how you look at it. From one point of view, death is always bad news, but I know a few people who might regard this one as welcome.'

'Death?' Marguerite raised her eyebrows. Emily put a finger to her lips to hint to her they didn't want Charlotte to hear. 'Who is dead?' Marguerite asked in a lower tone.

'Janine.'

Marguerite clapped a hand over her mouth. 'How?'

'Hanged in her hotel bathroom. We're not sure yet if it's murder or suicide.'

Oscar stared open-mouthed. 'Murder? Right before our wedding?'

'Sorry 'bout that, buddy. Nobody consulted me. I would've told 'em the timing was lousy.'

Oscar gave his head a shake. 'Right. Sorry. It's just . . . Well, naturally we want everything to be perfect. That seems doubtful now.'

'I know. You two and Lauren are out of the picture, of course, since you didn't know the woman. But I have to ask – was Mrs Hsu with you all day?'

Oscar stared again. Marguerite said, 'Mrs Hsu? Of course, we were all in the same car. We drove between Tillamook, Cannon Beach, and Seaside. But why? She did not know this woman, did she?'

'Apparently she and her husband did know her, from way back, and there was bad blood between them. That's all you need to know. Anyhow, looks like we can rule her out, at least. I'll have to find out what Mr Hsu was up to this morning.'

Oscar dropped his head into his hands. 'Oh my God,' he groaned. 'My wedding's a week away and my father-in-law might be a *murderer*?'

'I'm not saying I suspect him. I just need to rule him out.' Luke looked around. The two older men were both still absent. 'Guess I better go find him.'

He stood, but at that moment Mr Hsu came through the door. 'I understand my wife is cooking dinner,' he said stiffly. 'Is it your custom to put guests to work in this way? On their second day in your home?'

Emily went to meet him. 'I assure you, Mr Hsu, this was not my idea. My housekeeper is indisposed, and I'm hopeless in the kitchen, so I called Oscar and asked him to bring home some takeout. Apparently your wife insisted on cooking instead.'

'Ah.' His expression softened into one of wry understanding. 'I see. I do apologize, Mrs Richards. My wife is a force of nature. When she has made up her mind, it is unwise, not to say impossible, to resist.'

Luke cleared his throat. 'Mr Hsu, can I talk to you for a minute?'

'Of course, Sheriff.' He cocked his head. 'Is this official?'

'I'm afraid it is.'

'Then let us go into the other room.' He led the way into the parlor and shut the door behind them.

*   *   *

Luke sat down across from Mr Hsu. 'I have something to tell you, sir. All your curses on Janine Vertue have come to fruition. She's dead.'

Mr Hsu stared at Luke for a moment, then rose to his feet and lifted his hands to heaven. 'Praise be to the ancestors!' he said, then stood a moment in quiet rapture.

Luke cleared his throat. In his years as a lawman, he'd run into many people far more entitled to the label of *evil* than Janine Vertue. Although she'd come close to ruining some lives, he was convinced she'd acted out of a sense of duty – if a highly exaggerated one. And even the truly evil people he'd known had not inspired him to outright rejoice in their deaths.

'Mr Hsu,' he said sternly.

The older man blinked and made a little bow, then sat down. 'Thank you for bringing me this news, Sheriff. Is that all you had to say to me?'

'Well, no. You see, it's possible Ms Vertue may have been murdered. I need to know where you've been all day and what you've been doing.'

Mr Hsu's eyes widened. 'Me? You want to know where *I* have been?' He gave a little laugh. 'I am flattered you think me capable of this deed, Sheriff. I fear my murdering days, if I ever had them, would now be far behind me.' He shook his head with a little smile. 'I don't believe you told me how she died?'

'No, I didn't. She was found in her hotel room. Suicide is still a possibility.' He eyed the older man narrowly, hoping he might give something away.

Mr Hsu nodded sagely. 'Ah. An overdose of pills, perhaps? It is true I might have the strength for that. Although I think I would have needed more time to plan and to obtain the drugs. It is only since last evening I have known she was nearby.'

Luke was getting annoyed. 'Mr Hsu. Enough of this – whatever it is. Please answer my question. Where were you this morning and what were you doing? Specifically between eleven twenty and twelve twenty.'

Mr Hsu stroked his chin, examining the molded plaster ceiling. 'Let me see. This is a little difficult, because I do not wear a watch. But I think . . . That would be about lunchtime, yes? I had been walking, on the beach and around the quaint little shops, and I became hungry and weary, so I suppose that was somewhere near noon. I stopped at an amusing café called the Crab Pot and had a surprisingly delicious lunch, served by a very rude waiter.' He held a conspiratorial finger to his lips. 'But do not tell my wife. She thinks it shameful that I sometimes enjoy American food. She is most insulted that I could prefer it to her cooking.'

At the mention of a Crab Pot lunch, Luke's stomach rumbled loudly. He'd never gotten around to having lunch himself. His mouth watered at the thought of Harriet's signature crab melt served up by her terse and sour-faced brother, Sunny.

He pulled his attention back to the matter at hand. 'Thank you, Mr Hsu. We can easily check on that. In case you've guessed wrong on the time, what did you do after lunch?'

'After lunch, I felt I had had enough walking, so I went only as far as the coffee shop – what is it called? Something to do with a whale, I think.'

'The Friendly Fluke?'

'Yes, that is it. I sat on the deck, ordered a large latte, and sipped it very slowly, watching all the people go by.' He smiled and lowered his voice. 'Another guilty pleasure – my wife drinks only tea.'

'And after that?'

Mr Hsu shrugged. 'After that, I came back here. I walked on the road, as I was tired and did not wish to descend to the beach again.'

'All right, thanks. You can go now.' Luke stood, but Mr Hsu remained seated. 'Or not.' Luke pulled out his phone and took a picture of Mr Hsu before the man could protest. Then he went upstairs in search of Moses.

The door of the Brontë room was closed. Luke knocked lightly and heard a groggy 'Come in.'

He pushed the door open and saw Moses sitting up in bed. 'What can I do for you, Sheriff?'

Luke sat in the desk chair opposite. 'Janine Vertue is dead.'

Moses' eyes widened till Luke thought they would start out of his head. '*Dead?*'

Luke nodded. 'I found her in her hotel room when I went to serve the warrant, shortly after noon. She won't be persecuting you anymore.'

Moses crossed himself with a slow, ponderous movement. 'Lord, have mercy. God knows I had no love for the woman, but I wouldn't have wished her dead.'

He sounded sincere, and Luke devoutly hoped he was. Not only would he hate to have to arrest a guest in his own home – one he had come to respect and admire, at that – but he shuddered to think what would happen to Charlotte if she lost her protector.

'Can you tell me what you were doing at that time, Moses?'

He seemed to come back from a great distance. 'What time, exactly?'

'Between eleven twenty and twelve twenty. That's the best we can narrow down the time of death for now.'

Understanding registered in Moses' eyes. 'So I'm a suspect.'

'Just need to rule you out. I have to do that for everyone who knew her.'

'Have you ruled Charlotte out?'

'Not completely. She hasn't been able to tell us what she was doing during that time.'

Moses' head dropped and his body sagged into the bed.

'So can you tell me where you were around noon?' Luke asked again.

'I'm sorry, Sheriff. I can't tell you that.'

Luke cocked his head at him. 'Can't tell me? 'Cause you weren't tracking time, or what?'

Moses shook his head. 'I just can't tell you. *No comment*, I think, is the phrase.'

Luke frowned. 'Moses, you realize this is serious? *No comment* makes it sound like you have something to hide.'

'I know that. But that's my answer, and that's the way it's gonna stay. No comment.'

Luke stood. 'I have to tell you, I'm beyond disappointed to hear you say that. You have the best motive I know of, and for all I can tell, you had the opportunity. I have no choice but to promote you from person of interest to chief suspect.'

Moses nodded, his mouth fixed in a firm line. He had become as mute as his ward.

THIRTEEN

Moses did not come down for dinner. Emily took up a tray and left it outside his door, but when she went back for it after they'd eaten, the tray was untouched.

That dinner, which happened roughly on schedule despite Oscar's dire predictions, was among the oddest Emily had experienced in her own home, and that was saying something. The food was delicious, though she didn't recognize most of the dishes or know how to eat them, since only chopsticks had been provided. Mrs Hsu sat at the head of the table, blandly receiving compliments, as if she were the mistress of the house. Mr Hsu ate with a beatific smile on his face that had nothing to do with the food. Oscar and Lauren spoke to each other in low, nervous tones, picking at their meal. Charlotte was subdued, Luke and Emily preoccupied. Only Marguerite ate and conversed normally, though Emily struggled to keep up her end of the conversation.

When dinner was over, the guests dispersed – Oscar and Lauren to the kitchen to clean up, the Hsus to the parlor, Charlotte upstairs, and Marguerite to the library. Seeing her friend absorbed in her volume of Hugo, Emily thought she and Luke could have the equivalent of a private conversation without having to go up to their third-floor domain.

They settled on the loveseat, and Luke blew out a long breath. 'It's a messy one,' he told Emily. 'I've cleared Mrs Hsu, and it should be easy to verify Mr Hsu's alibi.'

'What was he doing, out of curiosity? I couldn't imagine what could keep him out the whole day on his own.'

'If you ask me, he was mostly playing hooky. Enjoying a little holiday from his wife's supervision.' Luke related the gist of Mr Hsu's alibi, ending with his coming home by the road.

'That's odd,' said Emily. 'He came in by the French doors and went straight to the shower. I assumed he'd been on the beach.'

'Huh. Well, that's a small point, since it happened well after

the death. But I'll see if I can clear it up.' Luke snorted. 'Maybe
he has an even guiltier secret than crab melt and coffee – one
he didn't dare tell me.'

Now Emily's mind was filled with the fantastical image of Mr
Hsu consorting with a mermaid. No, that would never do.

'What did Moses have to say?' she asked.

'Nothing.'

'Nothing?'

'Conversation started naturally enough – he said although he
hated her, he wouldn't have wished her dead, which is what I'd
expect. But when I narrowed down the time and asked him where
he was around then, he went all funny and clammed up. First,
he said he couldn't tell me, and when I pressed him, he resorted
to "no comment." I never thought I'd hear that from a man like
him.'

Emily turned to face Luke fully. 'Luke, you don't really think
he killed her?'

'I'd hate to be forced to that conclusion, but I don't know
what else to think. His silence is beyond suspicious.'

'But you don't even know for sure it's murder yet, right? It
could still be suicide.'

He nodded. 'Could be. I saw some contrary indications, but
nothing definitive. Should hear back from Sam tomorrow. God
willing, we'll be able to track down some other suspect if it is
murder. I do still have the Hugheses to check up on, though their
motive seems slim. Otherwise . . .' He trailed off, but Emily
could finish the sentence on her own. Otherwise, he'd have to
arrest Moses. Charlotte would lose her protector and be easy
prey for Terry.

'If you could only get Charlotte to open up about what she
saw . . .' Luke said.

*Yes, that's crucial. Unless what she saw was Moses in a
murderous rage.*

That thought brought back a detail Emily had neglected to
mention to Luke when it happened. She'd have to mention it
now.

'Luke . . . the other day, when I saw Moses and Janine quar-
reling on the beach . . .'

'Yeah?' He was all attention.

'He . . . well, he sort of threatened her. Not in so many words, but . . .'

'What words, exactly?'

'I think he said, "I'll keep you away from Charlotte no matter what I have to do." Then he repeated "no matter what." He looked kind of terrifying when he said it.'

Luke blew out a long breath. 'Those words alone won't convict him. But thanks for telling me. It could be important to know.'

The next morning, Luke skipped breakfast at home and went straight to the Crab Pot. He ordered coffee and a Full Fisherman's (eggs, bacon, hash browns, tomatoes, and toast – no fish involved) and stopped Sunny before he could shamble off.

Sunny glared at him through bleary eyes over a scruffy day's growth of beard. A whiff and a glance told Luke that Sunny had probably slept in his clothes and come straight to work without wasting a minute on grooming. He liked the breakfast shift even less than the lunch and dinner shifts, which was saying something.

Luke pulled out his phone and showed Sunny the photo of Mr Hsu. 'Did you see this man in here yesterday lunchtime?'

Sunny squinted. 'Some old Asian guy. Maybe him. Don't memorize faces.'

'What about times? Any idea *when* he was here?'

'Early. First lunch customer. Eleven thirty, thereabouts.'

'Stay long?'

'Usual. Got his food quick, ate normal, paid and left.'

'OK, thanks, Sunny. Oh, one more thing – you seen a large black man in here any time in the last few days?' He didn't have a picture of Moses but was hoping it wouldn't be necessary.

Sunny shook his head and shuffled off, leaving Luke to calculate. With fast service, Mr Hsu could conceivably have been out of here by noon. But it was a fair walk from the Crab Pot at the southern end of town to the Stony Beach Inn downtown – half a mile or so, and Mr Hsu didn't strike Luke as a fast walker. That would leave him only a few minutes to confront Janine in her room, commit the murder, and disappear. Unless Mr Hsu was a secret parkour master who could have escaped over the balcony as Luke was trying to get in, it didn't seem possible.

Still, he'd check the rest of the man's alibi. He enjoyed his breakfast before moving on to the Friendly Fluke in the heart of downtown. He'd had enough coffee himself, so he ordered cups to go for Pete and Heather.

'Hey, Jessica,' he said to the barista when she gave him the drinks. 'Do you remember seeing this man in here yesterday, early afternoon?' He showed her the picture.

She took the phone for a closer look. 'Oh, him? Yeah, he was here. Stayed for ages on the deck, nursing a latte and watching the world go by.'

'Any idea what time he came in?'

'Mm . . . Maybe twelve fifteen, twelve thirty? I'd just come on shift at noon, and he was one of my first customers. Not a busy time for coffee.'

'That's great, Jessica. Thanks.' Again, the afterthought . . . 'Has a big, tall, gray-haired black man been in here at all?'

'Not when I was on duty. Only black man I usually see is Ben.'

Luke pocketed his phone and grabbed the coffees, realizing too late that he still needed to talk to Danny the desk clerk. By the time he got back to the office, the coffees would be cold.

As cold as the Hsu lead. There was no way an elderly man could have lunched at the Crab Pot, stopped off to murder Janine, and showed up at the Friendly Fluke within Jessica's time frame. Oh well, he'd never been a big contender anyway.

At the Stony Beach Inn across the street, Danny was again on duty. 'Got a couple more questions for you,' Luke said to him.

Danny pulled out his earplugs and sat to attention.

'Heather told me you saw "some dude" come in after Janine Vertue yesterday. Any chance he could've looked like this?' He showed Danny the picture of Mr Hsu, to cover all the bases.

Danny made a face. 'I don't think so. The memory's pretty vague, but I feel like it was a younger dude, from the way he moved. Maybe lighter hair, too?'

'So it wasn't a gray-haired black man, about six foot seven with shoulders to match?'

Danny's eyes went wide. 'No way. *That* I would have noticed.'

One point in Moses' favor, anyway. Not to say he couldn't

still have come in when Danny was on his restroom break. Or much earlier, and waited around upstairs until Janine returned.

Luke drove around the corner to park in front of his office, reminding himself that negative results were still results. But he was going to need something far more definitive if he was going to solve this case.

Katie was still unwell on Friday morning. Emily did not feel up to finding out what a Chinese breakfast might be like, so she got into the kitchen ahead of Mrs Hsu and managed a simple spread on her own – scrambled eggs, bacon, French toast, and berries. Back when she had to cook for herself, breakfast had been the meal she was best at. It turned out well enough, but she hoped fervently that Katie's current indisposition was only morning sickness and she would feel better by lunchtime.

After breakfast, Lauren and her mother disappeared upstairs. It turned out the embroidered satin Mrs Hsu had been working on was the Chinese-style dress Lauren would wear for the reception, and it was time for a fitting. Mr Hsu retired to the parlor with a book, leaving Oscar, Marguerite, Charlotte, and Emily to sit restlessly in the library, feeling they should be doing something but with no idea what. Moses still did not appear.

Emily and Charlotte settled to knitting, which seemed to be the best way for Charlotte to stay calm; she was showing a decided tendency to skittishness in Moses' absence. Oscar prowled around the shelves, pulling out first one book then another, before he finally gave up and went back to the first one he'd selected. Marguerite was the calmest person in the room, curled up on the window seat with *Nôtre-Dame de Paris*.

After a while, she looked up at Emily. 'I have been thinking, *chérie*.' Emily put down her knitting and went to sit next to her so as not to disturb Charlotte.

'Reading Monsieur Hugo, I have been put in mind of his masterpiece, *Les Misérables*. Has it occurred to you that some of our new acquaintances resemble the characters in that story?'

Emily thought about that. 'You're right. Moses is the strong protector with a shady past, like Jean Valjean, and Charlotte is his fragile, formerly abused ward, like Cosette.'

'And Mademoiselle Janine was relentless like Javert. And you know what happened to Javert.'

'He committed suicide.' Emily looked intently at her friend. 'Are you saying you think Janine committed suicide, too?'

Marguerite shrugged. 'It is a possibility, is it not? The personality type is the same – obsessed with one goal. If she saw that she would never succeed against Moses, she could have despaired, lost all sense of purpose. What then would be left to her but *suicider*?'

Emily clung to that thought. Although, as an Orthodox Christian, she feared for the eternal fate of a suicide, she couldn't help but rejoice if Moses were freed from all danger of being convicted as a murderer.

'It's not for us to decide, though,' she said. 'There's bound to be some kind of evidence one way or the other. Luke just doesn't have it yet.'

'How long will that take, do you know?'

'Not long, I hope. He should have autopsy and forensics results today or tomorrow. They may or may not pinpoint a murderer, but they should be definitive on the suicide question.'

'*Bon.*' Marguerite returned to her reading. This question, so crucial to the fates of Moses and Charlotte, was a purely academic one to her.

When Luke got back to his office, Pete and Heather were hard at work reviewing Janine's files. They received the cooling coffees gratefully.

'Anything interesting come up for you two?'

Pete shook his head. 'All these files relate to one case – Moses Valory's proposed adoption of Charlotte Lovelace. Seems like a lot of paper with very little content of any significance. Like she was scraping the bottom of the barrel to find something against him.'

Luke nodded. 'That about sums it up. Heather, any luck?'

'A little. Like Pete, I found a ton of stuff relating to Moses Valory. Including some emails from the guy who hired her, Terry Garner. They start out normal enough, but the later ones get a little . . . personal.' She pulled up a message and sat back so Luke could see.

'Dated June fifteenth. That's a while ago.' Luke read, *Janine, since we met in person I can't think of anything else. I must see you again. Tell me you feel the same, Terry.*

'Now, that is interesting,' Luke said. 'Are there more like this?'

'This is the last one. Maybe she had a separate personal email account I haven't found yet. Or, my guess, he started calling or texting after this so as not to leave a trail on her work email.'

'Good thinking.' Luke drummed his fingers on the desk. 'We need that phone. Any word from forensics?'

'Not that we've seen. Could be something on your email.'

Luke went into his office and brought up his email. There it was – the forensics report. A note in the body of the email said the phone was proving troublesome to unlock and they would need more time.

'Damn,' Luke said under his breath. Then he opened the report itself.

It was short. Fingerprints and DNA had been collected from a number of surfaces. The prints of the victim and the hotel staff had been ruled out, leaving at least two other people who had not yet been identified. DNA results, of course, would take some time, but, again, samples had been taken from the cleaning staff for elimination. The samples on the toothbrush and water glass were assumed to be from the victim, but several hairs had been found that did not match hers in color or length. Most of them were brown and short, like a man's cut, found on the bedspread and carpet, but one, found on the victim's jacket, was long and pale blond.

The shadow of a shoe print Luke had thought he could see on the rim of the tub turned out to be real. It had been enhanced, extrapolated, and determined to belong to a man's athletic shoe, around size ten or eleven. That was way too small for Moses – he must take about a size fifteen – and Luke had only seen him in work boots with a different kind of tread. That was encouraging. The victim's shoes, for comparison, were women's size seven, and no athletic shoes were found among her belongings.

One oddity appeared: in that bare, meticulously kept room, the guys had found a crumpled-up gas station receipt on the floor under the desk. A snapshot of it was attached to the email. The station was in Portland, and the date was in the previous week.

But the ending digits of the credit card number did not match any of Janine's cards. Hell. He'd have to get numbers from all the suspects and compare them. Ordinarily, that would be a job for his deputies, but since most of the suspects were staying in his house, it would be easier for Luke himself to do it.

Luke considered all this. Fingerprints could come from anywhere – a previous guest, for instance, if the cleaning staff wasn't too thorough. Ditto the hairs in the room. But in addition to the receipt, two things stood out as unaccounted for: the shoe print on the tub, which was strange in itself and pretty much had to be recent to have not been cleaned off, and the long blond hair on Janine's jacket.

The shoe print was unspecific. Even in a tiny place like Stony Beach, during the tourist season there could be hundreds of men wearing size ten or eleven athletic shoes. The print could be a match for the Mystery Man desk clerk Danny had glimpsed coming in after Janine, or it might not. But the long blond hair called to mind only one person: Charlotte. At some point in the last few days, Charlotte must have come into close personal contact with Janine. And based on what Emily had told him of the period of Charlotte's disappearance, it could have happened on the morning of her murder.

Luke went to the incident board. He crossed out Mr and Mrs Hsu and wrote *Hair?* outside Charlotte's circle. Above Moses' name, he wrote *No comment*.

The desk phone rang behind him, and he turned to answer it.

'Sam here. Need you to come down and take a look at this body.'

Luke called out a quick update to his deputies, grabbed his cap, and headed out to the mortuary in Tillamook.

FOURTEEN

When Lauren and her mother had been sequestered for a couple of hours, Emily got a text from Lauren asking her to come upstairs with Marguerite and Charlotte but definitely not to bring Oscar. Emily concluded the grand secret of the dress was about to be revealed.

Mrs Hsu met them at the door to the Forster room with a finger to her lips, as if it would be bad luck even to let the spirits of the house know what was going on. The three of them filed in silently, then Mrs Hsu stepped aside to afford them a direct view of Lauren, standing in the middle of the room.

Emily gasped. Lauren was a lovely woman to begin with, but in this dress, she became a classic Chinese beauty. The deep red satin cheongsam was cut close to the body through the hips, then spread into a flared skirt that pooled slightly on the floor and was slit to the thigh on one side. Along the hem and up the front side of the slit coiled a dragon embroidered in gold. The dress had cap sleeves and the traditional mandarin collar with side frog closures made of gold braid. Lauren turned to reveal a golden phoenix that spread its wings from shoulder to shoulder across the back of the dress. Between the two majestic mythical creatures, miniature golden lotus flowers dotted the fabric. Emily had never seen anything so intricately beautiful.

'Did you make this all by yourself?' she said, turning to Mrs Hsu in awe.

The older woman smiled condescendingly. 'This dress has been in my family for generations. I wore it and my mother before me. I repaired the embroidery in places where it had become worn, and I fitted the dress to Lauren's figure, but that is all.' She sighed. 'The dress was much longer on my grandmother. Lauren is so tall, it barely brushes the floor on her. If she has a daughter, she may not be able to fit into it at all.' The implication being that Oscar's ungainly Anglo-Saxon genes might prevail and produce a girl closer to average American size. Such a woman would certainly burst the seams of this slender garment.

'It's all about good luck,' put in Lauren, as if she felt she needed to justify this extravagance. 'The colors red and gold, the dragon, the phoenix, the lotus flowers – all symbols of good luck.'

Emily nodded. 'It sure beats our American good-luck traditions for show value. All we get is something old, something new, something borrowed, something blue.'

'It is stunning,' said Marguerite. '*Très élégante*. I can see why you would not wish the groom to see it ahead of time – he might become too dazzled to play his part.'

Charlotte simply gazed at the dress in rapture. She went close and put out a hand to touch the dragon, but Mrs Hsu caught her wrist with surprising gentleness. 'We must not touch,' she said. 'The silk is very delicate.' Charlotte nodded contritely and stepped back.

'Can I take this off now?' said Lauren. 'I've been standing like a mannequin for hours and my feet are getting numb.'

Mrs Hsu rolled her eyes – a reciprocal family reaction, apparently. 'Very well. You may change.' She ushered the visitors out of the room.

Luke walked into the mortuary, tying on his green scrub coat. The body of Janine Vertue lay on the table, covered with a sheet as far as her shoulders. 'What've you got for me, Sam?'

'Haven't opened her up yet. Surface examination so far. But I think I've got your cause of death.' She beckoned Luke to stand at the opposite side of the table and indicated the victim's neck. 'See this semicircular mark that runs under her chin and up under her ears? That's the noose. The mark is wide and indistinct, consistent with the rolled-up sheet.'

'So she did die from hanging? Wasn't expecting that, tell you the truth.'

'Didn't say that. This isn't a true bruise, see? More of an abrasion. But look down here on her neck.' Luke leaned in closer. 'These bruises just starting to come up? Marks of hands around her throat. Strangled before she was hanged.'

'So not suicide.'

'Nope. Not possible to manually strangle yourself.'

'Any ideas what kind of person could have done it?'

'You mean man or woman? Probably man. Bruises look like bigger hands. Plus, takes a lot of strength and endurance to strangle. Most women don't have that in their hands.'

'Can you be absolutely sure it was the strangling that killed her and not the hanging?'

'Neck's not broken. Too short a drop. If she'd been conscious, she'd've been clawing at the noose, trying to get free. No sign of that. Possible she was strung up unconscious, but with the neck intact, she'd've taken a few minutes to die. Looks like you found her not too long after it happened.' She shrugged. 'Can't say for sure either way.'

Luke nodded. 'Anything else? Defensive wounds?'

'Not wounds per se. Did get some material from under her fingernails – looks like skin. Have to send that out for DNA.'

Luke groaned inwardly. DNA results could take weeks – he needed to solve this murder in days.

Sam picked up a scalpel. 'Time to open her up. You want to wait around for that?' She stared at him from under her shaggy brows.

'I'll leave her in your capable hands.' Luke grinned. 'You'll let me know if you find anything else?'

Sam nodded her agreement.

Luke left the mortuary in a puzzled frame of mind. On a purely physical level, he could easily imagine Moses strangling Janine and then hanging her. Charlotte, he was convinced, could never have managed it. But there was no evidence of Moses in the room.

And who the heck was Mister Size Ten?

After viewing the amazing dress, Emily went to check on Katie. If she was still indisposed, Emily would need to rustle something up for lunch.

But Katie was in the kitchen, looking slightly green but functional. 'I'm feeling much better,' she assured Emily. 'Mornings are bad, but I'm OK now. I'm going to try to get some extra baking and stuff done today so you'll have something to fall back on if I lose it again.'

'That's great, Katie, but don't overdo it. You'll likely land yourself in bed.'

She looked around the uncharacteristically disordered kitchen, with clean pots, dishes, and utensils scattered about the counters and table. 'Did you hear about last night?'

'No. But I guessed something other than takeout had happened here. For one thing, it doesn't smell like my kitchen.'

Emily rolled her eyes. Apparently that gesture was contagious. 'You can say that again. Mrs Hsu decided she was going to cook for us all – a proper gourmet Chinese feast. She must have used every pot and dish we own. Oscar and Lauren tried to clean up, but they didn't know where to put things, so this is the result.'

'Oh, boy. I get it. Was the meal at least good?'

'Fabulous. What I could eat of it, that is. She only put out chopsticks, not forks or knives, so I could only eat the things I could manage to get into my mouth.' They both laughed.

'Well, I should have all this sorted out in time to produce a decent lunch. And with any luck, Mrs Hsu won't have to invade my kitchen anymore. But I think I may need help with breakfasts for a while. Not only are mornings bad, but the smell of coffee does me in worse than anything.'

Emily quailed. Mornings without coffee were unthinkable, and her own attempts were not up to Katie's standard by a long shot. 'Do you have anyone in mind?'

'My sister Abby could do it. She's at a loose end this summer.'

'Call her in, by all means. In fact, if you want to have her around to help out on a regular basis, we can swing that. Between the wedding and Lizzie and the pregnancy, you may need more help than you think.' She suddenly realized Katie didn't know about Janine. 'And also a possible murder in town. But that shouldn't affect you directly.'

'Murder?' Katie went pale. 'Who?'

'Janine Vertue. Moses and Charlotte's nemesis. But I'm still hoping it was suicide, because if not, Moses could be the main suspect.'

'Holy cow. Don't take this the wrong way, Mrs R, but – you and murders . . . Is this ever going to stop?'

'I hope so, Katie. I really do.'

*   *   *

While Luke was at the mortuary, Nate the forensic technician texted him. *Got the phone unlocked for you. Can you pick it up?* Luke texted back, *Be right there.*

He drove straight from the mortuary to the main sheriff's office there in Tillamook. Nate met him in the lobby and handed over the phone. 'Sorry it took us so long. The guys tried every conceivable combination connected with anything we knew about her, but that wasn't much.'

'Sorry 'bout that,' said Luke. 'I didn't know that much either. I gave you all I knew.'

Nate acknowledged that with a nod. 'Finally got it by accident. The passcode is eight-three-seven-seven-nine.' He shrugged. 'No idea where she got that.'

'Who knows,' said Luke, entering the number in a note on his phone. 'Maybe it's her childhood phone number or something. I wouldn't have expected her to get clever, based on her leaving her laptop unlocked. But the main thing is you got it. Thanks.'

Luke was tempted to find a chair and look through the phone there and then, but he still had an interview to check off his list – Adrian and Polly Hughes. He drove back to Stony Beach and straight to the cottage they were renting from Emily, but no one was home. If they were out on the beach, he'd never find them. Before leaving, he stood by an open window and took a deep sniff of the air coming from inside. No trace of marijuana, thank God.

Chances were good that Adrian, at least, would be at work on the church window, so Luke drove up there. Sure enough, he saw Adrian on the outside scaffolding and Polly playing with bare-assed Raphael nearby. No law against public indecency for two-year-olds, more's the pity, he thought.

He approached Polly first since she was on the ground. She watched him cross the lawn with her hand shading her eyes. 'What's up, Sheriff?' she called. 'Come to arrest us for excessive sun exposure? I promise you we're all lathered up with SPF seventy-five.'

Luke managed a tiny smile. 'Bit more serious than that, I'm afraid. There's been a murder in town. I have to check up on the whereabouts of everyone who knew the victim.'

Polly's eyes grew round. 'Murder? Who? We hardly know anybody here.'

'Janine Vertue.'

Polly instinctively gathered her son close. He squirmed, not understanding this sudden solicitude. 'Oh. Goodness. Janine.' She kissed Raphael and let him go. 'I couldn't stand the woman, but I wouldn't have wished her dead. I'm sorry.'

'Have you had any contact with her since you've been in Stony Beach? Other than at Windy Corner, I mean.'

Polly grimaced. 'She did come around the cottage the other night. Not to speak to us, but Adrian caught her trying to peer in the windows. Like she was trying to catch us out in something. By the time he got outside, she was gone.' She shook her head. 'We considered complaining to you, but in the end, we decided to let it go unless she came back. Which she didn't.'

'I see.' Luke made a note on his phone. 'When was this exactly?'

Polly screwed up her eyes. 'Wednesday, I think? Around eight or nine.'

'And where were you yesterday noon?'

'Right here. I brought lunch and the three of us ate together. Then Adrian went back to work, and I took Raph to our cottage for a nap.'

'What time did you leave?'

She shrugged. 'I don't know. I don't wear a watch. But we weren't in any hurry. Raph and I probably stayed an hour or so.'

Luke noted that and called up to Adrian, who had noticed his presence and was looking down at them from the scaffold. 'Can you come down here a minute, please?'

Adrian descended carefully. 'I heard a bit of what you were saying. Something about a murder?'

Luke nodded. 'Janine Vertue was killed yesterday.'

'Janine?' Adrian's eyes went wide. 'Wow. I wouldn't have thought it, but I guess if you make enough of a pest of yourself, you're liable to get exterminated.'

Luke eyed him narrowly at that, but from Adrian's expression, the comment seemed more like a thoughtless play on words than an outburst of ruthlessness. 'I have to establish the whereabouts of everyone she interacted with in Stony Beach.' Luke placed himself between Adrian and Polly to forestall any attempts at signaling. 'Can you tell me where you were around noon yesterday?'

'Sure, I was right here all day. I started work at nine, broke for lunch when Pol and Raph came up, then went back to it till about five.'

'All right, thank you.' Luke stole a glance at Adrian's feet. He was wearing rubber-soled boat shoes that looked to be at least a size eleven or twelve. Nevertheless, he should verify Adrian's alibi with the vicar. 'I'll be in touch if I need anything else from you. Is Father Stephen around, do you know?'

'I don't think so. I saw his car leave a little while ago.'

Luke would have to check with Father Stephen later. He tucked his phone in his pocket and turned to go, only to find Raphael taking a leak in the grass right in front of him. The boy looked up at Luke with a cherubic smile. Luke stepped to the side and gave Raphael a wide berth as he walked to his car.

Back in his own office, Luke pulled out Janine's phone and unlocked it. But before he could look at anything, his own phone rang. Colin.

'Hey, Colin, what've you got for me?'

'Got a few things. Not sure how helpful they'll be.'

'I'll take what I can get.'

'Here goes. No next of kin; she was an only child, unmarried, and her parents are dead. Could be a cousin or something, but nobody I've been able to trace so far.'

'Well, that saves me one unpleasant interview. What else?'

'No criminal record, but like you thought, she has accrued a few complaints for unfair harassment. She used to work for the CPS, but they got rid of her 'cause she was too much trouble. Then she got a job with . . .' A pause while he presumably consulted his notes. 'The Happy Home Adoption Agency, here in Portland. Been there about six years. She was assigned to a case in June . . . a Terry Garner, male, hoping to adopt his step-daughter. No other cases since then.' Colin made an indistinct noise. 'I talked to her boss, and I wouldn't go so far as to say he's glad she's dead, but I think he's glad she's out of his hair. Looks like she was headed for the unemployment line if she'd lived.'

'Thanks, Colin. Anything else of interest?'

'I did get a hint that her boss thought her relationship with this Garner dude might've gone beyond the professional. That's one reason she was for the chop.'

'That fits with something on our end. That it?'

'That's all I've checked on so far. You want me to go interview her neighbors or anything?'

Luke pouched his lips. 'Might be a little premature for that. I may end up coming up there myself next week sometime, depending on how things go here. I'll let you know if I need any more.'

'Gotcha. Call if you do come up – we can do lunch or something.'

Luke hung up, made notes of what Colin had told him, and turned back to Janine's phone, which had gone black again. He woke it up and saw the screen to enter the passcode. As he punched in the numbers Nate had given him, 8-3-7-7-9, he realized the letter equivalents could spell out 'T-E-R-R-Y.' Those hints of a growing relationship between them looked like being confirmed.

Once in, he went straight to her call log. Dozens of unanswered calls to 503-552-4601, identified as the number of Moses Valory. Various calls to other numbers, none of which were remarkable in their frequency or duration. One more number came up time and time again: Terry Garner. These calls went both directions and lasted anywhere from a few seconds to half an hour. That was a lot of communication between two people who were essentially client and service provider.

He checked her text messages. She didn't do a lot of texting in general, but here again, Terry's number revealed a huge history.

Terry's messages to Janine started out businesslike, setting up in-person meetings to discuss the case. After they'd met, the texts became first inappropriately friendly, then flirtatious, then mildly suggestive, and ultimately outright lewd. Janine's replies were more subdued but revealed no discomfort with the trend the relationship was taking. When he got racy, she got lovey-dovey. No indecent pictures, thank God. Maybe they were too old for that.

Toward the end, Garner's texts veered toward the abusive because Janine was not getting results. Her apologies were first plaintive, then groveling, and finally desperate: *Don't leave me, my darling. I can't live without you. I'll nail him, I promise you. I'll get Charlotte for you if I have to kidnap her.*

Then one final text from him: *I'm coming down there tomorrow.* That had been sent the day before. *Tomorrow* was today.

Luke checked Janine's photos. No selfies, but a dozen or so pictures of what looked like the same man – in all of which he was turning away or shielding his face with his hand. Luke frowned. He needed a clear photo of Terry to show to Danny the desk clerk and to other potential witnesses as well.

He called Colin back. 'Can you check on Terry Garner for me? He may or may not have a record, but what I really need is a clear photograph. Janine tried to snap him with her phone, but it looks like he wasn't too keen on having his picture taken.'

'I'm on it.'

'And if you can, find out whether and when he left Portland. He told Janine he was coming down here today. I need to know if he came down yesterday instead. I'll be checking on my end, too.'

'Will do. And hey, Uncle Luke?'

'Yeah?'

'It's cool to be working with you.' Luke could hear the smile in his nephew's voice.

'Back atcha,' he replied.

FIFTEEN

After lunch, the wedding-prep party seemed to be at a loose end, and Emily needed a diversion from worrying about the murder investigation. So she suggested they all go up to St Bede's to see how the work was progressing.

Mr and Mrs Hsu declined to come. Lauren explained that, in their view, the ceremony at the church would be meaningless; their daughter would not be truly married until the banquet was over. They would attend for Lauren's sake, but they were uninterested in seeing the venue ahead of time. Emily was a bit relieved, as she feared the state of the church would not live up to Mrs Hsu's exacting specifications – certainly not now, and possibly not on the wedding day either.

So Lauren, Oscar, and Marguerite piled into Emily's car along with Charlotte; Emily did not feel right leaving her behind with Moses still incommunicado. Charlotte's gaze was glued to the window throughout the short drive. Emily couldn't be sure whether she was enjoying scenery that was still new to her or scanning the environs for danger. Surely with Janine out of the way, though, she should feel safer?

Oscar and Lauren chatted cheerfully in the back seat, but when the car came in view of St Bede's, they fell silent. Emily's spirits fell as well.

The church was entirely surrounded by scaffolding. Men swarmed over the roof like wasps at a picnic, but whether they were making any progress was unclear. With any luck, Father Stephen would be around and could update them on the situation.

They parked and left the car. Oscar and Lauren gaped at the scaffolding and traded glances full of trepidation. Marguerite merely rolled her eyes, while Charlotte waved to Polly and Raphael, who were playing on the lawn at the apse end of the building.

Emily looked around for the priest. A gap had been left in the scaffolding around the front door, so she cautiously made her way inside, feeling as if she ought to have a hard hat merely to step on to the property.

The nave was empty. 'Father Stephen?' she called, moving toward the vestry at the back of the church. On the third call, he emerged, smoothing his hair, which seemed noticeably grayer than when she'd last seen him, and straightening his cassock. Had he been grabbing forty winks? Or perhaps grabbing his hair in frustration?

He pulled himself together and put on a smile. 'Ah, Emily, good to see you. I suppose you've come about the wedding arrangements?'

'I do have the bridal couple with me.' She gestured toward the back of the church, where Oscar and Lauren hovered uncertainly. 'But our first object was to see how the work is coming along.'

'Of course.' He looked past Emily to the others with an outstretched arm. 'Welcome, welcome! I'm Father Stephen. I'm delighted you've chosen Saint Bede's for your big day.'

The rest of the party met them in the aisle, and Emily made the introductions as Father Stephen shook each person's hand in turn. When he came to Charlotte, though, the girl whisked her hands behind her back. The priest shot Emily a questioning look. *I'll explain late*r, she mouthed.

'Is one of you the maid or matron of honor?' Father Stephen asked, looking from Emily and Charlotte to Marguerite.

Lauren spoke up. 'No, that will be a friend of mine from Portland. Marguerite's helping plan the flowers, and Charlotte came along for the ride.'

'Of course.' He turned to Oscar. 'And your best man?'

'Luke.' Oscar shot a worried glance at Emily. 'That is, provided . . . he's not otherwise engaged.'

'Don't worry about that,' Emily said with a hand on her brother's arm. 'I'm sure he'll have the investigation all wrapped up by then.'

'Investigation?' Father Stephen said. 'Oh, yes, I did hear something about another murder in town.' He crossed himself, being a High Church sort of clergyman. 'I will pray for those involved, and especially that everything will be over with well before next

Saturday. Now, I expect you'd like to hear how the repairs are progressing.'

'Yes, please,' Emily, Oscar, and Lauren all said together. 'It looks pretty far from done,' Lauren added. 'Do you really think a wedding in a week is feasible?'

The priest cleared his throat. 'I can't promise every bit of the scaffolding will be gone. But the foreman has assured me the roof will be watertight by that time. And Adrian is making good progress with the window.' He gestured toward the indoor scaffolding in the apse, where the glass artist was working high above the floor.

Adrian turned and waved with a grin. 'I'll have this beauty back in top form by next Saturday, I promise.'

'And a temporary carpet will be laid tomorrow, in time for Sunday service.' Father Stephen gestured toward the bare wood floor of the aisle, which was bleached and warped from the flood. 'Unfortunately, we won't be able to get the floor completely replaced before the wedding. But at least you won't trip on the boards walking down the aisle.' He gave a small deprecatory smile.

Oscar and Lauren traded looks, which Emily read as Oscar imploring Lauren to regard this level of readiness as acceptable. She gave a small sigh, and Oscar said, 'I think we can live with that. Thank you, Father.'

The priest's relief was palpable, almost as if he feared Emily might demand a refund of her contributions should the church prove unfit for her brother's purpose.

Meanwhile, Marguerite had been making a circuit of the front pews and the area before the altar. Now she turned to the others and nodded. 'We will have bouquets on the ends of the first two pews, here,' she said, gesturing. 'And large arrangements there, at each end of the altar rail, yes? And another in front of the pulpit?' She addressed her query to Father Stephen.

He blinked. 'Yes, that will be fine.'

'And the church will be clear for me to work on Saturday morning?'

'Of course.' He ran a finger under his clerical collar.

'*Bon.*' She turned to Lauren. 'I have it all planned, *chérie*. We can discuss specifics *chez* Emily.'

Thank goodness for Marguerite's unflappability, at least.

'Now, as to a rehearsal . . .' Father Stephen began.

'Can we do that Friday evening?' Lauren asked. 'My maid of honor won't be arriving until Friday afternoon.'

'Perfect.' The priest gave a genuine smile at last. 'I look forward to seeing you all then.'

Emily said a silent prayer that everything would indeed work out as planned. Hosting a wedding on relatively short notice in a storm-damaged church was tricky enough. Doing it during a murder investigation could prove to be daunting indeed.

Detective Colin Richards put down the phone with a frown. Terry Garner wasn't in the system, and Colin hadn't been able to reach him at the cell number Luke had given him. It wouldn't do to call his uncle back with no information. He left word with another officer and headed out to search for Garner in person.

Thank goodness his old boss, Sergeant Wharton, had retired and Colin was now serving as acting sergeant. Wharton would never have allowed this unofficial excursion into another department's business. But, Colin reasoned, if Garner did turn out to be shady, nailing him would constitute protecting the residents of Portland. And Janine Vertue had been a Portland resident, too, so getting justice for her was his business on a moral level if not a legal one.

Garner's address was in Sellwood, a once nice-enough neighborhood in southeast Portland that had gone somewhat downhill since the racial troubles of the last few years. The house turned out to be a small one-story with peeling paint set in an overgrown yard. So Garner was part of the downhill slide.

Colin shivered slightly in the warm afternoon as he approached the front door. This place had a bad vibe. He wasn't a fanciful person in general, but in his years on the force, he'd come to realize that people left impressions on the places they spent time in. He could often predict with accuracy on entering a property whether the person he'd come to interview would turn out to be a perpetrator, victim, or witness.

Garner, or someone who lived here, was a perp, for sure.

Colin mounted the rickety steps and knocked on the door with normal force, then harder. No response. There was no bell, and the house was too small for anyone inside not to be able to hear. The driveway was empty of cars. He looked in the front windows through the crack left in the closed curtains and could see dirty dishes on the coffee table, but the flies feasting on them suggested they had been there a while. No one appeared to be home.

With a huff, Colin turned to the houses on either side. In the window of the well-kept bungalow to his right, he saw a curtain twitch. Aha, the policeman's best friend – a nosy neighbor. He crossed Garner's overgrown yard into the neighbor's freshly mowed one, mounted their solid stone steps, and knocked on their recently painted door.

The answer was almost immediate. The door was opened by a tall, solidly built middle-aged man with the 'high and tight' haircut of an ex-serviceman – the sort who was only 'ex' on paper. He said gruffly, 'You police?'

Startled, Colin flashed his badge and said, 'Yes, sir. Acting Detective Sergeant Colin Richards. I'm hoping to get some information about your neighbor, Terry Garner.'

The man humphed and stood back to let Colin in. ''Bout time somebody put the cuffs on that lowlife. Coffee?'

Colin blinked. 'If it's no trouble.'

His host gestured with the mug he held in his left hand. 'Fresh pot. Name's Miller, by the way. Sergeant Major, US Marine Corps, retired.'

Colin shook Miller's extended hand, then followed his wave into the kitchen. 'It looks like Garner's away right now,' he said. 'Would you know?'

Miller nodded as he took a second mug from a cupboard and filled it. 'Saw him take off yesterday morning. Woman he lives with left shortly after. Neither one's come back.' He handed Colin the filled mug. 'Black?'

Colin had the distinct feeling that asking for cream or sugar would sink him in Miller's estimation. 'Fine, thanks,' he said, accepting the mug. 'This is the first I've heard about a woman living with him.' Something of a surprise, given what Janine's boss had told him about her relationship with Garner. But maybe that wasn't exactly as it appeared.

Miller gave a disgusted grunt. 'Painted trollop. Bleached hair practically glows in the dark. Makeup so thick she could take it on and off like a mask. And clothes? Everything the good Lord gave her, right out there on display for all to see.' He shook his head. 'Course, he's just as bad, in his own way. Quite a pair they make.'

'Do you know the woman's name? I'd like to check on her, too.'

'Rodeen, I've heard him call her. Hell of a name. Don't know her surname. Not his wife, that much I know. He's not the marrying kind.'

'Has Garner lived here long?'

'Too long. Already stuck in when I came back from Iraq in 2012. I was gone four years, so do the math.' Miller sipped his coffee, leaning against the counter, and Colin followed suit. He had to stop himself from grimacing at how strong the coffee was.

'What about Rodeen? How long has she been with him?'

'Year or so, I guess. Had another woman before that,' Miller said. 'She was all right. Real beauty, and sweet with it. Never could figure what she saw in Garner. But she got out, her and her daughter. Glad for her sake, though she was a decent neighbor – kept the place up, had a friendly word now and then. All went downhill after she left.' He sipped meditatively. 'Hope she landed on her feet.'

The daughter must be the 'stepdaughter' Garner was hoping to adopt – not his actual stepdaughter at all, apparently. And what had happened to the mother? Luke had been a little stingy with the background on this case.

'Tell me more about Garner,' he said. 'Do you have any reason to suspect him of illegal activity?'

Miller puffed out his cheeks. 'Illegal? Hard to say. No sign of drugs or guns or stolen property. Lazy bastard, though – no job, far as I can tell, so he could have some shady operation going on. Or maybe he just lives off his women.' Another disgusted grunt.

'I did see Faye – his previous girlfriend – with a black eye once or twice,' he continued. 'Rodeen could have a black eye every day and I'd never know, with all the makeup she wears. And the girl, Faye's daughter – oh, what was her name? Something old-fashioned – she was like a scared rabbit the whole time. No telling what goes on behind closed doors in that house, but I'd bet my Silver Star it's nothing good.'

Colin pulled out his phone to take notes. 'Can you tell me what kind of car Garner drives?'

'Do better than that. Give you the license number.' He rattled off the digits. 'Beat-up old Toyota pickup. Used to be red. Rodeen, now, she drives a little light-blue Ford coupe, few years old. Give you that number too.'

Colin recorded both license numbers and descriptions in case Luke needed them. 'One more thing. I know it's unlikely, but you don't happen to have a photo of Garner? Or Rodeen, for that matter?'

'Funny you should ask that.' Miller pulled out his phone and swiped through his photos. 'Security camera caught him rummaging through my recycling bin one night. Wouldn't have found anything – I shred every bit of paper before it goes in. But this could be evidence if you go after him for identity theft or credit card fraud or something.'

Miller held up the phone for Colin to see and pressed play on a brief video clip. The image was fuzzy and dark, and the man had his head bent over the bin, so his face was mostly hidden.

'Thanks,' Colin said. 'I don't think that'll help us right now, but if you could hang on to it for a little while just in case?'

'Sure thing.' Miller put his phone away.

Colin pulled out a business card. 'Thank you, Sergeant Major. You've been very helpful. If you see either of them come back, or if you think of anything else that might be helpful, would you please give me a call at this number?' He handed Miller the card.

Miller took the card, scrutinized it, and stowed it in his shirt pocket. Then he extended his hand. 'Will do. Glad to be of service.' He walked Colin to the door. 'Anything I can do, let me know. I'd be glad to see the back of those two.'

From his car, Colin called Luke. He had some information to impart but even more to receive. He had a feeling there was a great deal about this case that he didn't know.

SIXTEEN

L ater in the afternoon, Emily was left alone with Charlotte in the library while the others went off to visit a florist. (Mr Hsu, as the gardener of the family, took an active interest in this one part of the preparations.) Emily decided it might be worth another shot at getting the girl to draw what she'd seen on the beach.

Charlotte was sitting on the hearthrug, dangling a spare piece of yarn for Levin and Kitty to bat at. Emily swallowed her qualms at the cats getting the idea that it was ever OK to play with yarn. 'Charlotte,' she said in as neutral a tone as she could manage, 'how would you like to draw me another picture?'

Charlotte immediately dropped the yarn, got up, and went to the window seat, where she had left her sketchpad on the table. She flipped to an empty page and looked up at Emily, as if to ask what she should draw.

Emily scooted on to the seat a couple of feet away from her. It might be better to approach her goal sideways. 'How about a beach scene? You do such nice ones.'

Charlotte frowned slightly but selected one of her colored pencils and began to lay in the background of sand, then the sea and the sky. She made the surf high for the time of year, even higher than it had been the day Janine was killed.

She finished the background and paused, as if waiting for Emily to tell her what to draw next. Emily made her voice as gentle as she could. 'Can you draw what you saw the other day? When you were so frightened?'

Charlotte shivered and put down her pencil. It must be too soon. Emily hoped she hadn't jinxed the entire idea with her impatience.

But then Charlotte picked up another pencil and began to draw a figure at the far left of the scene – a slender girl with a long blonde braid, her back to the viewer. The girl was hiding – no, more like cowering – behind an outcropping of rock, peering out at something that had not yet taken shape.

Charlotte was drawing herself. This suggested she'd only been a spectator in whatever happened, not a participant.

She finished sketching her self-portrait, if it could be called that, and picked up a plain pencil to draw an outline. She started with a head in profile at the level of an adult's, roughing in short hair like a man's. Then she dropped the pencil and a violent shudder went through her.

Emily slid closer and put an arm around her shoulders. 'It's all right, Charlotte. You don't have to draw it if you're not ready. Maybe you can finish later.'

Charlotte shook her head briskly and flexed her elbows. Emily took the hint and moved away to give her space.

She picked up the pencil again and made the hair long, blowing in the wind. With a few strokes, a female form took shape, holding a beach ball as if about to throw it. A couple of yards away, the pencil created a little naked boy, arms out, ready to catch the ball.

Polly and Raphael.

'Did you see Polly and Raphael on the beach? That same day?'

Charlotte nodded eagerly, her eyes on Emily's, as if she were calling on the two figures she'd drawn to bear witness to the events she couldn't bring herself to express.

Emily laid a hand on her shoulder. 'That's good, Charlotte. That's really good. You finish that now, and I'm going to call Luke. He can talk to Polly.'

Charlotte smiled her relief and thanks and turned back to her picture, now fully engaged in the healing act of creation.

Late in the afternoon, several hours after Luke had talked to Colin, Colin called back. 'I couldn't reach Garner himself,' he reported. 'But I did get some intel from his neighbor. Apparently he left home yesterday morning and hasn't returned.'

'Neighbor seem reliable?' Luke asked.

'Very. Retired Marine, name of Miller. He has no time for Garner. Thinks he's a total lowlife.'

'That I can believe. Anything else we can use?'

'Maybe. Garner has a live-in girlfriend. Pretty trashy by Miller's description. Name of Rodeen. He didn't know her surname, but he gave me the license numbers of both their cars. I looked hers up, and it's registered to Rodeen Norman. She's away too, apparently.'

Luke whistled. 'So looks like he was stringing Janine along with no real intentions. No big surprise there.' He drummed his fingers on the desk, thinking. 'Did you manage to get a photo?'

'Unfortunately, no,' Colin said, sounding almost like a teenager telling his dad he'd wrecked the car. 'Miller did have a video clip of Garner rummaging in his recycling, but you couldn't see the face. There's probably something in Garner's house, but I don't think we have enough to go on for a search warrant, do you?'

'Not at this point, no.' Luke sighed. 'If only we could get Charlotte to draw a picture. That'd be as good as a photograph.'

'Charlotte?' Colin asked.

Luke realized he hadn't given his nephew much of the back-story. 'Daughter of Garner's ex. He was working with Janine to try to adopt her.'

'Oh, that must be the old-fashioned name Miller couldn't remember. He mentioned a woman named Faye and her daughter who used to live with Garner. But something must've happened to the mother if he's trying to adopt?'

'Yeah. She died a few months back. Cancer.'

Colin tched. 'Too bad. From what Miller said, it sounded like Garner was the last person the girl ought to be placed with.'

'I'd say so, yeah. With Janine out of the picture, I doubt he'll have much of a chance.'

'Anything else I can do for you?' Colin said. 'I asked Miller to let me know if they come back.'

'Give me those license numbers, and I think that's it for now. Thanks a bunch, Colin. I'll keep you posted.'

Luke had just hung up with Colin when his phone rang again. Emily.

'I tried one more time with Charlotte,' she said. 'She drew a beach scene with herself hiding off to one side. She started to draw a man, but she couldn't go on with it. She seemed terrified.

Then she turned the figure into Polly and added Raphael. I think she really did see those two on the beach at some point that morning. Maybe they saw something useful?'

'It's worth checking out. I've got little enough to go on otherwise. I sure could use a picture of Garner, though. He seems awful camera-shy.'

'I wonder if Moses would have one,' Emily said.

'Possible, I guess. If you can get him to open his door and talk to you.'

'I'll give it a try. Maybe he'll come down for tea since there's only me and Charlotte here. I don't suppose you're coming home?'

'Not yet. I'm going to talk to Polly again. After that, maybe I can wrap it up for the day.'

At teatime, Emily went upstairs and knocked on the door of the Brontë room. 'Moses? It's Emily. There's only Charlotte and me here, and I think she's pining for you. Won't you come down for tea?'

Emily heard a loud creak as of a large man getting up from an old bed. A minute later, the door opened, revealing a figure Emily hardly recognized. Moses was slumped down almost to normal height, and his grayish, sagging skin added a decade to his apparent age. 'Yes, ma'am,' Moses said. 'I'll come down and see Charlotte.'

As they descended the stairs, Emily told him about Charlotte's drawing. 'Do you think she could have seen Terry Garner on the beach? That would account for how frightened she was.'

Moses nodded slowly. 'It's possible. If he thought Janine wasn't getting the results he wanted, he could've come down here to put a burr in her tail.' He straightened to his full height. 'If that's the case, my girl's gonna need protecting.'

They reached the landing, and Emily stopped. 'Oh, that reminds me – Luke wanted me to ask if you by any chance have a photo of Terry. Best not to do that in front of Charlotte.'

'No, indeed, ma'am. Best not mention that name in her hearing.' He dug his phone out of his pocket – an outsize phone to match his outsize fingers. 'Faye sent me a picture when she first came to the shelter so we could be sure to keep him away.

Must still have it somewhere.' He scrolled back through his
photos, stopped on one, and showed it to Emily. 'That's the
lowdown skunk there. It's an old picture, but I don't reckon he's
changed too much.'

The snapshot showed a nondescript man of medium height
and build with medium-brown hair, pushing a much younger
Charlotte on a park swing. He wasn't looking toward the camera,
and Emily suspected Faye had caught him unawares. But at least
his face could be clearly seen. 'That's terrific, Moses. Could you
send this to Luke?'

'Yes, ma'am. He can make a poster and plaster it all over the
county, far as I'm concerned. I want that dirty dog far away from
my little girl.'

They paused on the landing while Moses sent the photo, with
a message that simply said, *Terry Garner, around 2016.* Then
they continued down to the library.

Moses went in first. When Charlotte saw him, her eyes lit up
and she flew into his arms. He held her for a long moment, then
finally pried her arms free. 'It's OK, sweetheart. I'm not gonna
disappear again. Let's have something to eat. I'm starved.'

Luke drove back up to the church, but Polly wasn't there. Adrian
said she and Raphael had gone to their cottage.

He drove to the cottage and knocked on the door. After a
couple of minutes, Polly answered, with no toddler shadowing
her. Maybe Luke had gotten lucky and the boy was taking a nap.

'Oh, hi,' she said casually, pulling the door open. 'Come on in.'

Luke stepped into an atmosphere heavy with air freshener, but
he couldn't catch whatever smell it was meant to mask. He'd
give them the benefit of the doubt for now and assume a Raphael
bathroom accident rather than illegal use of marijuana in a rented
dwelling. Potty, not pot. He had bigger issues to deal with.

Polly waved him to a chair and sat on the small couch. He
checked that the upholstery was dry before sitting down.

'What can I do for you, Sheriff?'

'A few more questions, if you don't mind. Were you and
Raphael on the beach yesterday morning?'

'Yeah, that's right. We were there for a couple hours before
we took lunch up to Adrian. Is that a problem?'

'Not at all. I'm just wondering if you might've seen something there that could be helpful.'

Polly's eyebrows went up. 'Not that I know of. Like what?'

'Did you see Janine Vertue at all? You told me you hadn't had a run-in with her that day, but maybe you saw her from a distance?'

Polly frowned into the air. 'Come to think of it, I probably did. We were too far away to see faces, but I do remember seeing a woman in stupid clothes for the beach – like a skirt suit and heels. Could've been Janine.'

'What was she doing?'

'I didn't pay much attention, honestly. I was playing catch with Raph. But I think she was with somebody.' She scrunched up her eyes. 'Yeah, she was talking with some guy.'

Luke pricked up his ears. 'Could you describe this guy at all?'

Polly shook her head. 'Too far away. I couldn't even be totally sure it was a man – just an impression I got.'

Luke suppressed a sigh. Garner was starting to seem like the invisible man, or as good as. 'Did they seem friendly to each other? Hostile? Any impression at all?'

'I'd say the guy – if it was a guy – was kind of agitated. Waving his arms around, that sort of thing. Couldn't catch their voices.'

'Did you see them leave?'

'Nope. Like I say, I wasn't watching them. I caught a glimpse of them, paid attention to Raph and our game for a while, looked back, and they were gone.' She shrugged – a shrug of monumental indifference. Janine was no longer either a part of Polly's world or a threat to it; why should she care how the woman had met her death?

No matter how often Luke met with that attitude, it still got under his skin. But it was his job to care about justice for the dead, and to get it if he could. It wasn't Polly's. He thanked her and took his leave.

SEVENTEEN

Luke got home as all the wedding folks were climbing out of Oscar's car. 'How'd it go today?' he asked the groom.

'Pre-e-tty well, I think,' Oscar replied, in a tone that suggested just the opposite. 'Marguerite and Mr Hsu both have very definite ideas about flowers, and they aren't exactly the same. But I think we reached a workable compromise.'

Luke gave him a sympathetic clap on the shoulder. He'd counted himself lucky that he and Emily'd had no preferences but their own to consider in planning their wedding. And since he had no opinions to speak of on things like flowers and center-pieces, Emily pretty much had it all her own way. 'You'll end up married, and that's all that counts.'

Oscar grimaced. 'Yeah, about that . . . We went to the church and talked to the priest, and there's a ton that needs to be done for the place to be ready for a wedding. Way too many impon-derables, as Jeeves would say. Including whether you'll be through with this investigation in time. I'd hate to have my best man get a call and have to dash out just as he's handing me the ring.'

'You can set your mind to rest on that score. I promise you we'll have this case wrapped up before next Saturday.' Luke was going out on a limb to make that promise, but he knew if he hadn't solved it by then, his chances of ever nailing the culprit would go down to almost nil.

They followed the others into the house, and everyone dispersed to their own rooms. Luke found Emily alone in the library. He took the opportunity to give her a proper greeting. With all the extra people around, they'd hardly had a moment to themselves all week.

'How's it going?' she asked after a suitable interval.

'Got a lot of people ruled out. Nobody ruled in as yet.'

'Did you get that photo from Moses?'

'Yeah, saw it after I left Polly's. Wouldn't have helped to show it to her anyway – she said she saw a couple of people who might have been Janine and Terry, but they were too far away to make out faces. I'll send Pete and Heather around town tomorrow with copies, see if we can track this guy down.'

'Anything else you want to share?'

'It's mostly all negative. Oh, I talked to Colin – got him to check out some stuff in Portland. He sends his love.'

Emily smiled. Luke knew she'd grown fond of his nephew when they worked together the previous winter. 'Send mine back if you talk to him again.'

'Will do. Listen, there's something I have to do that might not seem like playing the gracious host. I have to get credit card numbers from some of our guests.'

'That shouldn't be too offensive. But whatever for?'

'Forensics found a receipt in Janine's room. Number doesn't match any of her cards.'

'How bizarre. All right, I'll back you up if necessary.'

The wedding shoppers trickled in, and Emily served a pre-dinner sherry as they chatted among themselves. Moses and Charlotte did not appear.

Luke went up to the Hsus as they were talking with Oscar and Lauren. 'Beg pardon, Mr Hsu, but there's one more thing I need from you. Could I please see your credit cards?'

Mr Hsu stepped back, looking indignant. But before he could protest, Oscar whipped out his own wallet and handed it to Luke. 'Here, you can see mine,' he said.

Luke didn't need Oscar's numbers, since he wasn't a suspect, but he appreciated what his brother-in-law was trying to do. He took the wallet with a nod, extracted one debit card and one credit card, and jotted down the numbers in his notebook. Then he restored the cards and handed the wallet back to Oscar.

Mr Hsu frowned but pulled out his wallet as well. 'Oh, very well, if you must.' He removed several cards and handed them to Luke. 'I suppose I can trust the law not to steal my identity.'

Luke recorded the numbers and handed the cards back to Mr Hsu. 'Thank you, sir. I appreciate your cooperation. Just routine, you understand. I've already verified your alibi.'

None of the women in the room had ever been on the suspect

list, since they were all out of town together at the time of the murder, so Luke didn't have to pester them. He decided to find Moses upstairs instead of waiting for him to come down. Charlotte was too young to have a bank account or even to drive, so she was out of the picture for this item at least.

Moses opened his bedroom door to Luke's knock. Luke glimpsed Charlotte behind him, sitting in a chair near the window. 'Almost dinnertime,' Luke said casually. 'I hope we can count on your company.'

Moses looked at his watch. 'Goodness, is it that time already?' He turned to address the girl, who was absorbed in drawing. 'Charlotte, honey, let's go get some supper.'

Luke put up a hand. 'Before you go, I need to take a look at your credit cards.'

Moses' eyebrows rose. 'My credit cards? I reckon that's all right. Can you tell me why?' As he spoke, he took his wallet out of his pocket and extracted three cards.

'Just routine.' Luke took the cards and wrote down the numbers. He hadn't memorized the number on the receipt, but one of Moses' numbers looked like it might be close.

He handed the cards back. 'Thanks. I'll see you down there in a minute.' Luke stepped aside and watched Moses and Charlotte down the stairs until they turned at the landing. Then he went back into the room and over to the chair where Charlotte had been sitting.

There on the back of the chair, held by the low pile of the upholstery, was exactly what he needed. He took his tweezers from his pocket and pulled out a long blonde hair.

Dinner was dominated by wedding talk. Emily tried to draw Moses into neutral conversation, but he was monosyllabic, seemingly constrained by Luke's presence across the table from him. Emily could hardly discuss the case with Luke in full company, so their end of the table remained mostly silent.

They were all on their way into the library for after-dinner coffee when the doorbell rang. Katie was busy clearing the table, so Emily called, 'I'll get it,' and went to the door.

When she opened it, she thought Matilda Wormwood's mother had stepped out of the Roald Dahl book and on to her doorstep.

Every part of a woman that could be painted, curled, bleached, enhanced, squeezed, lifted, or otherwise altered had received the full treatment. The result was a grotesque parody of glamorous femininity in a skin-tight hot-pink jumpsuit and stiletto heels.

The apparition extended a hand with surprisingly short but rhinestone-encrusted nails that Emily had no desire to touch. 'Hey there.' The shiny red lips parted to reveal gleaming teeth that were whiter than ever nature intended. 'I'm Charlotte Lovelace's auntie. Her poor mama's sister. I've come to collect the little orphan.'

Emily couldn't stop herself staring. She could find no point of resemblance between Charlotte and this woman except that they both had blonde hair – but there again, Emily couldn't believe this woman's shoulder-length platinum locks were attributable to natural causes.

'Her aunt? I never heard she had an aunt.'

The woman blinked rapidly. 'Well, see, I been livin' out o' the country. In Canadia. Me and Faye lost touch years ago. Poor Charlotte prob'ly don't even know she's got an aunt.' Again the dazzling toothy smile. 'But I just know she'll be tickled pink to find out she's got some family after all.'

Emily was debating where to start in challenging this improbable yarn – Canadia, indeed! – when Luke came up beside her, still wearing his uniform. 'Lieutenant Sheriff Luke Richards,' he said, also avoiding her still-extended hand. 'I didn't catch your name.'

On seeing Luke, the woman underwent a subtle but unmistakable whole-body transformation and became a femme fatale – out of some sex-starved adolescent male's fever dreams. 'Why, Sheriff, you startled me,' she purred, batting her eyelashes. 'Big hunk o' manhood like you oughta warn a woman when you're gonna sneak up on her. You might give some poor girl a heart attack.'

Emily thought she might be sick. A glance at her husband assured her his reaction was similar. She stepped back and let him take the lead – and sneaked a photo of the woman while she was focused on Luke.

'Can I see some ID, ma'am?' Every inch the impervious officer of the law.

The woman made a show of lifting her arms as if checking

for a purse that wasn't there, then patting her several zippered pockets, none of which showed any sign of containing so much as a tissue. She gave a girlish giggle. 'I seem to've left it in my car, Sheriff. Which I parked at the top of that lo-ong drive.' She batted her eyelashes again. 'I'm Teresa Lovelace. Charlotte's long-lost auntie? And I've come to take her home.'

Luke gave her his patented truth-extracting stare. Emily watched in fascination as the femme fatale withered and a frightened rabbit in pink faux leather took her place. 'M–maybe I'll come back tomorrow,' she stammered. 'You'll tell my niece I came? Give the girl a chance to get used to the idea. It's late, anyway.' She backed down the steps, one stiletto giving way beneath her. 'Bye now!' She turned and scurried up the drive.

Luke snorted. 'Aunt, my foot. Did you hear the name she gave? Teresa – like Terry. Couldn't even think of something original. That's Terry Garner's girlfriend, or I'll eat my hat.'

Emily stared at him. 'Terry Garner's girlfriend? Luke, I get the feeling there's a fair bit you haven't told me about this case.'

He gave her a deprecatory grin. 'I guess you're right. I kinda wanted to keep you out of it as much as possible – for your sake, I mean. You don't need all this on top of the wedding and everything.'

'Luke.' She put her hands on her hips and gave him a modified Aunt Beatrice glare. 'You know I'm in it already. I've practically become Charlotte's adopted aunt, and I've come to care deeply for her and Moses both. I can't have them staying here and be "out of it."'

He put his hands on her shoulders. 'You're right. I'm sorry.' He planted a kiss on her forehead. 'Let's see the others off to bed, then go upstairs and have a powwow. I'll tell you all I know.'

As they were about to reenter the library, Luke snapped his fingers in frustration. 'Shoot! I shoulda got a picture of that woman. Moses might be able to confirm her identity.'

Emily gave him a sly smile and held up her phone. 'For once, I'm ahead of you.'

He took the phone and saw a clear photo of their visitor. 'Emily Richards, I'll make a tech-savvy detective of you yet,' he said, giving her a squeeze. 'Mind if I send this to myself?'

'Go right ahead. Anytime you want to give yourself nightmares, you can pull it out and stare at it for a while.'

He chuckled as he completed the send, then handed her phone back to her. 'I'll send it to Colin as well. He can confirm with the neighbor if Moses can't.'

They went in and accepted a cup of coffee each from Katie, who had been serving in Emily's absence. Luke took a few sips, then set his cup down and went over to Moses, who was standing alone in front of one of the bookshelves.

'We just had an unexpected visitor,' he said to Moses in a low voice as he brought up the photo on his phone. 'Anyone you know?'

Moses stared at the photo, his face registering first baffled surprise, then alarm. 'That's Rodeen,' he said. 'Terry Garner's girlfriend. Current, far as I know, though he does tend to go through 'em like a fox through a henhouse.' He looked at Luke with troubled eyes. 'She came *here*?'

Luke nodded as he put the phone away. 'Claimed to be Charlotte's aunt. Wanted to take custody of her.'

'But you sent her packing?'

'*Oh*, yeah. I don't think we'll see her here again.'

'Thank God.' Moses crossed himself. 'So you know, Charlotte has no living kin of any kind. Definitely not an aunt.'

Luke nodded. 'That's what I figured. I'll make sure Rodeen doesn't bother Charlotte.'

Moses shook his head. 'I appreciate that, Sheriff, but you do realize Rodeen won't be acting on her own. She'll be scouting for Garner. I'd lay odds he's not more'n a few miles away, maybe less. He musta got wind somehow of Janine's death and decided it's time to act outside the law.'

'I realize that. And first thing in the morning, I'm gonna start a manhunt for Terry Garner.'

Later that evening, Luke and Emily settled in their private third-floor sitting room with a bedtime glass of wine. Luke gave Emily a summary of everything his investigation had uncovered so far.

'So I don't have any strong leads. I have one long blonde hair from the scene that could be Charlotte's, but it doesn't seem likely she'd have had time to do the murder. Nor strength, for that matter. At most, she might be a witness to something that would give us a lead.

'Then there's this gas station receipt.' He smacked the side of his head. 'Shoot, I got those numbers but I never got around to comparing them.' He pulled out his phone and notebook and searched in both while Emily sat in suspense.

Finally he stopped scrolling and stared at the screen. 'Oh, crap.'

Emily leaned forward. 'What? What is it?'

He looked up at her with pain in his eyes. 'The credit card number on the receipt. It's Moses'.'

They shared a long look that held everything they both hated about murder investigations: the intrusions into people's privacy, the atmosphere of suspicion, and, most of all, having to face up to the fact that someone they liked and trusted might be a murderer.

Emily spoke first. 'No. Surely not. Not Moses.'

'You've got to admit he had the strongest motive. And definitely the physical strength. And what would Janine be doing with his gas receipt?'

'Yeah, but . . . Where exactly did they find it? Where in the room?'

'Crumpled up under the desk.'

Emily slapped the seat beside her. 'See? Now what kind of sense does that make? Does a murderer come into a room, do his horrible deed, and then start throwing the contents of his pockets around? If it'd been found out in the room somewhere, it maybe could've fallen out of his pocket when he took out something else – a handkerchief, say, to wipe off fingerprints. But under the desk? That sounds like somebody was aiming for the wastebasket and missed. Moses is not stupid. He wouldn't be careless enough to leave behind something that could identify him so easily.'

Luke scratched his chin. 'You've got a point there. So what's your explanation?'

'The real murderer planted the receipt. Trying to frame Moses. And who would do that?'

'Terry Garner, for choice. But why would he kill Janine? She was his best hope of getting hold of Charlotte.'

'You said he was getting frustrated with Janine, didn't you? Maybe he figured she was never going to get any dirt on Moses and it was time for him to take matters into his own hands.'

'But kill a woman who's done you no harm just so you can frame somebody else for it? It's possible, o' course, but . . .'

Emily leaned forward and put a hand on his arm. 'Luke. If he can abuse a little girl for years on end and knock her mother around into the bargain, he can kill for no good reason.'

EIGHTEEN

The next day was Saturday, but weekends were nonexistent when Luke had a murder investigation in hand. His plan was to canvass all the hotels in the area, now that he was armed with photographs of Terry and Rodeen.

He went first to the Stony Beach Inn. Danny the desk clerk looked up from his phone and greeted Luke like an old acquaintance. 'Hey there, Sheriff. Catch the bad guys yet?'

'Not yet. Got a couple pictures for you to look at, and I need to check your guest register.'

'Gotcha. Bring 'em on.'

Luke brought up Terry's picture first. 'Could this be the person you saw come in after the victim on the day of the murder?'

Danny screwed up his eyes in an unaccustomed effort at concentration. '*Could* be. But I can't say for sure. I barely saw the dude.'

Luke swallowed his frustration and scrolled to the photo of Rodeen. 'What about this woman? Ever see her?'

Danny's eyes went wide and he gave a low whistle. 'Now *her* I'd remember. But no.' He glanced up at Luke. 'Hold up, though. Is that a real woman or a dude in drag?'

Luke snorted. 'I can see why you'd think that. But it's a real woman, I'm pretty sure.' He put his phone away. 'Now for that register.'

'Oh, yeah. You'll need to come around here – it's on the computer, and I can't turn the screen.' He hopped off his stool and lifted the counter hatch for Luke to pass through.

'Now what day was that again?' Danny asked, scrolling.

'Thursday the twenty-first.' Only two days ago, and this kid had already forgotten when a murder happened in his own hotel? He must go through a formidable quantity of weed in his off hours to kill that many brain cells.

'Got it. What names are you looking for?'

'Terry Garner or Rodeen Norman.'

Luke scanned the list over Danny's shoulder. 'Nope. Not here,' the boy said.

'Look at Wednesday and Friday.'

Danny scrolled back, then forward. The names did not appear.

Registering under a false name was tricky these days, since most places asked for ID and most people paid with a credit card. But given Danny's lackadaisical approach to his job, it was worth asking. 'You had anybody pay with cash the last few days?'

Danny's eyebrows went up. 'Cash?' he said, as if it were a word in a foreign language. 'No way, man. We don't do cash.'

'All right. Thanks. If you should happen to see either of those people, you let me know right away.'

'Sure thing.' Danny was already back on his phone. Luke let himself out through the hatch and went on his way.

The scene was repeated, with variations in the character of the desk clerks, at every other hotel and B&B in town. No one recognized Terry or Rodeen. Their names did not appear in any register. Luke trudged home at teatime, weary of foot and discouraged of heart.

Emily greeted him at the door with a kiss, which lifted his heart but did nothing to advance his investigation. 'How did it go?' she asked as they walked back to the library.

'No joy. Those two must be invisible,' he said. 'I can see it with Terry – he's pretty generic-looking – but Rodeen? Not a person you'd easily overlook.'

'No,' Emily said. 'Unless she sometimes goes around in civvies, as it were. Without all the armor and warpaint. I'd be willing to bet she looks like a different person in her own proper skin and normal clothes.'

'That's a point. Unfortunately, it doesn't get us anywhere, since we don't have a picture of her in that state.'

Emily led the way into the library, which was empty except for the cats. 'And honestly, I can't see her ever leaving the house without the full getup. She'd feel naked. I don't think she's bright enough to figure out that it would make an effective disguise.'

'Yeah, I bet you're right.' He sank into a wing chair, laid his head back, and put his feet up on a footstool.

'What's the next step?' Emily asked, sitting across from him.

'I honestly don't know. It's possible they blew in and out of town without checking in anywhere, or they could be staying in Seaside or Tillamook or Timbuktu. I'll get Pete and Heather to call around on Monday, but something tells me we're not going to find them.'

'I could check with my property manager. They could easily be in a private rental, and an awful lot of those belong to me.'

Luke sat up. 'That's an excellent point. Yet another reason for me to be glad I married you.' He was about to demonstrate how glad when the hall door opened and the wedding party trooped in, with Oscar in the lead.

'Got the cake ordered,' he said. 'Piece of cake.' He grinned at his own joke.

'So we're going to have a traditional American wedding cake along with the Chinese feast?' Emily asked.

Lauren put a finger to her lips. 'Don't tell my mom,' she whispered. 'We're keeping it dark until the last minute. She will *not* approve. I wouldn't put it past her to smash the thing if she sees it before the guests arrive.'

'What about after?' Luke was envisioning a public order incident in his own home.

'She cares too much about propriety to make a scene with all those people around. We're going to keep the cake at Katie's place and have her bring it in after everybody's here.'

Luke shook his head. Thank goodness being best man did not require him to get involved in all these machinations. All he had to do was remember the ring and give a toast, which he could do impromptu.

And host a bachelor party. Which he had completely forgotten about in the midst of the murder investigation.

Luke pulled Oscar aside. 'Listen, about your bachelor party . . .'

Oscar shook his head briskly. 'Don't give it another thought. I have no desire to go out carousing the night before my wedding. Anyway, we'll be having the rehearsal dinner that night.'

'Yeah, but we ought to do something. Let me take you to dinner another night, just the two of us. Thursday, maybe. You can pick my brain about the whole husband gig. Given my extensive experience of seven weeks of marriage.'

Oscar grinned. 'That sounds perfect. Emily's obviously happy, so you must be doing something right. Thursday it is.'

Which gave Luke an even earlier deadline for solving this murder.

Since there seemed to be little Luke could do on Sunday to advance his investigation, he took the day off. Emily talked him into attending church at St Bede's along with her, Oscar, and Lauren. The bridal couple's goal was to assess the temporary carpet and see how it would stand up to use. The Hsus and Marguerite had no interest in church, and Moses felt it was unwise to take Charlotte out in public while Terry might be in town.

The scaffolding around the door had been removed, so Emily no longer felt the need for a hard hat as she entered the building. The new carpeting, which extended into the narthex, was a pleasing deep red and substantial enough not to betray its make-shift character. The four of them walked up the aisle to a pew near the front, and no one tripped, even though the unevenness of the floor was not entirely smoothed out by the carpet. So far so good.

The scaffolding in front of the apse window had also been removed temporarily. Emily squinted up and could see patches where the sunlight streamed in undimmed by colored glass, but the repaired area had certainly grown. She glanced up at the ceiling. No interior signs of the damaged roof remained.

They had arrived early, and Emily discreetly watched as others trickled in. Even halfway into the service, the congregation was not large; she supposed many parishioners were using the repairs as an excuse to enjoy lazy Sunday mornings for a few weeks. The brunch places in town were probably packed.

When the dismissal had been said, Emily signaled her compan-ions to hold back until everyone else had left. Then she paid close attention to the carpet as the four of them walked out. No buckling or trip hazards appeared until the end of the aisle, where the narrow strip they'd been walking on met the larger expanse behind the pews. There one corner of carpet was rucked up.

Emily pointed it out to Father Stephen, who had come up behind them. 'This could be a problem for the wedding,' she said. 'Lauren won't be able to watch her feet that carefully under a big dress. Could the corners be fastened down better?'

'Of course,' Father Stephen said. 'I'll see to it first thing tomorrow.' He turned to Oscar and Lauren. 'What do you think otherwise? It's coming along.'

Oscar nodded with a slightly nervous smile. 'Yes, I can see the progress since we were here on Friday. I'm sure everything will be fine.' He exchanged glances with Lauren, who responded with a squeeze of the hand.

'As long as nobody trips on the carpet or gets hit on the head with falling tiles walking into the church, we'll be good,' she said with a mischievous grin. 'We'll be married, and that's what counts.'

Father Stephen visibly relaxed. 'Yes, indeed. The ceremony is the important thing.'

Luke whispered to Emily, 'I need to ask Father Stephen about something. Meet you outside.'

Emily, Oscar, and Lauren went out on the lawn, where people were milling around, talking. Judging from their gestures, the main subject of conversation was the progress of repairs. But when Luke appeared a few minutes later, silence rippled through the group as eyes turned toward him. Emily was sure they were all dying to ask about the murder, but there wasn't much Luke could say at this point. She crossed her fingers and prayed no one would break the silence with an indiscreet question.

They headed straight toward the car, trying to avoid eye contact, and had almost made it to the parking lot when a voice piped up. Of course, it was Rita Spenser, the local wannabe paparazzi. This week, her hair was neon chartreuse, clashing unbearably with her hot-pink and purple floral-print muumuu.

'Sheriff Richards!' her strident voice called out. 'What's the news on this murder? Have you caught the culprit yet? Are we all in danger of being murdered in our beds?'

Luke heaved a sigh before turning to face Rita. 'We're following several lines of inquiry. But we're sure the motive was personal. We do *not* have a homicidal maniac on the loose in Stony Beach, I promise you. My department is fully committed to keeping the public safe.'

Rita snorted. 'Come now, Sheriff. You can do better than that.

What leads do you have? Is it a man or a woman? A local or an outsider? Could we pass the murderer on the street without realizing it?'

'I'm not at liberty to share any details at this time.' He turned away and shepherded the rest of the party to the car, while Rita shouted questions after them. Fortunately, she didn't try to physically obstruct their departure.

Once they were on the road through town, Emily asked Luke, 'Could it help to show Terry's and Rodeen's pictures around? Not to Rita, of course, but to people we trust?'

'Yeah. I thought about showing them there at the church, but Rita would probably have found a way to grab the pictures and put them in her rag. I don't want Terry and Rodeen to find out we're looking for them and get spooked into leaving town. That is, if they haven't already.'

Emily was silent, torn between wanting the pair apprehended and wishing them as many miles away from Charlotte as they could get without a spaceship. She settled for simply praying that justice would be done and Charlotte would be safe.

'What did you want to talk to Father Stephen about? If it's not confidential.'

'Just needed to verify Adrian Hughes's alibi. Turns out the vicar can't vouch for him being here every minute of the day on Thursday like he claimed. I may have to talk to him again.'

NINETEEN

On Monday morning, Emily entered the kitchen and was surprised to see a blonde head bending over the counter instead of Katie's brunette ponytail. 'Abby?' she said. 'I didn't realize you were starting already.'

Katie's younger sister turned to greet Emily. 'Yeah, Katie's feeling pretty rotten today, so here I am. I'm not quite as good a cook as she is, but I do a pretty mean breakfast.'

Enticing odors of bacon and baking confirmed this claim. 'It smells wonderful. I'm sure you'll do fine. I really appreciate you stepping in like this. If it were only Luke and me here, I could cope, but with all these people . . .' She spread her hands helplessly.

Abby grinned. 'No problem. I can use the work, anyway. Win-win.'

Emily left her to it, grateful that Katie came from a large and capable family.

At breakfast, Lauren announced that she was going to Portland for the day. 'I have to pick up my church dress,' she explained. 'And take care of a few odds and ends.'

Emily had been wondering whether Lauren would be wearing the gorgeous embroidered red dress for the church ceremony. The clash of cultures might blow the newly repaired roof right off again.

'Do you wish me to accompany you?' Marguerite asked. '*Évidemment*, Oscar must not go.'

'Thanks, but Josie, my maid of honor, is meeting me there. And I suspect she may be planning something.' Lauren's eyes twinkled.

'Like a shower, you mean?' Emily asked.

'Or something.' A mischievous smile played about Lauren's mouth.

'Sure you don't need a designated driver to get back here?' Oscar put in with a worried frown. 'You are coming back tonight, aren't you?'

She leaned over and pecked him on the cheek. 'That remains to be seen. But I promise I won't do anything stupid.'

His frown did not lift. Emily knew that Lauren's playful, impulsive side was one of the things Oscar loved about her, but that didn't mean he was entirely comfortable with what might happen when that side took over.

After breakfast, Mr and Mrs Hsu retired to the parlor, and Moses and Charlotte announced they were going for a walk. 'Are you sure that's a good idea?' Luke asked. 'You know it's likely Terry Garner's in town.'

Moses gave a small smile. 'I may be gettin' on, but I can still handle a no-account like Terry if it comes to a fight. We won't go toward town, and Charlotte'll stick close to me. Won't you, sweetheart?' He gave her a squeeze. Charlotte nodded emphatically.

'We've been cooped up too long,' Moses continued. 'We need some fresh air. Don't you worry, Sheriff. We'll be fine.'

They left, and Emily walked Luke to the door. 'What's your plan for the day? Are you going to keep looking for Terry and Rodeen?'

'Yeah, I'm gonna show their pictures around and see if anybody's seen them. And you said you'd talk to your property managers, remember?'

'Right. I'll call them now and let you know as soon as I hear anything.'

She kissed him goodbye and checked the time. Eight thirty. The office wouldn't open till nine. She'd have to remember to make the call then.

Oscar and Marguerite were sitting in the library, books in hand but not looking very engaged. 'What will you two do with yourselves all day?'

Marguerite closed her book with a sigh. 'I ought to be glad for a day off from all the preparations. Instead, I feel at a loose end – I have nervous energy with no place for it to go.'

'Same here,' Oscar said. 'I feel like there must be something I should be doing, but I can't figure out what.'

Emily had a similar feeling. 'How about we play hooky? Walk into town and pretend to be tourists? We can drop in on all our shopkeeper friends, get coffee at the Friendly Fluke, maybe even have ice cream for lunch. What do you say?'

Oscar and Marguerite exchanged glances, then stood. '*Bon*,' said Marguerite. '*Allons-y!*'

They took the road into town, for a change, and by the time they reached the Friendly Fluke, they were all ready to sit down. Several people were enjoying their coffee on the deck as Emily and company went in. One was a young man alone, talking on his cell phone. As she passed his table, she heard him say in a stage whisper, 'Dude! The bitch is dead!'

Surely *the bitch* could only refer to Janine. Emily had no idea who the young man was, but his tone was that of a person deeply interested in the fact of Janine's death. She examined him closely, attempting to memorize his face, before turning to follow the others into the coffee shop.

After they had ordered and found a seat, at an inside table with a view of the deck, Emily asked Oscar and Marguerite whether they recognized the young man on the phone. They both shook their heads. Emily pulled out her phone, took a stealthy and poor-quality photo of him through the window, texted it to Luke, and then called him.

'Did you get that picture I just sent you?'

'I'm driving. Heading to Tillamook.'

'Can you pull over and look at it?'

'That urgent it can't wait till I get there?'

'I think it might be, yeah.'

'All right.' A pause of several minutes while Luke pulled off the road and brought the picture up on his phone. 'OK, I see the photo. What about it?'

'Do you recognize the guy?'

'Looks like Danny, the desk clerk at the Stony Beach Inn. Why?'

'Because I overheard him on the phone to someone. He said, "Dude, the bitch is dead."'

Luke swore under his breath. 'Dagnabbit, I told that kid to keep his mouth shut. Now he's blabbing all over town.'

'But he didn't say it like gossip. It sounded like it meant something to him. Something the person he was talking to would understand.'

A pause. 'Huh,' Luke said. 'I wonder. Sounds like it's time

for a background check on young Danny. Thanks, beautiful. This could be a lead.'

'I hope it helps.'

'Oh, by the way, did you call your property manager yet?'

Emily struck her forehead with her free hand. 'Shoot, I forgot. We set off for town before they were open. I'll call them now.'

She ended the call and glanced at Oscar and Marguerite, who were looking at her questioningly. 'Sorry,' she said. 'I have to make one more quick call. Then I'm all yours.'

Marguerite raised an eloquent eyebrow. 'Let us go sit outside, Oscar. We will give Emily her privacy.'

Emily shot them an apologetic smile as she raised the phone to her ear again. 'Justine? Emily here. Listen, have we got anyone on our books right now named Garner? Or maybe Norman?'

'Let me check.' A pause, then, 'I don't see either of those names.'

Emily wasn't willing to give up that easily. 'These people are shady. They might have used a false name. How about the first names – Terry or Rodeen?'

Another pause. 'Nope. Don't see those either.'

Emily drummed her fingers on the table. Something in her gut told her they were out there, hiding away in one of her properties. 'Read me off the names of everyone who checked in last Thursday. The twenty-first.'

'Okey-doke. Thursday's not a popular day, so the list is pretty short. We have a Joshua Campbell, a Marilyn Liebowitz, an Amin Hassad, a Faye Lovelace . . .'

Emily broke in. 'Did you say Faye Lovelace?'

'That's right.'

'Well, she's dead, so I'd lay odds those are the people I'm looking for. Where are they staying? Are they still there?'

'The cottage on First and Seaview. They reserved for a week.'

'Thanks, Justine. Let me know if they check out early, will you? Or if anything funny happens there at all.'

'Will do. Should we be concerned about illegal activity?'

'I'm getting Luke on to it right away. If there is anything, he'll take care of it. No need to worry on your end.'

She called Luke again. 'I think I found them. Someone checked into a cottage on Thursday under the name of Faye Lovelace.'

Luke whistled. 'That's a bold move. Or a very stupid one. If you were going to pick a false name, wouldn't you pick one nobody could connect you with?'

'Maybe Terry had an old ID of Faye's and Rodeen looks enough like her to pass?'

'Could be. I'll get on it as soon as I'm back in town. Which cottage?'

She gave him the address, then resolutely put her phone away. She'd done her share of sleuthing for the morning. This could be her last opportunity for quality time with her brother before his wedding, and she didn't want to waste it.

After he hung up with Emily, Luke drove on to the lab in Tillamook, where he handed over the hair he'd collected from Charlotte's chair. 'Need this compared with the one found at the crime scene,' he told Caitlin, the tech on duty.

'Gotcha,' Caitlin replied. 'Got some fingerprint reports for ya. Just sent 'em over to your email.'

'Thanks.' Luke found a quiet corner to sit down and opened the email on his phone.

All the fingerprints found in Janine's hotel room had been identified as belonging either to her or to someone on the hotel staff. The list of staff members included Danny, which Luke thought a little odd; what business would a desk clerk have in a guest's room? And his prints were not only around the door, which could make sense if Janine had needed help getting into the room. No, Danny's prints had also been found on the desk and on some of Janine's belongings. Very odd. Given those prints and what Emily had overheard, Danny was looking decidedly suspicious. Luke would have to question him again ASAP.

As for the absence of other prints, it was frustrating but not surprising. Anybody entering a hotel room with murder on his mind would be almost certain to come equipped with gloves.

Luke hesitated as to where to stop first – the cottage that most likely housed Terry and Rodeen, or the hotel, where Danny was probably at work by now. The cottage was closer, so he headed there.

He recognized the cottage as the same one he'd searched back at Christmastime, when Oscar's mother was staying there. Not that they knew at the time that she was his mother. Was there something about this particular cottage that attracted the criminal element?

Luke dismissed the thought as fanciful and strode up to the front door. He pounded on it briskly, waited, but got no response. A glance in the windows showed similar litter to what Colin had described finding at Terry's house in Portland. But in addition to the dirty dishes, he saw jackets and shoes strewn about the living room, showing that unless they'd found it necessary to depart in an almighty hurry, the tenants had not left for good. And since they had no reason to guess that Luke was on to them, an almighty hurry seemed unlikely.

Luke had no sufficient grounds for a search warrant at this point. In the past, he'd used the fact that Emily owned the cottage as justification for entering without the tenant's permission. But he knew Terry, at least, must be adept at using the law to his advantage, since he'd escaped arrest so far, and Luke didn't want to leave him any legal loopholes. If he were to find any evidence of wrongdoing, it would be vital that it not be ruled out in court. He'd have to wait till they returned.

Since he couldn't accomplish anything at the cottage for the time being, he drove on into town to the Stony Beach Inn. Danny was just taking over from the night clerk, coffee in hand. Probably his second or third coffee, since it had been nearly an hour since Emily had seen him at the Friendly Fluke.

Danny set his coffee on the counter and settled into his spot, apparently ready for another thrilling day of playing on his phone with occasional brief interruptions for doing his job. He glanced up as Luke approached, and a shade of something crossed his countenance that Luke hadn't seen there before. Nothing as definite as guilt, but maybe a little wariness or discomfort. Of course, that could be accounted for by any number of things, such as his having partaken of a joint on the hotel premises at some point in the last twenty-four hours. Or, on the other hand, it could be significant.

'Need another word with you, Danny,' Luke said, leaning his elbows on the counter so that his face was close enough to the boy's to make him even more uncomfortable. 'I get the distinct feeling there's something you haven't told me about all this.'

Danny swallowed visibly, his hand shaking slightly as he picked up his coffee again. 'All this? What do you mean?'

'You know what I mean. About Janine Vertue's murder. About what you were doing leaving your fingerprints all over her room and her stuff. And why you were gloating about her death on the phone to somebody this morning.'

Danny's mouth and eyes opened wide, as if he suspected Luke of clairvoyance. 'You were overheard,' Luke added. 'By someone who passed the tidbit on to me. You ought to watch what you say in public.'

Danny gulped coffee and then gasped, as though he'd burned his mouth. 'I didn't mean anything, Sheriff. Honest I didn't. I was just shooting my mouth off. I wasn't serious.'

'Shooting your mouth off. Exactly like I told you *not* to do.'

'Yeah, I know, but . . . it was only my brother. It's not like I put the murder on TikTok or something. It wasn't gossip. It was . . . news. Important news.'

'Why would Janine Vertue's death be important to your brother? If you didn't know her, how would he?'

'I, uh . . . well, I may have forgotten to tell you something about that.' If the boy had been wearing a collar, he would no doubt have loosened it at this point. Instead, he held on to his coffee with both hands, as if it might have the power to save him. 'I . . . well, I did sort of know her. From a long time ago. And my brother did too.'

Luke sighed. 'I think you better come down to the station and tell me the whole story.'

'The station? But I can't leave here. I'm on duty.'

'Get somebody to fill in for you. We need to do this in private.'

TWENTY

Emily, Oscar, and Marguerite finished their coffee and strolled down the street, looking into every shop if only to marvel at the vulgarity or strangeness of its contents. Several of the shopkeepers were friends; they stopped to say hello to Devon and Hilary at Remembrance of Things Past, Ben at the bookstore, and Beanie at Sheep to Knits. Finally, they came to Lacey Luxuries, owned by Emily's closest local friend, Veronica Lacey.

Emily chatted with Veronica while Marguerite and Oscar browsed the shop. After a few minutes, Emily heard a loud gasp from Oscar. She rushed over to him. 'Oscar, what's wrong?'

Oscar was staring at a grainy black-and-white photograph of a wedding couple in an antique silver frame. Emily could see nothing alarming about it, but her brother had gone white.

He turned to her with horror in his eyes. 'I forgot to hire a photographer. It was my one job – well, the one I was in sole charge of – and I forgot.'

Emily was momentarily as flabbergasted as Oscar. Competent wedding photographers booked up for summer weekends months in advance. Finding one on less than a week's notice could prove not merely difficult but impossible.

Veronica and Marguerite had come over to see what the fuss was about. 'Veronica, you know the locals. Is there anybody we could ask who might be free this Saturday? A talented amateur, maybe? I'm sure there's zero chance of a pro being free on such short notice.'

Veronica whistled. 'I'll have to give that some thought. No one comes to mind, but in a town like this, there's bound to be somebody. Stony Beach is a postcard waiting to happen.'

'We'd better head back and start making calls, just in case. Somebody might have a cancellation. Let me know if you think of anything.'

'Will do.'

Now wishing they'd brought a car, the three companions walked back to Windy Corner as quickly as they could. Marguerite, whose phone skills vastly exceeded Emily's and whose composure remained unruffled in the face of Oscar's panic, took charge, looking on Google for area photographers and assigning a list to each of the three to contact. Abby, who was still on duty, provided a steadying cup of tea, and they dug in.

An hour later, they had proven to themselves that not one professional photographer within a hundred miles was free on Saturday.

'*Dommage*,' said Marguerite. 'But do not despair. I will take the pictures myself. I have a camera, and I am not bad.'

Oscar lifted his head from his hands with an expression somewhere between incredulity and hope.

Emily simply stared. 'Margot – you already have a thousand things to do at the wedding. How can you possibly fit in picture-taking? And remember, Katie can't be relied on to help in her current condition.'

Marguerite shrugged. 'I will manage.'

Emily shook her head. Her friend's optimism and confidence were nearly boundless, but in this case, she feared they were misplaced. She was not going to give up on the quest for a dedicated photographer yet.

For one fleeting moment, the image of Rita Spenser's tame photographer flashed into her mind. But she immediately dismissed it. If he came to the wedding – Emily didn't even know his name – Rita would follow in his wake. That would be a result far worse than having no pictures at all.

But there had to be someone. Emily wracked her brain, but with no useful result. Luke should be home for lunch soon. Maybe he would be able to think of something. If they didn't have a photographer lined up by the time Lauren got back from Portland, the question could be moot. If Oscar was nervous about Lauren's impulsiveness, she was apt to get frustrated with his passivity. She might simply call the wedding off.

At the station, Luke parked Danny in his office while he filled Pete and Heather in. 'I need you two to get out there and find Terry Garner and Rodeen Norman. I'm texting you their photos.

I'm pretty sure they haven't left town. They may or may not be involved in the murder, but as long as they're here, I'm afraid Charlotte may be in danger.'

'On it, boss.' The two deputies checked their phones for the photos, then headed out. Luke went into his office and shut the door.

Danny sat in the visitor chair, fidgeting and shooting nervous glances toward the incident board in the corner. Luke turned the board around so its back faced the room. In the past – before Emily came back into his life – he'd rarely felt the need for an official interview room, but the way things had been going, he might be able to justify the expense in the eyes of the main sheriff's office.

He sat across from Danny and leaned back. The boy was so nervous already that any further attempt at intimidation was likely to backfire and make him clam up. Luke set his phone to record and said, 'Now. Tell me how you knew Janine Vertue.'

Danny made a helpless gesture. 'Me and my brother – we're twins, but not identical – she took us away from our dad when we were twelve.' His voice choked and he stopped.

Luke got him a cup of water from the cooler and sat down again. Danny drank gratefully.

'What was the situation?'

Danny shrugged. 'No different from a lot of other families. Mom died of cancer when we were ten. Dad had PTSD from Iraq, and after Mom died, he got worse. When he had a bad episode, he was kind of scary. If we got in his way, he might think we were enemies and lash out. But it didn't happen very often. The rest of the time, he was a good dad. He did stuff with us, and he was a good provider. We loved each other. Donny and I never thought we had it that bad.' He stopped, sniffling. Luke handed him a box of tissues.

'So how did Janine Vertue enter the picture?'

'A couple of times we had bruises that showed when we got into shorts for PE. One time the coach noticed and reported it to the counselor, and she reported it to the CPS. And they sent Janine.'

Luke groaned inwardly. 'I think I can imagine how it went down from there. You ended up in a foster home?'

'Worse than that. They separated us. Dad lived in North Plains. Donny went to a family way south in Woodburn, and I got sent east, to Gresham. We didn't see each other for years. The family I got placed with wasn't too bad, but Donny's . . . Let's just say he was a whole lot better off with Dad.'

Luke clenched a fist on his leg, out of sight. Bad foster homes were a real bugbear of his, and he knew the bad ones outnumbered the good. That was part of what made zealots like Janine so dangerous.

'So I'm guessing it's safe to say you both hated Janine for putting you in that situation.'

'Yeah. Hate's a strong word, but . . . yeah.'

'So how did you feel when she showed up at the hotel?'

'I didn't recognize her at first. It's been a while, and I was only a kid. And I wasn't the one that checked her in. But when I saw that name in the register . . . Well, it isn't a name you forget, y'know? I remember thinking at the time how ironic it was that somebody intent on destroying people's lives should be called Vertue. Even if she did spell it with an E.'

'So what did you do then?'

'I didn't want to confront her or anything. I mean, what good would it do? But I couldn't leave it, either. So I waited till she was out and I went up to her room. I didn't have a plan or anything, I just . . . I don't know. Maybe I was thinking about playing a trick on her or something. Nothing really bad. Short-sheeting her bed or putting a toad in it or something. Kind of childish, I know, but the whole thing made me feel like I was twelve again.'

Danny paused, and Luke prompted him. 'So what did you actually do?'

He stared at his hands. 'I looked around, and all her stuff was so neat, y'know? So kind of . . . impersonal. Like she had no real life. I mean, sure, it was a hotel room, but most guests leave some kind of personal stuff lying around. Even if it's only a book on the nightstand. But with her, there was nothing. It made me feel . . . a little sorry for her, you know? All of a sudden, I didn't hate her so much anymore.'

'But you didn't just leave. You left fingerprints on her computer, on the desk.'

Danny glanced up sheepishly. 'I had to snoop a little. I opened her computer, thinking it'd be shut off or at least protected, but it came to life right away. Open to her Messenger account, no less. I saw all these texts from some dude called Terry. It was totally obvious he was using her, leading her on, and she didn't get it. She was practically begging for his affection. Sickening, really. At first I felt like it served her right, but after a while, it made me even more sorry for her. She didn't just have *no* life, she had something she thought was a life, but it was totally fake. I mean, Donny and I got through our hard times, a little scarred maybe, but now that we're independent, we at least have each other. Janine had . . . nothing.'

Luke blinked, surprised to find such insight and sensitivity in a young man he'd written off as an airhead. But he recalled Danny's initial reaction when he told him about her body. 'But you were still happy to find out she was dead.'

Danny sighed. 'Yeah, I still hated her enough for that. More for Donny's sake than my own, if you know what I mean. I guess I'd sort of forgiven her for my own part of it, but I couldn't forgive her for what happened to Donny.'

Luke knew that feeling. A couple of times in past cases, Emily had been threatened or even seriously harmed, and he'd put the perps away with unusual relish.

Danny's story rang true, and in his heart, Luke didn't believe he'd had anything to do with Janine's death. But he couldn't ignore the fact that Danny's were the only unauthorized fingerprints found in the room. Nor did he have any possibility of an alibi, since no one was around to see whether he left the desk at the time of the murder. Luke would have to do some further checking.

He leaned forward across the desk, impaling the young man with his gaze. 'Can you swear to me on whatever it is you hold sacred that you had nothing at all to do with Janine Vertue's death?'

Danny started, his eyes wide. 'Absolutely. I never went near her. Never let her know I knew who she was. All I did was go through her room. I swear it.'

'And you didn't call your brother – before she died, I mean – and let him know she was there?'

'Well, yeah, I tried, but I couldn't get hold of him. He's in Idaho for the summer, leading river rafting trips. Most of the time he's out of cell range. I couldn't get through to him till today, when he came back to town.'

Luke drummed his fingers on the desk. 'All right, Danny. I'm gonna let you go for now. But I want all your contact info, and you are not to leave town until I give you permission. You got that?'

'Yessir.' Danny took the notepad and pen Luke pushed over to him and scribbled furiously, then stood. He made as if to bolt for the door, then paused and turned back to Luke. 'Thanks,' he said.

'For what?'

'For . . . you know. Believing me or whatever. Understanding, I guess.'

Luke nodded briskly, but once Danny was out the door, he cleared his throat and blew his nose. The boy's story had gotten to him far more than he would have expected.

Nevertheless, he went over to the incident board, turned it back to face the room, and added Danny's name to those circling Janine's. He placed it in the middle, between the people with a current close connection to the deceased on the left – Moses, Charlotte, and Terry – and the more tangentially connected on the right – the Hsus and the Hugheses. He also drew a line out from Terry's circle and added Rodeen.

He stood back and contemplated the rough diagram, forcing himself to consider the names objectively, based only on evidence. With a red marker, he crossed out the Hsus. They were the only ones with completely solid alibis. Polly and Adrian Hughes alibied each other but had no other witness. Luke would need to do some more checking on them. But there was no physical evidence against them, and their motive was weak.

Moses had still produced no alibi, and the gas receipt was against him, regardless of the fact that it looked like a plant. Charlotte also had no alibi, and the question of the long blonde hair was still open. But it was hard to believe she could have had the strength to commit the crime alone. Moses and Charlotte together? Luke's less objective side kicked in and dismissed that idea. Even if Moses had been driven to murder, he would never have allowed Charlotte to witness it, let alone be involved. Unless he'd acted in defense of the girl? But Janine was a flea compared to Moses; he could easily have protected his ward against her without resorting to murder.

Terry. Luke kept coming back to Terry. He had definitely been in the area on Thursday. Physically, he was inconspicuous enough that anyone who might have seen him probably wouldn't remember him. He could easily be the 'some guy' Danny had mentioned to Heather early on – though Luke now felt he ought to take everything Danny had said about that day with a grain of salt. Terry no doubt had the strength for the crime; he didn't appear to be a big man, based on that one photo, but he surely outweighed Janine.

But the motive. Luke kept getting hung up on that. Janine had been Terry's best hope of getting Charlotte back, so why would he want her out of the way? If he'd decided she was useless, he could simply have fired her. Why kill her and put himself in danger of life imprisonment?

There was Emily's idea that he had done it deliberately to frame Moses, but Luke had his doubts. Terry didn't seem like an intelligent man, by all accounts, but he was cunning – cunning enough to have avoided arrest throughout his life of cruelty and petty crime. Savvy enough to wear gloves on a hot summer's day, if he had been in the room. Surely he would realize that dropping a receipt would not be enough to implicate a man who had never entered the room to leave any fingerprints or DNA.

Luke heaved a sigh. This case was not going to fall open with a touch on the right spot, like a Chinese puzzle box. It was going to require painstaking, thorough, exhaustive police work, talking to everyone he could find and evaluating every tiniest piece of evidence. And even then, he might not end up with a result he could believe in.

What he needed was a villain *ex machina*. But those only appeared in bad paperbacks.

TWENTY-ONE

L uke called the rafting company Danny had said his brother worked for and verified that Donny had in fact been on duty in the wilderness from Thursday through Sunday. That left the loose end of Polly and Adrian Hughes's unconfirmed alibis. Back to the church once more, this time to talk with the other workmen on site.

He was prepared to climb the scaffolding if he had to, but fortunately a man in a hard hat was descending as Luke came up. He had a foreman-ish look about him. 'Hey there,' Luke called. 'Got a minute? Coupla' quick questions for you.'

The man looked baffled but came to meet him. 'What's up?'

'Are you in charge here?'

'Yup, I'm the foreman. Joe Jenkins.'

'Lieutenant Sheriff Luke Richards.' Luke shook the foreman's proffered hand. 'Just verifying some people's whereabouts. I expect you've heard about the murder on Thursday?'

Jenkins nodded as he took off his hard hat and wiped his forehead. 'My daughter's a maid at the hotel.'

Of course she was. Everybody was related to everybody, and everyone was everywhere in a little town like Stony Beach.

'I'm checking on Adrian and Polly Hughes.' At the foreman's clueless look, Luke added, 'The stained-glass artist and his wife? Can you confirm they were both here around lunchtime on Thursday?'

Jenkins wrinkled his nose and squinted upward. 'Thursday? Heck, I don't know. One day's pretty much like another, y'know? And I don't pay much attention to what's going on down here when I'm up there.' He pointed to illustrate his prepositions.

'I see.' Luke contained his frustration. 'Is there anybody else who'd be more likely to've noticed and remember?'

'Maybe the guys working inside. I think they were measuring for carpet on Thursday.'

'And where would I find them?'

The foreman shrugged. 'On their next job, I reckon. They're not part of my crew.'

'Would you happen to know what company they were from?'

'Now, that I can tell you.' He grinned as if proud of the important knowledge he was about to share. 'Truck said "Seaside Flooring and Carpet."'

Great. A trip to Seaside was not what he wanted to be doing this morning, especially given that this inquiry was merely about tying up a loose end. He didn't expect to learn anything incriminating. 'Thanks,' he told the foreman and went back to his car.

From there he called the carpet company and asked who had been assigned to the church job on Thursday. He was given two names. When he asked the men's current whereabouts, he was told they were working in Astoria that day – even farther north from Stony Beach than Seaside. No way was Luke going to waste two hours driving there and back merely to confirm an alibi for someone he didn't genuinely suspect anyway. He got the names and numbers of the two workmen and made a mental note to call them when their workday was over.

Luke checked in with Pete and Heather. Pete's phone went to voicemail, suggesting he was talking to someone, but Heather picked up. 'Any luck?' he asked her.

'Nothing yet. It's kind of a needle-in-a-haystack situation with all the tourists around.'

'Yeah, I get that. I'll join in. Where have you two covered so far?'

She told him the areas she and Pete had focused on – mostly the businesses downtown.

'OK, I'll hit the stragglers to the north on my way home for lunch.'

Luke stopped at every business establishment between downtown and Windy Corner. These consisted of a few restaurants, a bar (closed this early in the day), and an outdoor décor shop. He showed Terry's and Rodeen's photos at each place that was open, as well as to any passersby he encountered along the way. But he didn't find a single person who remembered seeing either of them.

If only he had a picture of Rodeen looking like a normal woman, just in case – but chances were that, in that state, she'd pass as invisibly as Terry apparently did. And Emily was probably right that she would never go out in public without the full getup.

By noon, he'd reached the end of Stony Beach's version of civilization, so he drove on home for lunch. He needed a new strategy, or a new piece of information, or *something*. This puzzle box was not going to open itself.

Having hoped for an hour of respite and peace, he walked into the aftermath of the fruitless photographer search. 'A change of trouble is as good as a vacation,' he mumbled to himself after Emily explained the situation. But he didn't quite believe it.

'Do you have any ideas?' Emily pleaded. 'Anybody you know who's competent with a camera and might conceivably be free?'

Luke pondered for a minute. 'This is gonna sound pretty weird,' he said in a voice pitched low so that Oscar, who was across the room getting a pep talk from Marguerite, wouldn't hear. 'But the only person I can think of offhand is David Burkhardt.'

'Who?'

'You've seen him, but I guess you haven't been introduced. The department photographer.'

Emily's eyes went wide. 'You mean the *crime-scene* photographer?'

'Yup. I know he does some kind of art photography in his spare time. I don't know if he's ever done a wedding, but at least there's a chance he's available.'

'Oh my God.' Emily rested her forehead on her hand, elbow on knee. 'I guess we'll have to ask. But don't tell Oscar who he is.' She grimaced. 'I was thinking before you came home that if we don't find somebody, Lauren might make it a moot point by calling the wedding off. Now I'm envisioning a crime scene with Oscar as the body and Lauren standing over him, rubbing her fist.'

Luke suppressed a chuckle. 'I'm sure it won't come to that. I'll go out and give David a call.'

He went into the small office by the front door, where he wouldn't be overheard, and found the photographer on his speed dial. David picked up right away, no doubt thinking this was a work call.

'Hey, David. No crime scene this time – this one's personal. You ever photographed a wedding?'

'A wedding? Not for pay, but I did my brother's last year. He and his wife seemed to think it came out OK.'

'I've got a kind of emergency here, and I'm hoping you can help me out.' Luke sketched the situation. 'Any chance you could do Saturday? And maybe a pre-wedding shoot too – say, sometime Friday?'

A pause while David presumably consulted his calendar. 'Saturday's good. And I think I can squeeze something in on Friday afternoon – provided you don't hand me any more bodies before then.'

'I will do my level best to see that doesn't happen. I'm the best man for this wedding, so it's in my own interest to avoid any work calls over the weekend. Thanks a ton, David. I owe you one.' He paused, realizing how that might sound. 'Not that we don't intend to pay you. Name your price. But I still owe you a favor.'

'I'll have to get back to you on that. But hey, this should be fun! Documenting love for a change instead of death. I'm all for it.'

Luke went back to Emily and whispered the news of his success. She jumped up and hugged him. 'You are a lifesaver! I knew there was a reason I married you.' She kissed the tip of his nose. 'Do you want to tell Oscar? Just say David's a friend, though. No need to get specific.'

Luke nodded and went over to Oscar and Marguerite, who were conferring in the window seat. 'Hey, Oscar, I think we've solved your problem.'

Oscar echoed Emily's jumping up but stopped short of the hug, to Luke's relief. 'You have? How?'

'I have a friend who does some photography on the side. He hasn't done a lot of weddings, but he's really good in general. And the best part is, he's available. He can do you a pre-wedding shoot on Friday afternoon, if you want, and, of course, the wedding itself.'

Oscar turned his eyes to heaven and sank back down on the seat, hand on his heart. 'Hallelujah! Luke, you are a total lifesaver. The *best* best man ever. Lauren would totally have killed me if we hadn't found somebody.'

At that moment Mr and Mrs Hsu entered the room through

the parlor door. 'Why would my daughter have killed you?' Mr Hsu asked. 'It is true she has a temper, but I do not believe she is prone to violence.'

'Oh, nothing,' Oscar said with a meaning glance at the others. 'Just a little detail I'd forgotten to take care of for the wedding. But it's all sorted now. Nothing to worry about.' He smiled, a little too brightly.

Mrs Hsu looked skeptical, but neither she nor her husband chose to press it further. 'Is it lunchtime yet?' Mr Hsu asked. 'I am growing quite hungry.' As if in reply, the gong rang in the hall.

Talk centered on the wedding during lunch, but Luke's thoughts were all on the case. He was wracking his brain for some other lead to pursue with regard to Terry and Rodeen.

As they were leaving the dining room, it occurred to him there was one possible witness he hadn't yet consulted – at least, not about what he might have seen. He'd only asked about what he'd done.

Luke pulled Mr Hsu aside as the others entered the library. 'While you were people-watching on the deck at the Friendly Fluke on Thursday, did you happen to see either of these two?' He showed Mr Hsu the pictures of first Terry, then Rodeen on his phone. 'Or maybe both of them together?'

Mr Hsu scrutinized each photo in turn. 'This man I do not recall. He seems generic, not a person one would notice. But this woman – I certainly saw someone gotten up in the same style, though I cannot be sure about the face under all that makeup. I think the hair may have been different, too.'

'Where did you see her? Walking by, or did she go in somewhere?'

'She went into the hotel across the street. The name of it escapes me.'

'The Stony Beach Inn? Where the body was found?'

Mr Hsu shrugged. 'If you say so.'

'Was she alone, or was she with somebody?'

'Alone, I think. I remember I speculated she was probably going to meet a man. Perhaps in a professional capacity.' He raised a wry eyebrow.

Luke resisted the impulse to shake Mr Hsu heartily by the

hand. He had a vague feeling the man might not appreciate such gestures. 'Thank you, sir. That is extremely helpful. I can't tell you how helpful.'

Mr Hsu gave a little bow. 'I am happy to be of service.' He went on into the library.

Luke followed him long enough to pull Emily aside. 'Got a lead from Mr Hsu that should give me grounds for a search warrant. I'm gonna pick it up and go back to that cottage we think they're in. Wish me luck.'

Emily gave him a kiss on the cheek. 'Good luck.' Then she made the sign of the cross over him. 'And God bless you.'

Luke had a feeling he was going to need it.

Oscar went upstairs for a nap, worn out by all the adrenaline of the morning's panic. The Hsus retreated to the parlor, as usual; Moses and Charlotte went to sit on the patio; and Emily and Marguerite were left alone in the library.

Emily settled to her knitting. Marguerite picked up *Nôtre-Dame de Paris*, read a page or two, and set the book down with a sigh. Sighing was so unusual for Marguerite that Emily looked up with concern.

'What's wrong, Margot? At a loose end again?'

Marguerite came to sit across from Emily in Luke's wing chair, removing Levin from the seat and repositioning him on her lap. 'It is more than that. I am restless, yes, but it is not *seulement* about the wedding. It is about . . . my life, I suppose. I should be looking forward to the new school year, to being department chair. I have wanted that for some time – there are changes I would like to make, to shake things up *un peu*. But when I think ahead to the semester starting, all I feel is *fatiguée*. Exhausted before I begin.' She sighed again. 'Perhaps I am getting old.'

'Old, Margot? You? Never!' Emily said with a smile. 'But maybe you are having a midlife crisis. You are sort of overdue for one.'

Marguerite nodded. '*C'est vrai*. All has been on an even keel for me, and until now I have been content to have it so. But it begins to feel . . . empty, somehow. I cannot say why.'

Emily hesitated before treading on what might be forbidden

ground. 'Do you think it has to do with what we talked about the other day? About wanting a stable relationship?'

Another heavy sigh. 'I think that is part of it, yes. I look at the footprint I have left on the world, and I do not see much that seems worthwhile. A few students have kept in touch and have gone on to do good things, but most of them simply graduate and fade away. I have friends – *alors*, to speak the truth, I have you, *ma chérie*, and many acquaintances – but I am not necessary to them as I would be to a permanent partner. I have no children, and it is too late for that to change. I could die tomorrow, and the wind would blow away all trace that I had ever lived.'

Emily put down her knitting and reached across to touch her friend's arm. 'That is absolutely not true. You are necessary to me, and your passing would leave an enormous hole. But I do know what you mean, nevertheless. You need an anchor in your life, someone you can lean on when you need to, someone to remind you daily of how wonderful you are. You need a good man.'

'I do not *need* a good man,' Marguerite rejoined. 'But I would like one, *oui*. And I am *bien fatiguée* with the other kind.' She squeezed Emily's hand and stood. The time of confidence was over. 'Perhaps the universe will send me a good man. But for now, I have Monsieur Hugo. His company will have to do.' She returned to the window seat and took up her novel in earnest.

Emily was sorry there seemed to be nothing she could do to help her friend. But it was some consolation that in the course of the current visit, Marguerite had opened up to Emily more than in the entire duration of their friendship hitherto.

TWENTY-TWO

L uke obtained his search warrant with no trouble and drove
back from Tillamook straight to Terry and Rodeen's cottage.
Once again, he knocked loudly several times but got no
response. Having armed himself with a key from Emily, he
unlocked the front door and went in.

His nose was immediately assaulted with the stink of rotting
food and sweaty socks. These people lived like pigs. If he failed
to pin any crime on them, at the very least they'd be forfeiting
their cleaning deposit. Luke hated searches like this.

It would go faster with help. He called Pete. 'Any luck yet?'

'Nada. We're running out of people to talk to.'

'Let's forget that, then. I need some help over here searching
their rental. Then I'll post you two on guard till they come back.'
He gave Pete the address and ended the call.

It wasn't often Luke pulled rank to get out of the nasty jobs,
but he'd just eaten, and the smell down here was making him
retch. He decided to start upstairs in the bedroom and bathroom,
hoping at least the couple had confined the food to the ground
floor.

Chaos reigned in the bedroom, too, but it seemed his hope
was justified – no food. Clothes covered the bed and part of the
floor. Most of them were women's, with the requisite amount of
male socks and underwear thrown in.

He started with the bed and soon began to regret his choice
of search area. Heather would do better up here. But he'd begun,
so he soldiered on. He picked up slinky jumpsuits, miniskirts,
and low-cut tops in the style of what he'd seen Rodeen wear on
her visit to Windy Corner. But mixed in with these were items
of lingerie he'd only glimpsed in sleazy catalogs and didn't even
know the names of – if, indeed, they had names.

And weirdly, in among all the typical adult trappings of a
woman who lived by and/or for sex, he found a couple of baggy
T-shirts and a pair of well-worn bib overalls. Terry's, maybe?

But they looked too small for a man, and a cautious sniff revealed cheap perfume. Luke set these aside to contemplate later.

There must be more in this room than discarded clothing. He turned to the dresser. The corner of it had snagged a bra strap – Luke refused to think about how that could have happened – but otherwise the top was bare. The drawers also proved to be empty.

The desk held a neatly positioned array of makeup and a lighted magnifying mirror. Apparently the bathroom did not provide sufficient accommodation for Rodeen's warpaint. If there was anything suspicious to be seen in all those bottles and tubes, Luke didn't have the experience to spot it.

He turned to the closet, where the hangers were empty but the floor was full. The suitcase rack held an open carry-on bag with a crumpled pair of men's jeans, a couple of touristy T-shirts, and one pair of presumably clean briefs. It seemed Terry left as small a personal footprint on his lodgings as Janine did, though a far less orderly one.

On the shelf above the hanging rack, Luke found one item stowed with the care most women would bestow on all their personal things: a canvas wig head to which was pinned a long blonde hairpiece.

Luke carefully lifted the head down and took one strand of the wig in his fingers. Synthetic, if he was any judge, which he wasn't, but the strand seemed slightly thicker and stiffer than real hair. He set the head down on the dresser and pulled out his phone to call the lab.

'Caitlin? Luke here. You got any results on those hairs I asked you to compare? The one from the crime scene and the one I brought in?'

A light chuckle came over the line. 'Yeah, we have those results. They're not a match.' Luke felt an unprofessional relief wash through him – Charlotte was not involved. 'In fact, the one from the crime scene? It's not human hair at all. It's synthetic – from a wig, presumably. No root, but a kink on the end like it was knotted. Not getting any DNA from this puppy.'

Luke grinned in triumph. 'No DNA required. I think I found the source. I'll bring it by later to confirm the match.'

He stopped by the bathroom to collect toothbrushes in case

any DNA turned up from the crime scene later on. Nothing suspicious there – shaving gear, deodorant, and toothpaste in the medicine cabinet, suggesting that Terry's personal hygiene was at least a notch above his care for his surroundings. An array of salon-brand women's hair products stood on the shower shelf, and an even larger array of mysterious tubes and bottles, presumably related to skincare, littered the small counter around the sink.

Luke retrieved the blonde hairpiece on its head and carried it downstairs, where Pete and Heather were already on the scene, their faces contorted in disgust as they pawed through the mess. 'I found something I think will put Rodeen, at least, on the scene.' He held up the canvas head. 'You two keep going – you might find something on Terry. When you're done, work out a schedule and take turns watching this place. I'm gonna run this down to the lab.'

Emily returned to her knitting and Marguerite to her book. After a while, Moses came in through the French doors from the patio, nodded to them, and went on toward the bathroom. At the same time, Emily heard the crunch of tires on gravel. She assumed Lauren had returned from Portland and knitted calmly on. But when a minute passed and she didn't hear anyone come in, she began to wonder.

Then sounds of a scuffle arose from the patio, outside the bay window where Marguerite sat. Marguerite lifted her head in alarm. The blinds had been lowered against the sun, which was now, in the late afternoon, streaming in from the west. Together the two women raised the blinds to see a smallish man, presumably Terry, along with the woman they knew to be Rodeen, trying to drag Charlotte toward the drive. The girl clung for dear life to one post of a trellis, opening her mouth as if to scream, but no sound came out.

'Moses!' Emily yelled with all her might as she and Marguerite rushed out the French doors on to the patio. Moses was right behind them. He pulled Terry off Charlotte and held him in a vice grip. Emily grabbed on to Charlotte while Marguerite administered a karate-style chop to Rodeen's elbow, breaking her hold. Rodeen, seeing herself outnumbered, ran off as fast as her high

heels could carry her. Marguerite was after her in a flash, but
Rodeen managed to reach her car and lock the doors before
Marguerite could catch her. Instead, Marguerite planted herself
in front of the car, which had been turned to face the highway,
blocking its exit.

Meanwhile, Emily turned to see Terry wriggling like an eel
in Moses' grasp. Moses had been attempting only to restrain
him, not to harm him. But Terry was lithe and slippery, and
before either of them could stop him, he had slid out of the big
man's arms and run to the car. He clicked open the driver's door,
got in, and gunned the engine, as if daring Marguerite not to get
out of the way. She held her ground through the gunning, but
when the car actually began to move, she jumped aside, and in
a shower of gravel, the car sped off toward the highway.

Marguerite stood quaking on the grass verge, sending a volley
of French curses after the car. Charlotte ran to shelter in Moses'
arms, sobbing. Emily immediately called Luke. 'Terry and
Rodeen just attempted to kidnap Charlotte,' she told him. 'We
tried to stop them, but they got away. Late-model light-blue two-
door, I didn't catch the make or the license number. And no, I
didn't see which way they went.'

'Holy crap,' Luke replied. 'I was on my way to Tillamook,
but I'm turning around now. If they come south, I should be able
to intercept them. Pete and Heather are at the cottage, so they'll
get them if they go back there. And I'll call in reinforcements
from up north in case they head that way. We've got them for
attempted kidnapping now anyway, so we'll be able to hold them
until some evidence comes up one way or the other on the
murder.'

'Just catch them, Luke. Catch them and lock them up. Charlotte
needs this nightmare to be over.'

Luke thought fast as he drove back toward Stony Beach, keeping
an eye out for Rodeen's blue coupe. With the trackless coastal
range rising immediately to the east, there were two main routes
out of Stony Beach – Highway 101 to the north, toward Cannon
Beach and Seaside, or the same road to the south, toward
Tillamook. From Tillamook you could turn off on State Route 6
to get back to Portland – the quickest way. To the north, State

Route 53 turned off a few miles to the north to wind through hills and trees to State Route 26, or you could keep going along the coast and catch 26 halfway between Cannon Beach and Seaside.

He radioed the main office in Tillamook to have them alert other departments and get roadblocks set up north of Garibaldi on the southern route and before the turnoff to 53, praying they'd be in time to catch the culprits. But then he remembered there were two vehicles in play here. According to Colin's information from Terry's neighbor, the retired Marine, both Terry's and Rodeen's vehicles had left Portland on Thursday morning. Neither had been parked at the cottage, so Terry's pickup must be stashed somewhere. Chances were good they'd either transfer to the pickup in the hope of avoiding capture, or else split up and take both vehicles, one going in each direction.

Luke pulled over, checked his phone for the description and license number of Terry's truck, and radioed again to relay the information to the roadblock crews. With any luck at all, they'd intercept at least one of the vehicles.

As he continued on the road back to town, Luke attempted to put himself inside Terry's head. It was foreign territory, but Rodeen's would be such an alien landscape that he'd never find his way around. He envisioned her mind as barren and trackless as the dark side of the moon. Terry's, on the other hand, seemed more like Mordor – full of perils, with the Mount Doom of his ruling obsession looming in the distance. All Terry's energies were focused on his one goal of getting Charlotte back into his clutches.

Having failed in his last-ditch attempt to do that by force rather than by legal means, what would Terry do next? Luke could only imagine that he would head to some neutral ground – both to evade capture and to regroup. He probably had enough native cunning to realize that the police would be able to find him at home, so he wouldn't be likely to go there. But Portland was big enough that he could lose himself in it one way or another.

Would he guess it wasn't safe to go back to the cottage? As far as Luke knew, Terry and Rodeen had no idea who their land-lady was or that their false name registration had betrayed them.

They might think they could risk stopping by to pack up their things, especially if they also switched vehicles along the way.

In that case, Pete and Heather might need backup. Luke had no reason to think his quarry was armed, but they would be desperate, and that translated to dangerous.

With Luke on the trail of the would-be kidnappers, Emily shepherded her shaken guests back into the library. She made sure the doors and windows were locked before returning to hand around restorative glasses of sherry.

'Don't worry,' she said to Moses and Charlotte as she handed them each a glass, Moses having indicated his permission for Charlotte to have a tiny one. 'Luke will catch them. And even if he doesn't, it's hardly likely they'll try again. Not here, at any rate.'

Moses shook his head, looking suddenly a decade closer to his real age. 'If he doesn't, that means us going on the run again. Lord, have mercy, but I don't think I can take it. We can't live always looking over our shoulder for fear he's gonna turn up. And I can't be with Charlotte twenty-four seven forever. I've got through most everything I can teach her – she's gonna have to go back to school at some point.'

He swallowed his sherry, put the glass down, and rested his head on his hands. Emily thought she had never seen anyone look so thoroughly exhausted.

Charlotte, curled up next to Moses on the loveseat, still resembled a frightened rabbit. She'd taken one sip of sherry, made a face, and set it down again, and she was shivering. Emily pulled an afghan off the back of the couch and wrapped it around her. If she wouldn't drink the sherry, perhaps a nice cup of tea with plenty of sugar would do the trick.

Katie was in the kitchen, taking a tray of scones out of the oven. Emily realized with a start that it was almost four o'clock – their regular teatime. Perhaps there was no need to rush things after all.

Katie turned her head as Emily came in. 'What was all the commotion just now? I wanted to go see if I could help, but my hands were covered in dough.'

'It's just as well you didn't. Charlotte's – well, stepfather, I guess you could call him, though he never married her mother – showed up with his new girlfriend and tried to kidnap her.'

Katie dropped the tray of scones on to the waiting cooling rack and covered her mouth with her hands. 'Oh my God,' she said. 'They didn't get her, did they?'

'No. But we didn't get them, either. They got away. Luke's starting a manhunt for them now. I don't think they'll come back, but do be on the alert for any strangers on the property, OK? And tell Jamie, too.'

'I will. My goodness, Mrs R. This feels almost as scary as when we had actual murders in the house.'

'I know. I pray Luke's people will apprehend them quickly and it will all be over. It's not only Charlotte I'm concerned about – you don't need any trauma in your condition. How are you feeling?'

'I'm fine now. Mostly it's just the mornings. Abby's been a big help.'

'Good to hear. She did a fine job with breakfast this morning.' Emily glanced from the scones to the kettle on the stove, which was gearing up to whistle. 'Charlotte's in shock – she needs her tea. Can you hurry things along at all?'

'Sure thing. Be right there.'

Emily took her cue to get out of the way.

Back in the library, everyone had assembled ahead of the tea gong. Marguerite was explaining to Oscar, who had slept through all the drama, and to Mr and Mrs Hsu, who had simply ignored it, what had happened. The doorbell rang as Katie was bringing in the tea tray.

They all stared at each other in horror. Who could it be? But Emily admonished herself to be reasonable – it was hardly likely Terry and Rodeen would return and ring the bell. 'I'll get it,' she said to Katie and went to the door.

At first, looking through the door's high windows, she thought no one was there. But then she glimpsed an unknown young woman standing off to the side.

The bell rang again, this time accompanied by a familiar voice. 'Hey! What's with the locked door? Let me in!'

Emily sighed in relief. Lauren. She was too short to be seen through the high window. And the other young woman must be her maid of honor. She unlocked the door and let them in.

'What's up?' Lauren asked. 'For a minute I thought nobody was here. But it's teatime, so that didn't make sense.'

Emily held up a hand for patience. 'Welcome to Windy Corner,' she said to Lauren's friend.

'Oh, sorry,' Lauren said. 'I forgot to introduce you. Emily Richards, this is Josie Chung. My maid of honor.'

Josie shook hands, then said, 'I'm sorry to barge in on you like this. I know I wasn't supposed to show up till Friday. But I got free unexpectedly, and Lauren insisted I come back with her.'

'It's no problem at all,' Emily said in her best hostess manner. 'But I'm afraid all our beds are full. I have nowhere to put you.'

'Oh, that's OK, I managed to get a room at the Stony Beach Inn. They had a last-minute cancellation or I never could have managed it.'

Emily wondered if that 'cancellation' could have been caused by the death of one of the guests. Would Janine's room have been released by the sheriff and put back into use so soon? She had no way of knowing, but in any case, it wouldn't do to tell Josie she'd be sleeping in the bed of a murder victim.

'Excellent. Come on into the library – tea is being served as we speak.'

The buzz of talk broke off as Lauren and Josie entered, and introductions were made all around. To Emily's immense relief, the conversation immediately turned to what Lauren had been up to in her time away. Moses and Charlotte put their tea things on a tray and quietly slipped out of the room – a move Emily heartily approved.

'I know I'm not allowed to ask about the dress,' Oscar said. 'But did it go OK?'

Lauren twinkled at him. 'Perfect,' she said. 'But more than that I will not say. Josie's taking the dress to the hotel with her so you can't sneak a peek.'

'As if I would!' Oscar replied, hand on heart. 'So what did you get up to all day? Surely the fitting didn't take four hours.'

Lauren shot a conspiratorial look at Josie, who drew herself up and said, 'What happens at a bachelorette lunch stays at a bachelorette lunch. I will say only that a very good time was had by all.'

Oscar cleared his throat with a nervous glance at his bride. 'Well, you're back safely, anyhow.' He gave her a quick kiss on the cheek.

They got through tea with no further explanations of the afternoon's events being required. Then Lauren drove Josie to the hotel to check in and get settled, promising to retrieve her in time for dinner. When she got back to Windy Corner, Emily filled her in.

'Holy cow!' Lauren said. 'I go away for one day and all hell breaks loose!' She turned to Oscar, grasping his hand. 'But you're OK, right? You don't look too shaken up.'

He blushed deeply. 'I slept through the whole thing. We walked to town in the morning, and I was wiped out, so I went to bed right after lunch and slept almost until you got here.'

Lauren put her head back and laughed. 'I should have guessed. Well, anyway, I'm glad it all turned out OK. Will they catch them, do you think?' she asked Emily.

'I hope and pray they will. Though it's been long enough, I'd think a roadblock would have caught them by now if it was going to. I'll have to hope Luke hasn't called because he's too busy booking them, not because there's nothing to report.'

TWENTY-THREE

Luke got back to the cottage to find Pete and Heather on the alert – Heather in her car and Pete hiding in the bushes by the front door. He parked his own SUV around the corner, facing toward the front of the cottage, where he could see but was unlikely to be noticed. He radioed Heather to get her vehicle out of sight as well. The last thing they needed was for Terry to drive up, get spooked, and tear off again before they could catch him.

They didn't have long to wait. In a few minutes, an old, beaten-up, faded red Toyota pickup came around the corner toward them. Luke waited till the driver had parked in the cottage driveway and gotten out. Then he pulled his SUV out of the side street and across the road, blocking any exit. Heather did the same at the next intersection down.

Terry, who was heading toward the front door, turned at the engine noises and froze like a cornered animal. Pete jumped out from the bushes and almost managed to grab him, but Terry turned and ran across the street, past the opposite house, and along a track that led down a steep rock stairway to the beach. All three cops were after him in a flash, though Pete's and Heather's flashes moved quicker than Luke's.

Pete was big – twice the size of their quarry – but Heather was fast. She pulled ahead as they reached the stairway, and as soon as Terry dropped on to the sand at the bottom, she leaped from the last rock straight on to his back, pinning him to the loose sand. Pete was right behind her, and the two of them had him up and cuffed before Luke had time to worry about Terry being able to breathe with his face in the sand.

Terry coughed and spluttered as Luke read him his rights, arresting him on suspicion of attempted kidnapping. He was tempted to throw in the murder charge, but he reminded himself he didn't have enough evidence for that yet. He would have to get Terry to talk.

They got their prisoner back up to the street with difficulty, Pete having to half drag, half carry him up the rock steps. 'Take him to HQ and book him,' Luke told his deputy. 'I'll be right behind you. Heather, hang on a minute while I check in with the roadblock crews.'

His first call, though, was to Emily. 'We got Terry,' he told her. 'They'd split up – Rodeen wasn't with him. But Charlotte can breathe easy. I highly doubt Rodeen will try anything more on her own. And with any luck, we'll get her soon, too.'

'Thank God,' Emily breathed. 'I'll let them know right away. There's no danger he'll wriggle out of it, is there?'

'Not a chance. We're doing everything by the book, and you all can provide plenty of eyewitness testimony to the kidnapping charge. Whether we can get him for murder is another question.'

After that, Luke radioed the roadblock crews to tell them not to watch for a red pickup anymore but to concentrate on the blue coupe. If only he knew which direction Rodeen was more likely to go! If she knew the roads, she'd realize 53 was the fastest way to get off 101, and if she got through that junction, she'd be able to lose her pursuers on side roads. But Luke was betting she didn't know the area well and would be driving in panic mode, taking the most obvious route and not thinking through the consequences. His money was on her heading south.

Depending on where she'd dropped Terry to retrieve his pickup, she could be halfway to Garibaldi by now. Whether Luke's goal was to pursue her or to begin interrogating Terry, Tillamook had to be his destination.

He told Heather to patrol the main roads in Stony Beach, in case Rodeen tried to hide there instead of heading directly out of town. Then he started off for Tillamook.

Luke's call came in as Emily finished filling Lauren in on the situation. She told the others briefly, 'They got Terry,' then sped up the stairs to Moses' room.

Moses and Charlotte were sitting together on the small balcony outside his room that overlooked the driveway, presumably so Moses could keep a lookout in case the would-be kidnappers returned. Charlotte sat with her feet tucked under her, hugging a quilt around her. The empty tea tray lay on the floor between their chairs.

'You can end your vigil now,' Emily told Moses. 'Terry has been apprehended.'

Moses stood, color and life returning to his face. 'Luke got him? And Rodeen?'

Emily shook her head. 'Rodeen is still at large. But I don't think she's much of a threat on her own, do you?'

'No, ma'am. Not much. But I still want to see her behind bars for what she tried to do to my girl.'

'Of course. That's what we all want.'

Charlotte, still seated, tugged on Moses' sleeve with a question written on her face. Emily couldn't read the content of the question, but Moses apparently could.

'What about the murder? Can Luke get Terry for that?'

'That I don't know. I don't think he has any real evidence against him.' Emily bit her tongue, knowing she mustn't divulge the little physical evidence Luke did have, all of which still pointed toward Moses and Charlotte. 'In fact, the only reason he suspects Terry at all is that we all want him to be guilty. You know as well as I do that's not enough even for an arrest, let alone a conviction.'

Moses closed his eyes for a moment and made the sign of the cross ponderously over his massive chest. 'Yes, ma'am. I know. It's in God's hands.' He turned to smile at Charlotte, giving her hand a reassuring squeeze. 'You're safe, sweetie. They'll put him away one way or another. You and I will be able to go on with our lives.'

Charlotte returned his smile, but her eyes still held a shadow of worry. Emily knew this wasn't a final resolution for this beleaguered pair. She retreated to her private sitting room to do some serious praying of her own.

When Luke reached the northern outskirts of Garibaldi, he found the roadblock still in place. 'No sign of a blue coupe?' he asked the officer in charge.

'Nope. Not much traffic through here, either. No way we could've missed it.'

'Damn,' Luke muttered. Had he miscalculated? Had Rodeen

gone north after all? Surely she couldn't have eluded the road-block at the 53 junction; after dropping Terry at his truck, she wouldn't likely have been able to get there ahead of the block being set up. She must be driving around or hiding out somewhere in between.

'Listen, can you spare one car to go back to Stony Beach? I feel like if she was coming this way, she would have gotten here by now.'

'Sure thing.' The officer called one of his men over and gave the order. Luke continued on his way, radioing Heather that he was sending reinforcements and the ball was most likely in her court. He was tempted to join the manhunt – in this case, woman-hunt – personally, but Rodeen was at most an accessory. Terry was the one Luke really had to nail. And that meant interviewing him before he had too much time to concoct a story.

He didn't have time to get official witness statements from Emily and the others, but he called her as he drove and recorded her detailed account of what had happened. Once they had Rodeen in custody, he'd get Pete or Heather to take statements in the usual way.

When he pulled into the parking lot of the main sheriff's office, the evidence bag on the seat beside him reminded him that his first stop needed to be the lab – to confirm whether the blonde hairpiece he'd taken from the cottage matched the synthetic hair from the crime scene. He could see virtually no chance that it wouldn't, but he had to have the official word.

He dropped off the bag with Caitlin. 'Compare this to that synthetic hair you found.'

She nodded with a smirk as she took the bag. 'I'd say this is a very likely culprit. I can probably get you results before you leave the building.'

'I'll be here a while – got somebody to interview. Text me when you know.' He started to leave, then checked himself and went back. 'And get the shoes from the man Pete brought in – Terry Garner. Compare his soles to that print from the side of the tub.' They might have some physical evidence against him after all.

He checked in with Sheriff Tucker before going to the interview room. Pete had already booked Terry and had him waiting there for Luke. 'You want to sit in, sir?' Luke asked.

'Nah, you got this,' the sheriff replied. 'Good work. Can you get him for the murder, too?'

'Not yet, but I'm hoping to get him to confess now that he's in custody. Wish me luck.'

Luke stopped by the coffee machine and poured two cups. Outside the door of the interview room, he paused and took a deep breath. He had no illusions that Terry would be an easy nut to crack. Training in advanced interview techniques had never been considered necessary for his job, though the events of the past year might change that. Luke was going to need every brain cell and every ounce of native cunning he possessed to get the truth out of this slippery devil.

He entered the room and set one of the coffees down in front of Terry. 'Hope black's OK.'

The man's expression shifted from a mix of fear and defiance to a crafty smirk. 'Actually, I take three sugars.'

Of course you do, Luke thought. He poked his head out the door and asked the nearest officer to fetch the sugar. Then he sat down, turned on the recorder, and introduced himself.

'State your name for the recording,' he told Terry.

'Terence Garner.'

'Now, Terry – can I call you Terry?'

He shrugged.

'I think you know why we're here.'

'I'm not talking till I get a lawyer,' Terry said.

'I haven't asked you anything yet.'

'I want a lawyer. That's my last word.' He leaned back in his chair with his arms crossed over his chest.

Luke weighed his odds of getting a public defender there on short notice at quitting time. He could only try. He paused the recording, then poked his head out again to see the officer returning with the sugar. Luke took the three packets and said, 'Any lawyers in the building that you know of?'

'Yeah, just saw Mitchell on his way out.'

'Grab him, will you? Quick as you can.'

The officer sprinted off, and Luke shut the door again. He tossed the sugar on to the table in front of Terry. 'Lawyer'll be here in a minute.'

Terry made a slow business of ripping open each packet and

dribbling the sugar into his coffee, the smirk never leaving his face. 'Stirrer?'

Luke pulled a ballpoint pen out of his pocket and tossed it across the table. 'Use that.'

Terry quirked one eyebrow. 'Hardly sanitary, Sheriff.'

Luke choked down the reply that judging by the state of his lodgings, sanitation did not appear to be a high priority for Garner. 'Best I can do at the moment.'

Terry left the pen where it fell and gently swirled the coffee in his cup. He sipped it and made a face. 'You sure this is coffee? Tastes more like engine oil.'

'Gourmet coffee's not one of the perks of the job. Take it or leave it.'

Terry set the cup down at arm's length.

A knock came at the door, and Luke got up to let Arnold Mitchell in. Mitchell wasn't bad as public defenders went, but he'd been in the job too long, and it showed – in his stooped posture, skewed tie, and the bags under his defeated eyes. He nodded to Luke, who introduced him to Garner.

'Can I have a few minutes alone with my client, please?'

Luke handed him the charge sheet and stepped out. Barely two minutes elapsed before Mitchell opened the door and said, 'We're ready.'

Luke settled himself in his chair and restarted the recording, adding Mitchell's name to those present.

'All right, Terry. We have eyewitness testimony that this afternoon at three forty-five, you and your accomplice, Rodeen Norman, attempted to kidnap Charlotte Lovelace from my home in Stony Beach.'

'Wasn't me.'

Luke frowned. 'One of the eyewitnesses, Moses Valory, knows you well. There's no chance at all that he could've been mistaken.'

'Wasn't trying to kidnap her. Just wanted to have a chat.'

Good grief, how much obvious truth could one man deny? 'You were seen grabbing her and trying to pull her toward your car against her will.'

'Friendly hug, that's all. Hadn't seen my stepdaughter in a while.'

'She's not your stepdaughter. You and her mother were never married.'

'Common law. Same thing.'

Luke wasn't sure of the exact duration of their relationship, so he let that go. 'The point is, Charlotte was not in the least happy to see you and had no desire whatsoever to go with you. That constitutes attempted kidnapping.'

'Wasn't my idea. All Rodeen. She always wanted a daughter and took a fancy to the girl. I told her it was a bad thing to do, but she insisted.'

Luke swallowed his irritation. This fellow was something else. 'Now, Terry, you know that's not true. God knows why Rodeen went along with you on this, but we all know you've been trying to get Charlotte back ever since her mother died. You tried legal means, hiring Janine Vertue to block Moses' adoption. But with Janine dead, you got desperate and took matters into your own hands by trying to kidnap the girl.'

A sly grin turned Terry's already unattractive face into that of a scary clown. 'You've got it all wrong, Sheriff. Charlotte wants to come back to me. Always has. She's Daddy's little sweetheart. But Valory won't give her up. Now, why would an ugly old black ex-con like him want to hold on to a pretty little white girl who's in no way related to him? I can only think of one reason.' Terry leaned forward till he was practically spitting in Luke's face as he said, 'He wants himself a sweet little piece of lily-white ass.'

At that, Mitchell looked as if he'd bitten into a piece of rotten meat. Luke choked down the bile that rose in his own throat. If being disgusting were a crime, this man would qualify for capital punishment. But Luke couldn't let the interview be derailed by any attempt to address the underlying issues, which he had only Moses' third-hand testimony to confirm. Unless by some miracle Charlotte finally managed to talk.

'I have the word of three people, two of them completely disinterested, that Charlotte was resisting being taken away by you and Rodeen. Let's drop all this prevarication, shall we? We all know what really went down at my house a couple hours ago. You and Rodeen attempted to kidnap Charlotte Lovelace, and that's all there is to it.'

Mitchell, who had been sitting with his forehead in his hand, leaned across and whispered something in Terry's ear. Terry grimaced and leaned back in his chair. 'Well, if you know all about what happened, Sheriff, why are you asking me?'

Why indeed? This was clearly an exercise in futility.

'Let's leave the kidnapping for now.'

'Attempted kidnapping,' Mitchell put in, for form's sake. Clearly the lawyer was as disgusted with his client as Luke himself was.

'Attempted kidnapping. Thank you, Mr Mitchell. I'd like to ask you about another matter, Terry.'

Terry perused his dirty fingernails, his face a deliberate blank. Luke noticed his hands, underneath the filth, were red and raw – some kind of rash or allergy, maybe. 'What matter is that?' Terry asked conversationally.

'When did you arrive in Stony Beach?'

The man's stone face cracked, revealing surprise. He picked a biggish piece of grime out from under the nail of his left forefinger. 'Let me see. I believe it was Thursday afternoon.'

'Sure it wasn't Thursday morning?'

Terry shook his head. 'Checked into the cottage at three o'clock.'

'That would be standard check-in time, yes. But you were in town for at least a few hours before that.'

'What makes you say that, Sheriff?' Terry still did not look Luke in the face.

'You were seen. At least, Rodeen was seen. In downtown Stony Beach, between twelve and twelve thirty.'

Terry finally lowered his hands to the table and turned toward Luke. 'Oh, *Rodeen* was seen! In case you hadn't noticed, Sheriff, we are two separate people. We even drive two separate cars. *She* may've been there at noon, but that doesn't mean I was.'

Luke consulted his notes. 'We have information that you left your home in Portland before Rodeen did. I think you came down first, and she followed you.'

Another grin. 'You can think whatever you like, Sheriff. No business of mine.'

Luke gritted his teeth. 'Let's leave that point for now. Rodeen was seen entering the Stony Beach Inn, where Janine Vertue was staying. Where Janine Vertue was killed. And right around the time of her murder.' Terry's eyebrows went up in fake surprise. 'As far as we know, the two women were not acquainted. Can you think of any reason for Rodeen to go there other than to meet you? Or look for you?'

'Sure. Rodeen was jealous. She thought I had a thing for Janine. Went to confront her.' Terry leaned across the table with a repellent all-boys-together smile. 'In fact, it was Janine who had a thing for me.'

Finally – for the first time in the interview, Garner had said something true. 'Which you encouraged, because it made her more eager to help you.'

Terry sat back with a shrug. 'Why not? Stupid bitch. If she could fool herself into believing any male could be attracted to a dog like her, she deserved to be taken for a ride.'

Luke had next to no sympathy for Janine Vertue, but this barb awakened his chivalry toward women in general. 'She was a human being and therefore entitled to a certain amount of respect. I'll thank you to watch your language from now on.'

'Ooh, Sheriff, you surprise me. Don't tell me you liked the b— I mean woman? Now what would your lady wife say to that?'

Luke needed every ounce of training and experience to keep himself from rising to Garner's bait. It was time to cut to the chase.

'Were you or were you not in Janine Vertue's hotel room on Thursday the twenty-first between eleven thirty and twelve thirty?'

Once again Garner leaned toward him, his eyes full of challenge. 'Prove it.'

Unfortunately, that was exactly what Luke could not yet do – though the shoeprint might help. 'Let's see what Rodeen has to say.' Let the man stew, thinking they had his girlfriend in custody. Luke announced the suspension of the interview, clicked the recording off, and stood. 'This isn't over, Garner.'

A flicker of unease crossed Terry's face as Luke turned and left the room. They *had* to find Rodeen.

TWENTY-FOUR

n the hall outside the interview room, Luke checked his phone. A text from Caitlin read, *Two for two – hair and shoe both match.*

He now had confirmation of some sort of encounter between Rodeen and Janine, presumably in the hotel room. Terry could have been telling the truth when he said Rodeen was jealous. Luke envisioned a catfight, but Janine's body had no scratches or bruises beyond those associated with the actual strangling. Which Rodeen, being no taller than Janine herself and quite a bit lighter, would have been hard put to pull off.

But Terry – or someone with identical shoes to his – had definitely been the one to string her up. Whether Rodeen talked or not, Luke would now have something solid to confront him with.

He found an empty desk and made some calls. First to Colin. 'Did you by chance get any background on Rodeen Norman?'

'I did, since you ask. Just idle curiosity, but I found out she works as a massage therapist. The legitimate kind, believe it or not. Attached to a beauty salon there in Sellwood.'

'Oh, does she now?' A massage therapist would have strong hands. With a shiver of revulsion, Luke summoned up a memory snapshot of Rodeen as she had appeared at Windy Corner. Her nails had been fancy but not long, and he had an idea her hands might have been muscular-looking and large for her size. 'That fits.'

'Need anything else? I can dig some more.'

'That'll do me for now. Very useful – thanks.'

'Glad to be of service.'

Luke's next call was to Heather. 'Any joy?'

'Not yet. I've been driving around randomly, looking for the car. So far so— Wait a second. I just turned into the parking lot at Saint Bede's to turn around, and there's a light-blue coupe here. Stay tuned – I'm going to check inside.'

St Bede's was the last stop on a road going uphill from town.

Rodeen could have driven up there thinking she'd found an escape route, realized it was a dead end, and panicked. But where would she go from there? And how? She wouldn't get far on foot, given her usual choice of shoes; the woods closed in immediately past the end of the road.

He heard indistinct noises through the phone, and then Rodeen's voice came through, shrill with fear but resonant in the acoustic space of the church: 'I claim sanctitude. You can't touch me!' Good Lord, the woman must mean *sanctuary*. Luke envisioned her clinging to the altar like some medieval miscreant.

Heather spoke calmly in a reassuring tone. 'It's all right, Rodeen. No one's going to hurt you. We only want to talk.'

'No comment!' Rodeen shrieked. 'I won't discriminate Terry!'

That's the line, Heather. Go with that. Luke didn't dare speak in case Rodeen could hear him. He texted, *Tell her Terry's already thrown her under the bus.*

A pause, then, 'Terry doesn't deserve your loyalty, Rodeen. He's already told us you were to blame.'

A shocked silence, then Rodeen's voice, closer than before. 'I don't believe you! Terry would never do that. He loves me!'

With remarkable insight, given how little she actually knew, Heather responded, 'Terry only loves Terry. He's not going to help you. You need to help yourself. If you come quietly and tell us all you know, it'll go easier for you in the end.'

'No . . . You can't take me . . . I claim sanctitude!' The voice was quite close now. Heather must be nearly at her side.

'Oregon doesn't recognize that kind of sanctuary, Rodeen. This is the end of the line.' Luke heard the click of handcuffs. 'Rodeen Norman, I'm arresting you on suspicion of conspiracy to kidnap Charlotte Lovelace.' Directly into the phone, Heather said, 'I've got her, boss. I'm bringing her in.'

While he was waiting for Heather to arrive with Rodeen, Luke called off the roadblocks. Then he phoned Pete, who was on his way back to Stony Beach, and let him know the search was over.

'Sounds like Heather did us proud,' Pete said.

'She was an absolute star. Now I need you to go to Windy Corner and get official statements about the kidnapping attempt from Emily, Moses, and Marguerite.'

'Sure thing.' Pete sounded slightly wistful. 'Glad I can be of *some* use.'

Despite Pete being the muscle of the group, Heather had managed to apprehend both suspects in this case. Luke could imagine how his senior deputy felt. 'Hey, you can't hog the glory all the time. It was Heather's turn.'

Luke was going to be stuck in the office all evening, no doubt, trying to get a straight story out of Rodeen and Terry. Heather deserved a celebration. 'Tell you what – when you're done with those statements, how 'bout you take Heather out for a drink to celebrate? Put it on the department tab.'

Pete's voice brightened. 'Sounds good.'

Luke found an empty desk and got a start on the case paper-work in the ten minutes that remained. At last Heather walked through the door, Rodeen in tow. Once she got her booked in, Luke clapped his deputy on the shoulder. 'Good work, Heather. You handled her just right. I'm stuck here for a while, but Pete's gonna take you out for a drink when he's done getting statements. You can do your report while you wait.'

Heather flushed. 'I got lucky, is all. She was at the end of her rope. She didn't even resist.'

Luke shook his head. 'Don't sell yourself short. You used exactly the right approach. If you'd been rough and spooked her, God knows what might've happened.'

Heather blushed deeper. 'Thanks, boss.'

Luke squared his shoulders. 'My turn now. Wish me luck.' He strode off toward the interview room.

Inside, Rodeen shivered in her chair, hands wrapped around a steaming cup. Luke took his seat and looked her over. The woman was a mess. Runny mascara gave her eyes a raccoon look, while smeared lipstick turned her mouth into a clown's. Her hair would have made Phyllis Diller proud. But when she glanced up at him, her eyes were those of a frightened child. Weirdly, they reminded him of Charlotte's.

He got up and went to the door. 'Get me a blanket, would you?' he said to the officer outside. He hoped the blanket would be enough to deal with her shock for now. As a human being, he would have been happy to let her rest overnight before he interviewed her, but as a lawman, he knew he had to question her now, while she was vulnerable. Given time to pull herself together, she might clam up completely.

He waited till the officer returned, then shut the door and handed the blanket to Rodeen. 'Wrap up in that.'

She took the blanket with a smile that seemed to be trying for her old flirtatious manner but failed miserably. Her shaking hands fumbled with the fabric until Luke came to her rescue, unfolded it properly, and placed it around her shoulders. She pulled it tight across her chest.

Luke sat down, turned on the recorder, and made the necessary introductions. 'Now, Rodeen. Suppose you tell me all about it. In your own words.'

'All – all about what?' She tried an innocent smile this time, which also didn't come off.

'From the time you arrived in Stony Beach on Thursday. Why did you come?'

'I, um . . . Terry needed me.'

'Why didn't you come down with him in the first place, then?'

'Well, you see . . . He didn't know he was gonna need me at first. He called me from the road.'

'Are you sure that's what happened? I think maybe you came on your own.'

'Wh–why would I do that?'

'Maybe 'cause you thought Terry was coming here to meet Janine, and you wanted to keep an eye on him. You wanted to be sure they kept the relationship professional.'

'No! It wasn't like that. It was . . . Well, it was different, that's all. He needed help getting hold of Charlotte. I mean, talking her into coming back, away from that horrible Moses.'

'So that's why you came to my house the other day. To persuade Charlotte.'

'That's right. Only you wouldn't even let me talk to her.' Rodeen formed her mouth into a grotesque pout.

'To be fair, you did give me a false name. And lied about being her aunt.'

Rodeen rolled her eyes like a teenager.

'So what happened when you told Terry you'd failed?'

Her lip quivered, and her hand went to her cheek. Luke suspected her thick makeup covered a bruise. 'He . . . he wasn't happy. He wanted me to try again, but I knew it wouldn't do no good. You and that wife of yours'd never let me in.'

'So the two of you came up with another plan?'

'Terry did. He said we'd go get her together.' Her eyes darted toward him, then away. 'I didn't want to go. He made me.' She touched her cheek again.

So maybe Rodeen wasn't guilty of conspiracy to kidnap. Maybe Terry had coerced her. But according to Emily, she still played an active part.

'So you and Terry went back this afternoon. To take her, whether she wanted to go or not.'

'You make it sound so . . . criminal. We just wanted Charlotte to be back with her family. Terry's the only family she's got left. Moses ain't nothing to her.'

Luke let his eyes bore into hers. 'Now, you know that's not the way it is. Don't you, Rodeen? You know Terry's interest in Charlotte is far from fatherly.'

Her face crumpled into tears. And suddenly, several odd details of Rodeen's wardrobe and behavior clicked into place in Luke's mind. The long blonde wig, the overalls, the fragments of a girlish manner – she used them to try to look like Charlotte. So Terry would want her.

This woman was more pathetic than criminal. But she was guilty of attempted kidnapping, if not more – and possibly much more. He couldn't let her off. But he kept his voice gentle.

'Terry never did love you, did he, Rodeen? First, he couldn't get Charlotte out of his head. You told yourself he was concerned for her, he was the only father she ever had and he wanted to take care of her. But something inside told you that wasn't the real reason. Did he ask you to wear the wig and dress like a child? Was that the only way you could get him to respond to you?'

Rodeen answered only with louder sobs. Luke pushed the tissue box close to her, and she grabbed a handful.

He pressed on. 'And then Janine came along. At first, she was simply doing a job for him, trying to get Charlotte back. But then something changed. Did you get a look at his phone? See all those texts he sent her? Sexy texts. Like he was in love with her. Maybe you followed him when he went to meet her – saw

what an old frump she was. You could almost understand about
Charlotte – at least she was pretty – but Janine? She was nothing
like Charlotte, and not a patch on you. How could Terry prefer
her to you?'

'He never!' Rodeen exploded, slapping her wet palms on the
table. 'He didn't love her. He was just using her. He loved *me*!'

'I'm sure he told you that. But deep down, you didn't believe
him, did you? He didn't treat you like a woman he loved. He
was cruel, wasn't he? Insulted you, taunted you, even hit you.
Didn't he? Isn't that the way it really was, Rodeen?'

More sobs.

'So when Terry came down to Stony Beach to see Janine, you
followed him. You followed him all the way to her hotel room.'

She looked up at him, eyes wide with astonishment. 'How'd
you know that?'

'You were seen going into the hotel.'

'But I . . . I just . . . I just wanted to talk to him. To her. Talk
sense into her.'

'And did you talk to her, Rodeen? Or did you see them doing
something that drove all the sense out of your head?'

Rodeen's last vestige of control vanished. She fairly spat her
words into Luke's face. 'She was on her knees to him, that bitch.
Holding on to his belt. I thought she was about to – you know.
But I yanked her up and got my hands around her throat.' She
demonstrated the action in the air. In the process, her long sleeves
slipped down to reveal healing scratches on her forearms – no
doubt from Janine trying to fend her off. 'She wasn't gonna take
my Terry away from me. No way!'

Luke swallowed his surprise. Despite Colin's new information,
he hadn't genuinely expected a confession of murder. But if that's
where this was going, he'd certainly take it.

He spoke in a low, confidential voice, as if he were a priest
or a therapist instead of a cop. 'You have strong hands for a
woman, don't you, Rodeen?' Now that she was in front of him,
he could see the power in the long fingers as they returned to
twisting the wad of tissues. 'Masseuse's hands. You put them
around her throat and you squeezed. Did you squeeze the life
right out of her? Or did that come later?'

Rodeen was too far gone to scent the trap. 'I squeezed till she went limp. I let go and she just laid there on the floor like a rag doll.'

'And then Terry took over. Am I right? He knew you had to make it look like something else – suicide, maybe, or at least like someone else had done it. He stripped the sheet from the bed and used it to string her up from the shower rod. Is that how it happened?'

Rodeen nodded, all the energy drained out of her. 'He had some cotton gloves in his pocket. My Terry's a mortar to his ex*zee*mia, see, so he carries 'em all the time for when he puts the cream on. He told me not to touch nothin', so I didn't. I just sat in the chair and waited for him to get done.'

'And then he dropped a receipt under the desk.'

She looked puzzled. 'Yeah. I didn't get that. He said it'd point to Moses, but I don't see how.'

Luke had everything he needed now. 'Rodeen Norman, I'm arresting you for the second-degree murder of Janine Vertue. This charge is in addition to that of the attempted kidnapping of Charlotte Lovelace. You'll be held here overnight, then transferred to await trial.' Then to the recorder, 'Interview ended, seven forty p.m.'

Her bewildered eyes followed him to the door. Could it be that she didn't fully understand what she'd done? It wouldn't bother Luke if she were to plead diminished responsibility. Morally speaking, he held Terry Garner liable for the whole sorry mess.

He told the officer on duty, 'Take her to a cell and get her something to eat.'

He could use something to eat himself. But first, he had to tackle Terry.

They had only one interview room, so Luke had to wait while Rodeen was taken out and Terry brought in again. He told the officer to make sure the pair didn't see each other in the process. Poor old Arnold Mitchell shuffled back into the room and put his head down on his arms. Luke took him a fresh cup of coffee when he went back in.

After the preliminaries, Luke started off. 'We found Rodeen, Terry.'

The merest flicker of fear shot through Terry's eyes and was quenched. He shrugged. 'Never thought she'd get away. Terrible driver. No more sense o' direction than a rock.'

'The thing is, Terry, she had kind of a lot to say.'

His eyes darted around the room. 'Awful talker, that woman. Never shuts up. Don't mean you can trust a word she says.'

'On the contrary. I found her to be quite straightforward. Much more truthful than you, for example.'

Terry's raw, red hands, clasped on the table, started to shake. He scratched at them viciously, then shoved them under his armpits. 'Her word against mine. You know she's got the brain of a newborn chick? I'm telling ya, not a true word comes out of her mouth.'

Luke leaned forward. 'I've had about enough of you, Garner. You're a bully and a pedophile and a lying manipulator, and yes, I do have enough evidence to prove at least some of that. For the moment, I can put you away for attempted kidnapping, accessory to murder, and perverting the course of justice. And given a little time, I have no doubt we'll be able to add to that list.'

Garner stared at Mitchell as if challenging him to object to this speech. Mitchell sat up and cleared his throat. 'Can we stick to the known facts, please, Lieutenant?'

'OK. Fact. You coerced Rodeen into helping you attempt to kidnap Charlotte Lovelace.'

Terry rolled his eyes. 'Like I told you. It was all her idea.'

Luke let that lie. 'Fact. You helped Rodeen kill Janine Vertue and then tried to cover it up.'

At the word 'kill,' Terry's control snapped. He leaned forward, palms on the table. 'I did not kill that woman! Rodeen strangled her. She was dead before I strung her up.'

Luke had consulted his notes from the postmortem while he was waiting for Heather to bring Rodeen in. Dr Sam had expressed some uncertainty as to whether Janine had been killed by the strangling or the hanging. From Rodeen's description, it sounded as if she had let go as soon as Janine passed out. She didn't hang on long enough to be sure Janine was dead.

Luke would dearly love to be able to get Garner for second-degree murder, not just accessory. 'Are you absolutely certain she was dead? Did you check her pulse?'

'Well, no, but . . . I'm telling you, she was dead! All I did was set the scene. I was only trying to save the woman I love from being charged with murder. Any man would do the same.'

'Any man who was implicated on his own account, maybe. You never in your life cared about saving anybody but yourself. And as for loving that poor woman – you don't know the meaning of the word.'

Terry sat back with a scowl. Luke went on. 'And let's not forget that you used the situation to try to cast the blame on Moses Valory. Fact: it was you who planted that gas receipt. Moses was never in the room. Pretty clumsy the way you did it, Terry. Didn't have us fooled for one second.' Well, at least it didn't fool Emily. 'One thing I'm curious about, though – where'd you get that receipt? You go through his trash or what?'

Mitchell leaned toward Terry's ear, but he pushed him away. A crafty grin spread over Terry's face. 'Followed him around for a while. Thought he might try to leave town, and I wanted to be right behind him. He stopped for gas and didn't take the receipt, so I pulled up to the same pump and grabbed it.' He shrugged. 'You never know when something like that's gonna come in handy.'

'Turns out it's more handy for me than for you. Proves the charge of perverting the course of justice. You shot yourself in the foot with that one, Terry.'

Watching his self-satisfied expression crumble was worth all the time Luke had spent with the man. 'Terence Garner, in addition to the existing charge of attempted kidnapping, I'm arresting you for the second-degree murder of Janine Vertue and for attempting to pervert the course of justice. You won't be hurting any more women for quite some time.'

TWENTY-FIVE

Emily was knitting in their third-floor sitting room when Luke finally got home. Everyone else had gone to bed. She set down her work and stood to greet him.

'Have you got them? Really got them both?'

Luke nodded wearily as he sank on to the loveseat beside her. 'Drink?'

'Please.'

Luke didn't drink much beyond beer as a rule, but they kept a bottle of brandy upstairs for occasions such as these. She poured him a snifter, and he nursed it as they talked.

'Heather was the hero of the hour,' he told her. 'She nabbed Terry as he was running away, and later she found Rodeen trying to claim sanctuary at Saint Bede's. Talked her down and brought her in. I'm gonna have to see what I can do about a commendation. Maybe even a raise.'

'Good for Heather.' Emily had a soft spot for Luke's junior deputy as a fellow member of the elite society of redheads. 'Did they talk? Either of them?'

'Garner's the slipperiest fish I ever dealt with, but once Rodeen understood that he'd tried to shift all the blame on to her, she couldn't talk fast enough. The kidnapping was his idea, of course; he forced her to help. But it was Rodeen who strangled Janine. Terry strung her up to make it look like suicide and left the receipt as insurance in case that didn't fly. Sam couldn't be sure Janine was dead before she was hanged, though, and the way Rodeen tells it, seems more likely she'd just passed out. So I've charged them both with second-degree murder.'

'But . . . but why? Why would Rodeen try to kill Janine?'

'Jealousy. She thought Terry was seriously interested in Janine. I tell you, that woman doesn't have two brain cells to rub together. And the one cell she does have is one hundred percent focused on Terry. He's her whole world. It's pitiful to see, Em. I kind of hope she pleads diminished responsibility, 'cause Garner's been pulling her puppet strings from the word go.'

Emily snuggled up to her husband. 'The more I see of men, the more grateful I am to have you. You are one in seven billion, Luke Richards.'

He put his arm around her and pulled her close. 'And so are you, Mrs Richards. I never appreciated your intelligence more than I did today, seeing the opposite. Not that that's the only thing I love you for, by any means.' He set down his drink and proceeded to back up his statement with action.

In the morning before breakfast, Luke and Emily went together to see Moses in his room.

'It's over,' Luke told him when he opened the door. 'We've got Terry and Rodeen both in custody, and between them they've confessed to killing Janine.'

Moses closed his eyes and swayed slightly on his feet, then slowly crossed himself. 'Thank God. I've got to tell Charlotte.'

He started to exit, but Luke held up a hand. 'Before you do that, I'd like to go over a few things. Just to put my own mind at rest. If that's OK?'

Moses hesitated with his hand on the doorknob, then nodded and stepped back into the room. 'I guess I owe you that much.'

He sat on the bed, which groaned under his weight, while Luke and Emily took the two chairs. 'Can you tell me now where you were on Thursday?'

'Sure thing. I drove to Portland to see my lawyer. Find out if there was any stone we'd left unturned to help protect us against Janine's persecution.'

Luke and Emily exchanged glances of consternation. 'Why the hell wouldn't you say so?' Luke asked.

Moses sighed. 'As long as there was the slightest chance of Charlotte being accused, I had to leave myself the option of confessing. No way was I gonna let my girl be arrested for something she could never possibly have done. Or even if she had done it, I'd've felt the same. I survived prison once. I could do it again. But put Charlotte in some kind of institution, and she'd die.'

Emily thought to herself that perhaps Luke was one of two in seven billion, after all.

'Was there anything else?' Moses said. 'I don't want to keep Charlotte in suspense any longer'n I have to.'

'I thought you might have questions about how it all went down,' Luke responded. 'Wouldn't want to go through that in front of her.'

Moses shook his head. 'Don't need to hear it. I like to keep my mind on what's good and true, like it says in the Bible. Enough bad gets in that I can't avoid – I don't need to go seeking after it.'

Emily thought that was an excellent philosophy. She'd have to try it herself – at least until the next murder came along.

Moses stood. 'Can I tell her now?'

Luke and Emily stood as well. 'Absolutely. Let's tell her together.'

Moses knocked at the door of the Montgomery room. 'Charlotte, sweetie? You ready? Got some news before we head down to breakfast.'

She opened the door, fully dressed but with hairbrush in hand, her pale blonde locks cascading around her shoulders. She reached up to give Moses a good-morning kiss on the cheek, then looked questioningly at Luke and Emily.

'Sit down, sweetie. It's good news, but it's big.'

Charlotte sat on the edge of the vanity stool, her expressive face awash with expectation.

'Sheriff Luke here has arrested Terry Garner and his girlfriend, Rodeen. They've confessed to killing Janine. They'll both be going to jail for a good long time.' Moses glanced at Luke for confirmation, and he nodded.

Charlotte dropped her brush and her mouth fell open. A little squeak emerged from her throat. She flung herself into Moses' arms, and their tears mingled on their cheeks.

Then Emily heard a sound she could hardly comprehend, it was so unexpected – a slightly croaky but distinctly young and feminine voice. 'We're – free?'

Charlotte pulled back and clapped her hand over her mouth, eyes wide. The sound coming from her throat had surprised her as much as anyone else. Emily could barely imagine the revolution that must have happened inside Charlotte's mind to make speech possible for her at last.

Moses held his daughter at arm's length, quaking with amazement and joy. 'Yes, sweetheart. We're free.'

Charlotte hugged him again, then turned to Emily, who had joined in the happy tears, and embraced her in turn. 'Thank you,' she whispered. 'You've been so kind.'

Then she wrapped her arms around Luke, whose eyes were suspiciously moist as well. 'And thank you, Mister Sheriff. You saved us.'

Luke cleared his throat. 'It wasn't all me, but you're welcome.' He patted her shoulder awkwardly until she released him.

'Let's get some breakfast,' Charlotte said, as if her speaking out loud were the most normal thing in the world. 'I'm starved!'

The four of them were the first ones in the dining room for breakfast. Oscar, Lauren, and Marguerite followed soon after. The Hsus preferred to breakfast later, on their own, which was fine with Emily. She wasn't sure they would be as joyful at the news as the occasion demanded.

She looked to Luke to make the announcement as the others trooped in, but Charlotte spoke up before he could do so. 'Terry's in jail!' she cried, her voice now almost normal, lubricated with use and orange juice. 'We're free!'

The others stopped short with varying degrees of astonishment written on their faces. Lauren was the first to recover.

'And you're talking!' she said. 'So it *was* trauma, after all! I would love to have a good long powwow with the two of you.' She looked from Charlotte to Moses.

Moses opened his mouth to respond, but Emily forestalled him, lest he feel somehow duty-bound to accede to Lauren's thoughtless request. 'They need time to process everything, Lauren. Give them some space.'

Lauren dropped her eyes. 'Oh, right. Of course. Sorry.' She smiled at Charlotte apologetically. 'I'm really happy for you.'

'Thanks.' Charlotte grinned back.

Everyone got their food from the buffet and sat down. Lauren and the others pumped Luke for details of the arrest, while Moses and Charlotte spoke confidentially at the other end of the table.

Her curiosity satisfied, Marguerite murmured in Emily's ear,

'*Alors*, Jean Valjean and his Cosette will live peacefully together in his declining years. All we need now is a Marius to become her protector when Valjean is gone.'

Emily shook her head. 'Plenty of time for that. Charlotte is still very young – in some ways younger than fifteen, in other ways older. It'll be a few years before she's ready to trust a man in that way.'

When they'd all finished eating, Moses spoke up. 'Miss Emily, ma'am, Charlotte and I are as grateful as we can be for your hospitality. But we're missing our own home, and now that it's safe to go back there, we'd like to go.' He looked at Luke. 'If that's OK with you, Sheriff?'

'I'll need to get formal statements from both of you,' he said. 'If you could stop by the main office in Tillamook on your way? After that, you'll be free to go. We won't need you as witnesses until the trial, and that'll probably be months away.'

'Thank you kindly. We'll get packed up now.' Moses stood, and Charlotte followed suit.

'One thing before you go,' Emily said. 'Charlotte, if you can bear to talk about it now that you're safe, I'm dying to know – what was it you saw on the beach the day Janine died? What frightened you so badly?'

Charlotte shivered slightly in retrospect. 'I saw *him* – T–T—'

'Terry?' Emily supplied gently. That was one word Charlotte might never be able to utter.

Charlotte nodded. 'Arguing with Janine.'

'Just arguing?' Luke put in. 'He didn't attack her or anything?'

She shook her head. 'He was loud and wild. Like he used to be with Mom before he hit her. I thought he would hit Janine any minute, but he didn't.'

Probably restrained by being in public, Emily thought. That was why he'd followed her back to the hotel – so he could vent his feelings in private. But Rodeen's arrival had forestalled him once again.

'Thank you, Charlotte. I know that was hard for you.'

Moses and Charlotte turned toward the door, and Oscar sprang from his chair. 'Oh, but we hoped you'd stay for the wedding!' He glanced at Lauren. 'Didn't we?'

'Definitely. Please stay. Or come back on Saturday.'

Moses and Charlotte exchanged looks. Emily supposed they had perfected their wordless communication during the time Charlotte had been mute. Moses spoke for them both. 'We appreciate the invitation, and we'll consider coming back. But for the time being, we need to be in our own home. I reckon you can use the rooms for wedding guests, anyway.'

Charlotte nodded her agreement. Not everything needed to be spoken.

Luke stopped Moses on his way out the door, Charlotte having run ahead. 'Any chance she'll talk about the abuse?' he asked in a low voice. 'I'd sure love to add that to the charges against Terry. It would mean more years on his sentence, plus he'd be registered if he ever did get out. I guess you know what happens to men like him in prison.'

Moses shook his head. 'She may never want to revisit all that. We'll have to wait and see. At the least, it'll take time, and I'm not gonna push her.'

'No, of course not. But if she does want to talk, let me know. It's not my jurisdiction, but I have a nephew on the Portland force we can trust. We could get her testimony taped since she's a minor – she wouldn't have to appear in court.'

'As the Lord wills,' Moses said. 'I'm not one to seek vengeance, but I do want to be sure Terry never hurts another innocent again.'

'Amen to that.'

Half an hour later, Moses and Charlotte came down with their packed bags. 'Don't forget your knitting,' Emily said to Charlotte, handing her the bag she'd left in the library.

'Oh, thanks,' Charlotte said. 'I love knitting almost as much as drawing. I'll have that forever now. Thank you so much for teaching me.'

'I couldn't have asked for a better pupil. If you ever need help or just want to talk stitches, give me a call. Or next time I'm in Portland, maybe we can get together for a yarn crawl.'

'I'd love that!' Charlotte gave Emily an enthusiastic hug. 'You're like the auntie I always wanted but never had. Can I call you Auntie Em? Like Dorothy?'

Emily teared up at that. 'Absolutely.' She glanced at Moses,

who was waiting with a patient smile. 'And now I think it's time
for you to click your ruby slippers together and say, "There's no
place like home."'

TWENTY-SIX

W hen Abby had finished cleaning Moses' and Charlotte's rooms, Emily offered the Montgomery room to Josie, who had come over to help with the final preparations for the wedding.

'Oh, that would be terrific! Thank you!' Josie responded. 'I didn't want to say anything, but I got a kind of creepy feeling from that hotel room. Like maybe somebody died there or something.'

Emily glanced at Luke, who grimaced. So it appeared Josie had been given Janine's room, after all.

Lauren was agog. 'Did you see a ghost?'

'N–no. I didn't see anything exactly. Or hear anything, either. It was just kind of . . . a feeling. Oppressive and sad. And a smell – I couldn't identify it, but it was nasty. I'll be glad to get out of there.' She glanced at her watch. 'If we go now, we can beat checkout time.'

Josie and Lauren left their place cards half done and sped out.

Emily turned to Luke. 'A bad smell? They did get the room properly cleaned, didn't they?'

'That would've been up to your manager, but I assume so. I gave them the name of the best crime-scene cleaners in the area. And it's not like there was blood or anything, anyway. I think Josie's just the fanciful type. Or maybe something died on the beach outside her window.' He frowned. 'No, wait a sec. That window faced the parking lot.'

Emily crossed herself just in case. 'I'll have the manager comp Josie's stay. And I'll get her to air out that room for at least twenty-four hours. So the bad spirits can get out.' Luke looked at her quizzically. 'You never read any Tony Hillerman? When somebody dies inside a hogan, the Navajos break a hole in the wall to let the *chindi* – the bad part of the person's spirit – escape.'

'But you don't believe that stuff, do you? I thought you were a Christian.'

'I don't exactly believe it, but I leave room in the universe for things I don't understand. Evil does leave a trace, whether tangible or not. I don't think Josie was making things up.'

The rest of the week passed as smoothly as the week before a wedding ever does for the people intimately involved. Luke took Oscar out for his ultra-low-key bachelor party on Thursday night. On Friday afternoon, the wedding party got dolled up and went down to the beach for a photo session, while Emily drove to the church to make sure all was in readiness for the rehearsal in the evening.

Father Stephen met her in the parking lot. 'I hope you approve,' he said, gesturing to the scaffolding-free façade. 'There's still some scaffolding on the far side, but the guests shouldn't have any reason to go around there.'

'So far, so good,' Emily said. 'The roof looks great – what I can see of it, anyway.'

'Yes, I think they've done a fine job. At least, when we had that rain yesterday, nothing leaked.' He led her inside.

Emily kept her eyes on the carpet until they'd passed the join where the narrow strip covering the aisle began. No loose corners to be seen. Then she looked up, and her breath caught in her throat.

The inside scaffolding was gone, and the sun streamed in through the completed rose window. The glass was brighter and clearer than Emily had ever seen it. It looked as if Adrian had meticulously cleaned each of the old panes, perhaps replaced a few, to match the new pieces he'd put in. She could almost believe she'd been transported to the Cathedral of Notre Dame.

'Oh, it's beautiful!' she breathed.

'Thanks,' came a voice from the side of the altar area. 'Some of my best work, I think.'

Emily tore her eyes from the window to see Adrian packing his tools away. 'You've done a wonderful job. The window hasn't looked that good since – I don't know, probably since it was new. Thank you so much for finishing it in time.'

'Thank you for the work,' Adrian said. 'And for the cottage. Polly and Raph have had a great little vacation here.'

'We sure have,' Polly echoed from the back of the church.

She stood just inside the door, holding her little naked son by the hand. Raphael looked around curiously. Emily prayed hard he wasn't spying out the best place to take a pee.

'You're welcome to attend the ceremony tomorrow,' she said. With a glance at Raphael, she added, 'Properly dressed, that is.'

'Thanks, but we've got to get back,' Adrian replied. 'I'm starting a new job tomorrow morning.'

'I hope everything goes well,' Polly added.

Emily was secretly relieved that they had declined. They might have taken the invitation to extend to the reception, and she knew every place card was accounted for. Lauren's spontaneity did not go as far as adding last-minute guests to her list.

She thanked Father Stephen for all his work getting everything ready on time, then paused before the altar rail to say a last prayer that all would go well on the morrow. She'd learned from long experience that things going smoothly could never be taken for granted.

On Saturday morning, Emily and the men kept out of the way upstairs while Marguerite, Lauren, Josie, and Mrs Hsu transformed the ground-floor rooms into a Chinese banqueting hall. Katie was having a good morning and lent a willing hand, but Emily was glad the food would be catered so Katie could get a good rest later on.

Luke had invited Oscar and Mr Hsu into his half-finished hideout to watch a martial arts movie, having ascertained this was the one and only genre in which all their tastes converged.

Emily knew she would be more of a hindrance than a help downstairs, having less than no aptitude for draperies and table settings. But she couldn't settle to her knitting in her own sitting room, so she wandered the second floor like a ghost, catching snatches of conversation from downstairs and of martial music and exclamations from the men in the den.

The door to the Forster room was ajar, and she sneaked in to take another peek at Lauren's church gown, displayed on a dress form Emily had rescued from the attic. Oscar had been banished to the Brontë room for the night before his nuptials to keep up the pretense of the bride and groom coming together only at the altar.

Emily fingered the delicate chiffon of the full skirt gathered into the fitted, strapless bodice. Lauren had chosen an understated gown that would not overwhelm her tiny figure, but it still had enough skirt to trail behind her as she walked down the aisle. She would make a beautiful bride.

Emily drifted to the big bay window that looked out over the sea. It was a warm, sunny day with no more wind than was inevitable on the Oregon coast, and everything seemed in readiness for the wedding of Oscar and Lauren's dreams. Yet a wistfulness haunted Emily's heart that she couldn't account for.

She'd had her own lovely wedding a couple of months ago, so it couldn't be envy. Did she fear she'd be losing her newfound brother to some extent? That didn't seem likely, since he'd been in love with Lauren for as long as Emily had known him, and there was no reason the siblings wouldn't continue to see each other as often as before. In fact, everyone she cared about seemed set for a happy future – she and Oscar with their new spouses, Moses and Charlotte with their newfound security, Katie and Jamie with their coming baby . . .

Except Marguerite. Was it Marguerite's barely acknowledged unhappiness that kept Emily from entering fully into the joy of the day? She'd have to find a moment during the festivities to let her friend know that her feelings and needs were not forgotten.

The lunch gong sounded, and Emily shook herself from her reverie. The time had come for everyone to pull together to bring all the wedding planning to fruition.

Once again in the afternoon, all Emily had to do was get herself dressed, tie Luke's cravat (Oscar having opted for traditional English morning suits for the men of the party), and ask him fifty times if he was sure he had the ring. Since she wasn't needed to help dress the bride, she rode with Luke and Oscar to the church. The joyful sound of bells greeted them as they entered.

People were beginning to gather as Marguerite, with Abby's help, put the finishing touches on the flowers. Emily greeted the guests she knew, who were mostly from Reed as the bridal couple had little local acquaintance. When she came to Teresa Rivera, the Spanish professor, Teresa gestured up from her wheelchair to a tall, handsome, vaguely familiar-looking man beside her.

'The invitation said plus-one, and the only plus-one I have is my little dog, who I thought might not be welcome. So I brought Julian Wallingford, our new art history professor. I thought it would be a good opportunity for him to become acquainted with our set ahead of the rush of the semester beginning.'

So that was why he looked familiar – Oscar had shown them all his photo when the announcement of his hiring came out. She smiled and shook his hand. 'You're most welcome, Julian. I hope you'll have a wonderful time.'

He bowed slightly over her hand. 'I am already,' he said. 'Just admiring this little jewel of a church and watching the people. I don't suppose the florist will be coming to the reception?' He indicated Marguerite, who was stepping back to survey the final arrangement she'd completed.

Marguerite was dressed in red silk, to complement the colors of the reception. Red was her best color, setting off her dark hair and white skin, and her simply cut dress skimmed her slender curves alluringly. Emily smiled to herself as she replied, 'Oh, she's not a professional florist. She's my dear and multitalented friend Marguerite. Of course she'll be there.'

'Not Marguerite Grenier? As in the French professor and head of Lit and Lang?'

'That's the one.'

He straightened his tie with a sparkle in his eye. 'I look forward to meeting her.'

Emily made her way to the back of the church. As a sort of stand-in for the mother of the groom, she was to be seated formally by an usher shortly before the bride came in. She waited with the Hsus as the last of the guests filed in. A friend of Oscar's from Reed took Mrs Hsu's arm, then Jamie took Emily's and led her to the front pew. The organist launched into 'Jesu, Joy of Man's Desiring' as Lauren processed slowly up the aisle on her father's arm.

Lauren was radiant, shooting smiles and glances left and right as she approached. Emily glanced at Oscar, whose eyes were fixed immovably on his bride. She thought she'd never seen anyone so completely overwhelmed with joy and awe as her brother was at that moment. Of course, her sisterly thought was to hope that Lauren would prove worthy of such devotion, but she had no serious doubts about that. She looked forward to watching them fall more in love year by year and, God willing, produce at least a couple of babies for their dear old auntie to fuss over, knit for, and generally spoil.

She spared a glance at Luke, who gave her a nearly imperceptible smile and wink, so she knew his thoughts ran along similar lines. In that moment, Emily's happiness was complete.

Emily didn't recognize her own home when they returned from the church. She felt as if she'd been transported to Imperial China. The reception was a blur of red and gold and happy faces, of speeches and dances and unrecognizable dishes that proved delicious once Emily figured out how to get them into her mouth using only chopsticks. Lauren's gorgeous dress elicited oohs and aahs enough to satisfy even Mrs Hsu, who reigned at the top table in a more subdued red cheongsam of her own, completely in her element.

David Burkhardt, Luke's photographer, darted about among the tables, displaying a disquieting tendency to focus on small details such as the table centerpieces rather than on groups of guests. Apparently, you could take the photographer out of the crime scene, but you couldn't altogether take the crime scene out of the photographer. But as long as he didn't focus too much on body parts, the photos should turn out OK.

The event that stood out in Emily's later memories was the one that came as a complete surprise. After the bride and groom had changed into their traditional Chinese clothes, been welcomed, and taken their places at the top table in the library, the gong sounded from the hallway. Everyone turned to the hall doors, which were flung open to reveal two sets of dancers composing two Chinese lions, draped in gold silk with dozens of red and gold ribbons forming their manes and fluttering down their sides. The lions were accompanied by several men playing drums and cymbals. The procession snaked its way between the closely spaced tables, the lion heads bowing and rearing as the four legs of each moved in perfect synchrony, never faltering or bumping into anything. Everyone applauded as the lions danced through the library and into the parlor, which was also full of tables of guests, then toward the front door.

Emily, seated at the top table between Luke and Marguerite, turned to her friend, who she assumed had been in on this from the beginning, to ask what it was all about. But she found Marguerite deep in conversation with Julian Wallingford, who had pulled up a chair at the end of the table. His face revealed complete absorption in what she had to say.

Emily smiled to herself and turned to Luke instead. 'I suppose that was all about good luck, like everything else in this banquet?'

'I guess so,' he replied. 'I don't think luck has much to do with a good marriage, though, do you? I mean, maybe there's some luck involved in meeting the right person, but after that you make your own fortune, good or bad.'

'Absolutely. And I'm sure Oscar and Lauren will put in the work to make their marriage one of the best.'

'*One* of the best, sure,' Luke responded, sliding his arm behind her and drawing her close. 'But not *the* best. That place is already taken.'

She turned to receive his kiss, knowing all eyes were elsewhere at that moment. 'And as soon as we have our house to ourselves again, we can get started on making it even better.'